Stephen Crane's Novel of the Civil War
THE RED BADGE OF COURAGE
An Historically Annotated Edition

Stephen Crane's Novel of the Civil War

THE RED BADGE
OF COURAGE

An Historically Annotated Edition

by Charles J. LaRocca

PURPLE MOUNTAIN PRESS
Fleischmanns, New York

This book is dedicated to: Private Charles C. LaRocca, Co. D 146th Infantry, American Expeditionary Forces, wounded at the Meuse-Argonne; Tech Sergeant John S. Chumas, United States Army Air Corps, B-17 Waist-gunner, prisoner of war 1944/45; Chief Master Sergeant Joseph N. LaRocca, United States Air Force, Veteran of World War II and the Korean War. Like the old soldiers Stephen Crane talked to in the park, they answered their country's call.

Cover photo credit: Pvt. James Conklin, Co. K, 124th New York, from the Harry L. Murray, Sr. collection, courtesy of Betty Carey and Lillian Murray.

First Edition, 1995

Published by
PURPLE MOUNTAIN PRESS, LTD.
Main Street, P.O. Box E3, Fleischmanns, New York 12430-0378
914-254-4062

Annotations and original illustrations copyright © 1995
by Charles J. LaRocca

Manufactured in the United States of America. Printed on acid-free paper.

Library of Congress Cataloging-in-Publication Data

Crane, Stephen, 1871-1900.
    The red badge of courage : Stephen Crane's Novel of the Civil War.
- - An historically annotated ed. / by Charles J. LaRocca, 1st ed.
        p.   cm.
    ISBN 0-935796-67-3 (acid-free paper). - - ISBN 0-935796-68-1 (pbk.
: acid-free paper)
        1. United States- -History- -Civil War, 1861-1865- -Fiction.
    2. Chancellorsville (Va.), Battle of, 1863- -Fiction. I. LaRocca,
    Charles J., 1946-   . II. Title.
    PS1449.C85R3   1995
    813' .4- -dc20   95-22834
                                                                    CIP

ACKNOWLEDGMENTS

THIS VOLUME has been the work of many years. Through it all, my wife, Kathy, has been a constant source of encouragement and support. She also spent a great deal of time proofreading and giving sound advice on how the book should be composed. Her training as librarian and teacher have been invaluable in bringing the project to a successful conclusion. Without the confidence and foresight of Wray and Loni Rominger of Purple Mountain Press, this annotated edition might still be a jumble of papers under my desk. Their confidence is greatly appreciated. Many others deserve thanks for bringing this new edition of Crane's novel to completion:

Gary Farbman, a good friend and colleague, who gave technical advice and direction about the various computer programs used in production.

Chris Farlekas, feature writer for the Middletown *Record* and a Stephen Crane fan for many years, who has been a steadfast source of encouragement.

Peter Osborne, Port Jervis Historian, who also gave his support and encouragement to the project.

Mike McAfee of the United States Military Academy Museum, who critiqued the section on Civil War weapons.

Liz Weisz of the Pine Bush School District, who proofread the introductory material.

Lt. Mel Johnson, 124th NYSV, who discovered, among other things, the connection between editor John Hasbrouck of the *Whig Press* and Lt. Hasbrouck of Crane's 304th New York.

Charles Radzinski of the Middletown Historical Society, who helped by making original copies of the *Whig Press* available for examination.

Former students David Anderson, Greg Anderson, and Jon Lewis, who discovered Charles Weygant's obituary which clearly linked the historic 124th and the fictitious 304th. Former students Sheryl Lindros, Petra Carroll, Jean Ruckle, Jessica Bradbury, Heidi Nickish, and many others who contributed enthusiasm and hard work to this project.

THE ILLUSTRATIONS

MANY OF THE ILLUSTRATIONS in this book are original works done by two good friends who also serve in the 124th New York Civil War reenactment group. Sergeant Wayne Merrick and Corporal Dianne Drewes provided many pen-and-ink drawings, unique contributions that add immeasurably to the text. I am greatly indebted to these talented artists and teachers.

Some of the pictures not signed by Wayne or Dianne come from *Frank Leslie's Illustrated Famous Leaders and Battle Scenes of the Civil War*. The pictures, according to the book's introduction, ". . . were drawn and engraved directly from sketches made on the scene of battle by the most famous artists of the time, and can therefore be relied upon as absolutely accurate." Since most of the pictures are not signed, it is impossible to give individual credit where that credit is due.

Other illustrations came from *Battle and Leaders*, the very same source that Crane used in his search for realistic details.

Maps 1-3 are from *Chancellorsville and Gettysburg* by General Abner Doubleday, published in 1886 by Charles Scribner's Sons.

Maps 4-10 are my own creations, and I am responsible for any inaccuracies. They are done after those found in John Bigelow's *The Campaign of Chancellorsville* and are greatly simplified to give the reader a general idea of the battle. Those wishing a more detailed view should consult Bigelow or Ernest Furgurson's recently published *Chancellorsville 1863: The Souls of the Brave*.

INTRODUCTION

STEPHEN CRANE was born six years after the American Civil War ended. Except for some drill instruction at prep school, he had no military training and never served in any army. Lacking such personal experience, it is remarkable that he was able to write *The Red Badge of Courage*, a story of war so convincing that Civil War veterans corresponding with the young author in the late 1890s demanded that he name his regiment.

Some veterans even claimed to have served with Crane in the war. "I was with Crane at Antietam," was the proud, but incorrect, assertion of Colonel John L. Burleigh.[1] Many Civil War veterans who read Crane's novel found it to be a realistic, faithful rendition of a soldier's life, especially on the battlefield, and were sure it must have been written by someone who had been there. Stephen Crane had not. He was born in 1871, in Newark, New Jersey, led a somewhat bizarre life, made his mark early, and died young.

The Red Badge of Courage is the story of a private in the Union army named Henry Fleming who comes to grips with his fear on a Civil War battlefield. The strength of the novel is in its powerful descriptions of the chaotic terror and disorientation felt by the "common soldier" in battle.

When the novel was to be made into a movie in the early 1950s, the actor chosen to play Private Henry Fleming was Audie Murphy, one of America's most decorated World War II veterans. If anyone knew what soldiering was all about, he certainly did. When told that Crane had never been a soldier, Murphy was amazed. "But he knew," said Murphy, "that in a battle you are all alone."

How was Crane able to capture these experiences so well? Was he the reincarnation of a long dead warrior, as some claimed? Was he a genius who dreamed up what he wrote? "Crane's description of battle," said the *New York Press* (October 13, 1895), is so vivid as to be almost suffocating. The reader is right down in the midst of it where patriotism is dissolved into its elements and where only a dozen men can be seen, firing blindly and grotesquely into the smoke. This is war from a new point of view. . . One should be forever slow in charging an author with genius, but it must be confessed that *The Red Badge of Courage* is open to the suspicion of having greater power and originality than can be girdled by the name of talent."[2]

Crane addressed the issue of his "genius" in a speech to the Philistine Society after he had attained fame as an author: "I don't believe in inspiration. I am one of those who believe that an enthusiasm of concentration in hard work is what a writer must depend on to bring him to the end he has in view."[3]

The "hard work" that Crane was talking about was historical research. *The Red Badge of Courage* has been thoroughly analyzed as a work of literature. The realism and symbolism have been attributed to a wide variety of sources, but until now, the novel has never been adequately examined as a work of history.

This annotated edition has two purposes. The first is to describe the broad historical context in which Crane wrote *The Red Badge of Courage*. This includes a definition of terms, place names, and jargon as well as an explanation of the uniform and equipment of the Civil War soldier. This background should help the reader understand what Crane was writing about and what so appealed to the veterans who read his novel.

The second purpose of this edition is to link Crane's realism to the history of a regiment that actually went to war in the fall of 1862. Since Crane was familiar with the war record of the 124th New York State Volunteers, the famed "Orange Blossoms" of Orange County, it is logical to conclude that he based much of the novel on their actions.

Crane never acknowledged a historical source for his work. No record of a conversation, no diary entry nor letter exists in which the author credits his "inspiration." In fact, just the opposite is true: he avoided naming a source.

After *The Red Badge of Courage* was published, Crane was urged to write more war stories, but factual histories of battles rather than fictionalized accounts. A letter to publisher John Phillips explains one reason for Crane's reluctance to name his sources in the novel, but it also reveals something very important about the author's style: he was determined to learn as much as possible about what actually happened before he started his work.

> . . .[O]ne of the first things I would want to do would be to visit the battle-field—which I was to describe—at the time of year when it was fought. The preliminary reading and the subsequent readings, and investigations of all kinds, would take much time. Moreover, if I did not place the original crown of pure gold on the heads of at least twelve generals they would arise and say: 'This damned young fool was not there. I was however. And this is how it happened.' I evaded them in the Red Badge because it was essential that I should make my battle a type and name no names but in your case, it would be very different.[4]

About a week later, Crane wrote to Phillips that he wanted to start the Civil War project with an article on the Battle of Fredericksburg. "If you intend to have me do the thing, let me know soon. I want to understand Fredericksburg completely as far as the books will teach it and then after that, the other things."[5] What were the "other things?" Crane could find out all he needed to know about troop movements, battle plans, casualties, etc. from the numerous accounts then in print. The "other things" could only have been the firsthand accounts of soldiers who had been at Fredericksburg, the accounts that would contribute the same raw authenticity that Crane had achieved in *The Red Badge of Courage*. He sought them for his Fredericksburg article just as he had for his novel.

Among other sources, he referred to Century Publishing Company's *Battles and Leaders of the Civil War*, which contained hundreds of firsthand accounts, mostly by high ranking officers. He borrowed the books from a certain Mrs. Armstrong to whom he wrote on April 2, 1893: "I have spent ten nights writing a story of the war on my own responsibility but I am not sure that my facts are real and the books won't tell me what I want to know so I must do it all over again, I guess."[6]

Crane could have learned a great deal about Chancellorsville from several accounts found in *Battles and Leaders*. Major General Darius

Couch, commander of the Union Second Corps at Chancellorsville, wrote an article entitled "The Chancellorsville Campaign," which gave a particularly detailed picture of the event. At the very start of Couch's article, Crane would have seen pictures of the corps badges of the Army of the Potomac as well as an account of how they were adopted. From Couch's account he could have learned about the Union and Confederate pickets talking to each other across the Rappahannock River, the cavalry raid by General Stoneman, and details of the actions of May 2 and May 3, 1863, when most of the fighting took place.

Following Couch's article was one entitled "The Successes and Failures of Chancellorsville," written by General Alfred Pleasonton, a cavalryman. The article contains a good description of the charge of the 8th Pennsylvania Cavalry, the only notable cavalry action of the battle, as well as the fighting that took place at Hazel Grove, a strategically important clearing near Chancellorsville. Both the charge and Hazel Grove are described in the novel.

Certainly Crane relied on *Battles and Leaders* to research his novel, but this work alone could not have provided the kind of firsthand accounts of the privates in the ranks that made his work so believable. For that kind of information, he looked instead to a local source.

Crane spent part of his youth in Port Jervis, a small city in western Orange County, New York, where his father was a Methodist minister. Local tradition has it that Crane liked to go to the park and talk to the veterans who gathered there in the shadow of an imposing monument to the men of the town who had served in the Union army.

Company F of the 124th New York State Volunteers was raised in Port Jervis. No doubt some of the old-timers Crane talked to were members of the regiment. These men proudly wore the Kearny Badge, a red diamond signifying their regiment had been part of the First Division, Third Corps, of the Union Army of the Potomac. The red diamond was known during the Civil War as the "red badge of courage," and Crane, who first entitled his novel *Henry Fleming, His Various Battles*, most likely felt the reference to the Kearny Badge more inspiring.

In the novel, Private Fleming is a member of the fictitious 304th New York Infantry. No such unit took the field from New York during the Civil War. The novel provides many clues that indicate the 124th New York was the model for the 304th. The 304th was a new regiment on its way to its first battle, as the 124th had been. The battle described in the novel is without a doubt the Battle of Chancellorsville, the first major battle fought by the "Orange Blossoms."

An examination of the units that fought at Chancellorsville reveals that only one of the new regiments from New York ever wore the red diamond, then or later. That regiment was the 124th New York. At Chancellorsville, the "Orange Blossoms" were part of the Third Division, Third Corps, and wore the blue diamond-shaped corps badge of that unit. Soon after Chancellorsville, the Third Corps was consolidated into two divisions, so severe was its casualties, and the 124th went to the First Division. The insignia worn by that famous unit was the red diamond badge. In the winter of 1864, the Third Corps was dissolved entirely, and the 124th went to the Second Corps, where the men were ordered to give up their Third Corps badges and wear the trefoil badge of that corps. They refused and defied all efforts to force them to submit. Some even wore the trefoil badge on the seat of their pants to show their displeasure. Finally, the order came down to allow the former Third Corps men to keep their old red diamond badges.

In the novel, Jim Conklin was the best friend of Henry Fleming. He was shot early in the battle and died in a scene full of symbolism. There was a *real* Jim Conklin, a private from Orange County who served in the 124th and was present at Chancellorsville. He survived the battle and the war to live into this century. Some of his possessions are still in the hands of his descendants, and among his belongings are two red cloth diamonds and an enameled red diamond bearing the number "124." The real Jim Conklin did not keep his blue diamonds or his blue trefoils, only his red diamonds, clearly revealing the pride felt by this "Orange Blossom" for his red badge of courage.

There is no evidence that Crane ever talked to Private Conklin. However, in Crane's short story, "The Veteran," written after *The Red Badge of Courage*, he drops several hints clearly intended to add more information to the story. Henry Fleming is now much older in

"The Veteran," which takes place long after the war is over. Henry tells some friends that Chancellorsville is the battle where he ran away and where Jim Conklin died, leaving no doubt as to the historical setting of the novel.

This story also links Henry's regiment with the historic Third Corps of the Union Army of the Potomac. Three times Henry mentions a grazing horse called "Sickles' colt," an indirect reference to Major General Daniel Edgar Sickles, the flamboyant commander of the Third Corps at Chancellorsville and Gettysburg. The combination of the red badge and Sickles colt can only mean that Fleming's regiment was part of this famous Third Corps.

Another link can be found in Crane's short college career. Although he was an indifferent student, he did well at Hudson River Institute, a prep school in Claverack, New York. At HRI, Crane gained a reputation as a drill instructor, and he studied under "The Reverend General" John Bullock Van Petten. The popular teacher often told his classes about his war experiences at the Battle of Antietam and the Battle of Winchester. The rout of Van Petten's regiment at Antietam is sometimes cited as the source for the scenes of rout in *The Red Badge of Courage*.

The real importance of HRI to Crane, however, is that one of its alumni was Colonel Charles Weygant, the author of *The History of the One Hundred Twenty-Fourth Regiment N.Y.S.V.*, the regimental history of the "Orange Blossoms." He was also the last commander of that famous regiment. Weygant attended Claverack Collegiate Institute, the predecessor of HRI, just before the Civil War began. He published his history in 1877, eleven years before Crane enrolled at HRI and no doubt saw to it that his old alma mater had a copy of his book.

When Weygant died in 1909, his obituary filled the front pages of the Newburgh, New York, newspapers. He had been the mayor of the city, the sheriff, and a real estate developer. His obituary contains a startling assertion:

> It is also generally supposed that Col. Weygant's book suggested to Stephen Crane the writing of his most powerful story The Red Badge of Courage. Young Crane had a brother, William H. Crane, who was a practicing lawyer in Port Jervis and the author spent

much of his early manhood in that neighborhood. It is known that he was familiar with Col. Weygant's book.

Stephen Crane once remarked that he wrote *The Red Badge of Courage* because he wanted to portray what it felt like to be in battle. He complained that books like *Battles and Leaders* told of troop movements and the experiences of generals but did not convey the feelings and emotions of the privates who fought on the battle lines.

A source for this kind of firsthand information may have been a local newspaper printed in Orange County during the war years. *The Whig Press* was founded by John Hasbrouck in 1851 in Middletown and remained in circulation until 1865. Hasbrouck was a supporter of the war and filled his paper with accounts of battles that kept his readers current on the progress of the Union troops, particularly the local regiments like the 56th New York Volunteers, Regan's Artillery Battery, the 19th New York Militia, and the 124th New York Volunteers. The paper ran articles on the whereabouts and activities of these units in almost every issue, but what would have interested someone like Crane was Hasbrouck's practice of reprinting letters from soldiers.

The post-Chancellorsville issues are especially interesting. It was the first big battle for the 124th, and while the Orange County residents were anxious for casualty reports, they also wanted to know how the local boys did in their first engagement.

A close examination of the *Whig Press* reveals that Crane may well have used this local newspaper as a source for the novel. Many of the letters were printed unsigned, but in some cases it is possible to ascertain who wrote them. Hasbrouck was most interested in letters written by members of Company K and Company E. Both companies were raised in or near Middletown and "K" was commanded by a popular school teacher, Captain William Jackson.

On May 27, 1863, a letter appeared in the Whig Press. It read, in part:

Morning came and no orders were received to start, and we began to think that it was a false alarm, like many others we had had. In the afternoon, an orderly riding in at break neck speed, and the sound of bugles in the neighboring camps blowing the 'strike tents' announced to us that the Army of the Potomac was really under way. . . . At an early hour we started for the Ford, crossing the pontoons about 9 o'clock. About noon we halted in the woods and had a good rest. At 5 heavy firing being heard in front 1 1/2 miles off, we were ordered to fall in and move up ready to act as support.

Compare this with the opening passages of the novel. Crane used the idea of delay and false rumors to contribute to Henry Fleming's growing uncertainty about how he would act once in battle. Crossing the pontoon bridges at United States Ford and the firing that was heard are also part of the narrative to the novel.

A letter published on June 3, 1863, refers to the red badge. A soldier, describing Confederate prisoners, wrote, "They said it was no matter whether they lay or stood up, the fire of the 'red-taped devils' fetched them, alluding to the pieces of orange tape worn by us as a badge."

Crane, in his usual indirect manner, did acknowledge his debt to editor Hasbrouck. The young officer of Henry Fleming's company was none other than Lt. Hasbrouck.

When Crane talked to the soldiers in the park in Port Jervis, he was talking to men who wore the Kearny Badge, the "red badge of courage." A veteran of the great battle of Chancellorsville must have come away with images that he would long remember. Surely he would have recounted the bayonet charge of his regiment that was new to battle but determined and ably led. This was the charge that made the the 124th famous. It was at Chancellorsville that the men began the practice of wearing orange ribbons in the buttonholes of their uniforms both as a mark of distinction and for easy identification of their casualties on the field, and the newspapers back home picked up the name "Orange Blossoms."

Stephen Crane never did reveal if any one unit served as a model for the 304th New York, and it is well that he did not. A story of such universal appeal cannot be the story of just one man in one battle. It is, after all, the story of a boy who confronted his fear and overcame it. Crane might just as well have written a story about facing up to the town bully, but instead he chose a subject about which he had no firsthand knowledge. He drew upon the experiences of the old soldiers in the park and in retelling the events of those momentous days, he created a story that has inspired others for generations.

On Monday, August 22, 1983, the Common Council of Port Jervis, New York, voted to change the name of The Stephen Crane Memorial Park at Orange Square to The Orange Square Veterans Park. Some local citizens argued that *The Red Badge of Courage* was an anti-war novel that glorified cowardice and desertion and that "Stephen Crane did a disservice to the many honorable veterans when he wrote *The Red Badge of Courage*." His name, they insisted, should be removed from a park that honored veterans.

"Stephen Crane was not a veteran. He did not fight in the Civil War. He sat in the park and got information from the veterans that were there." When Wilson Turner, commander of the V.F.W. Post No. 161 in Port Jervis spoke those words, he may not have realized it, but he best summarized the tribute that Crane paid to local veterans in his classic novel that is based, at least in part, on the exploits of the 124th New York State Volunteers.

1. Robert W. Stallman, *Stephen Crane: A Biography* (New York: George Braziller, 1968), 181.
2. Ibid., 183.
3. Ibid., 168.
4. Ibid., 166-167.
5. Stanley Wertheim and Paul Sorrentino, *The Correspondence of Stephen Crane* (New York: Columbia University Press, 1988), 178.
6. Ibid., 666

HISTORICAL SETTING

THE SETTING of *The Red Badge of Courage* is the Battle of Chancellorsville, which took place in the spring of 1863. The battle was fought in the "Wilderness" of northern Virginia, so named because of the dense forests and tangled underbrush that covered much of the area. The movements of the Union army were hindered by the Wilderness and the primitive condition of the road system running through it; the Confederates, more familiar with the area, used it to conceal their whereabouts. The sense of darkness and foreboding of this locale adds a great deal to the sense of terror and confusion that pervades Crane's novel.

During the winter of 1862–63, the Union Army of the Potomac, numbering over 130,000 men, encamped on the north side of the Rappahannock River at Falmouth, Virginia. Starting his command in January, Major General Joseph "Fighting Joe" Hooker worked hard to revive the sinking morale of his men by improving their rations and by instituting corps badges, insignia for each corps and division to foster a sense of group identity and pride. Frequent drills, inspections, and parades helped the men to feel like soldiers. The desertion rate fell as soldiers in efficient units were allowed furloughs home to their families.

Hooker had been an able division and corps commander known for his hard drinking, handsome countenance, and huge conceit. In an army in which everyone wore a beard or mustache, he was clean shaven; it was said that he did not want whiskers to hide his good looks. In an army famous for political conniving and infighting, he excelled at cutting support from under his superiors. President Abraham Lincoln personally warned Hooker that this atmosphere of contention he had helped to create in the army might one day turn against him.

The Confederate Army of Northern Virginia, just over 60,000 men strong and commanded by General Robert E. Lee, was camped on the south side of the river at Fredericksburg. There were squabbles and personality conflicts in this army, too, but, unlike their adversaries, the Southerners all were united behind their commander. They were victorious through most of 1862, but the winter was hard on the poorly equipped, malnourished troops, causing a sharp increase in the number of deaths and desertions among them.

The two armies faced each other, much as they had done all winter since the Union defeat at Fredericksburg in December 1862. Major General Ambrose Burnside, Hooker's predecessor, had attacked Lee, and the resulting Battle of Fredericksburg was a disaster. Union troops crossed the river and assaulted Lee, who had taken a strong position on high ground outside of town. Wave after wave of Burnside's men were cut down in the futile attacks. In the end, Burnside withdrew to his camp at Falmouth.

Every soldier knew that spring would bring a renewal of the fighting, and each had his own ideas about where and when the inevitable offensive would begin. Hooker devised a bold plan. By moving a sizable force up the north bank of the Rappahannock River, he could cross his men at lightly defended upstream fords and then fall upon the rear of Lee's army. He would leave some of his men in the area of Falmouth to make Lee think he was about to attack at Fredericksburg again, while three full corps, comprising 70,000 men, would move on Lee's flank. Once those troops were safely across, the bulk that remained behind would march to join the men already south of the river. Hooker predicted that the enemy either would "ingloriously fly" or fight it out in the open. In either case, he was sure he could whip the Rebels.

Hooker's plan had merit and its opening moves were accomplished with such speed that, for once, General Lee was taken by surprise. Confederate General E. P. Alexander considered this the most dangerous attack ever launched against the southern army. Lee quickly recovered the initiative, however, and made none of the moves that Hooker expected. Instead, Lee divided his force in the face of a superior enemy, something soldiers were taught never to do, and moved to the attack. He left some of his men behind to prevent the

Union Sixth Corps from advancing beyond Fredericksburg and marched the rest of his army west to meet Hooker in the Wilderness.

In the opening passages of *The Red Badge of Courage*, Crane describes the encampment at Falmouth on the north side of the Rappahannock from where one can see the "red eyes" blinking across the river, the campfires of the Confederates at Fredericksburg. One morning, Private Henry Fleming finds himself in the dark in formation with his regiment, awaiting orders. Soon they are marching west, up river, with the rising sun to their backs.

The main action of the novel is based on the events of Saturday and Sunday, May 2 and 3, 1863. On Saturday, Lee, who quickly had taken the measure of his opponent, held Hooker in place and once again divided his own smaller force. He sent General Thomas "Stonewall" Jackson on his famous march by the back roads and trails of the Wilderness to gain the right flank of the Union army. The march and the attack that followed crushed the Union Eleventh Corps and drove in the exposed flank. Jackson's goal was to cut off the Union army from the river crossings and destroy it. Disaster for the North was averted only by the coming of night and by the timely arrival of backup units, including Major General Daniel Edgar Sickles' Third Corps, which blunted Jackson's drive.

Just before dawn on Sunday, May 3, the Confederates renewed their attack but were stalled by Sickles' men. All morning the Third Corps and parts of the Eleventh and Twelfth Corps battled the best units of the Rebel army to a standstill while thousands of other Union men, close at hand, did not fire a shot. These troops and their corps commanders knew that the fury of the Rebel assault had been spent; they were only awaiting word from Hooker to launch a counterattack.

On the eve of battle Hooker boasted, "My plans are perfect and when I put them into operation, may God have mercy on General Lee for I shall have none." But Hooker never issued the order that would put his plan in action. Instead he was wounded and his confidence was further shaken at being on the field against the legendary Robert E. Lee. Instead of sending his fresh troops forward, Hooker ordered the whole army to fall back and withdraw to the old camp at Falmouth. His plan had been a good one, but his execution was so flawed that it turned what should have been a stellar victory into another shameful defeat.

This dismal performance in the face of an enemy fewer in number brought about Hooker's rapid fall from favor. In June, as both armies marched north toward Gettysburg, Hooker argued with his superiors and submitted his resignation to President Lincoln, who accepted it only days before the Battle of Gettysburg.

As for General Lee, because of the audacious use he made of his troops, Chancellorsville is considered his greatest battle. It was not a decisive victory, however, as the Union army simply fell back to regroup and was soon ready to fight again. Casualties on both sides were heavy, but the North could draw upon far larger numbers than the South to replace its fallen soldiers.

Even though the Confederates repulsed the Union troops, they were seriously drained of manpower. Even worse, Stonewall Jackson was mortally wounded by his own men during the battle. His absence from the Battle of Gettysburg, less than two months later, may well have been the decisive factor in the Confederate defeat.

The Battle of Chancellorsville boosted the spirits of the South and encouraged Lee to launch his second invasion of the North. It further depressed the North and caused the removal of yet another Union general.

But the battle is no less important because it served as the setting for *The Red Badge of Courage*, which would come to be recognized as a classic of American literature. Stephen Crane's novel is based upon the experiences of real soldiers, including some "Orange Blossoms" who sat in the park in Port Jervis and told the young author about the day they twice charged the Rebs and earned the red badge of courage.

ARMY ORGANIZATION

THE UNION ARMY of the Potomac was restructured in the winter of 1863 while encamped at Falmouth, Virginia. The new commander, and the man who would lead the army at the Battle of Chancellorsville, was Major General Joseph Hooker, a graduate of West Point, class of 1837. He organized his army into seven infantry corps and one cavalry corps; the corps were referred to by number or by the name of the corps commander. Artillery batteries, usually six cannons each, were assigned to the various corps.

At Chancellorsville, each of Hooker's corps but one had three divisions; the 12th Corps had two divisions. Each division had from two to five brigades; obviously the corps were not of equal size. The brigade, composed of two or more regiments, was the basic fighting unit of the Union army. A brigade was supposed to be commanded by a one-star (brigadier) general, but promotion to such a rank was slow, so quite often a brigade was led by a colonel.

Colonel Emlin Franklin's Brigade was composed of the 86th New York, the 124th New York, and the 122nd Pennsylvania. On the eve of the Battle of Chancellorsville, Franklin's Brigade had not yet been tested as a fighting unit. The 86th was a veteran regiment that had been in battle before; the 122nd was a nine-month volunteer regiment with limited experience. The 124th had been present at Fredericksburg, but not engaged, so Chancellorsville was their first real taste of battle.

The 124th, like most regiments, had a strength of about 1,000 men when it went off to war; but many men proved to be physically unfit for duty and were sent home, others died of disease, some were transferred to other units, and some deserted. The regiment marched to Chancellorsville with about 560 men. The 124th started with ten companies of about 100 men each and a color guard, but by the time the regiment went into action, most of its companies were well below full strength. This was typical in the Army of the Potomac at mid-war. However, a 560-man regiment was still a big unit. In the novel, a veteran from another regiment, upon seeing the 304th New York, asked what brigade was marching past; he was told that this was not a brigade, but a regiment. "O Gawd!" the veteran laughed. He knew that they had to be a new unit to have so many men, and therefore deserved little respect.

In the summer of 1862, President Lincoln called for 300,000 three-year volunteers. Orange County, New York, recruiting mostly by town, was able to raise one regiment of local men. Company C, for example, was made up of men from Cornwall; Company K was recruited primarily from Middletown. Other companies were comprised of men from several towns, as there were not enough recruits from any one town to make a full company.

The companies were formed in line of battle to ensure that the left and right flank companies were commanded by the most senior officers and that there was always a balance of senior and junior company commanders next to each other. In formation, the left battalion of the 124th was made up of companies B, G, K, E, H and the right battalion was made up of companies C, I, D, F, A. The Color Guard, whose function was to protect the flag at all costs, stood between the battalions.

The 124th New York was commanded by Colonel Augustus Van Horne Ellis. He was not a professional soldier, but had been active in the militia made up of part-time soldiers much like those in the present-day National Guard or Army Reserve. He had been present at the First Battle of Bull Run in 1861 as part of the 71st New York State Militia. There he commanded a two-gun artillery battery in some very heavy fighting. It was agreed by the local recruitment committee that he had the experience needed to qualify for command. He chose as his second in command Lt. Colonel Francis Cummins, a veteran of the Mexican War who had served with the 1st Iowa and later with the 6th Iowa, which saw action at the Battle of Shiloh. Both Ellis and Cummins had commanded men under fire in battle; that kind of military experience was at a premium in the early days of the Civil War.

Charles Weygant of Newburgh, New York, was another story. He was able to gather enough volunteers quickly so as to have his group designated Company A. He had had no military experience whatsoever, but he was made the senior company commander, and therefore was first in line for promotion to the rank of major. At the Battle of Gettysburg, Weygant was the senior officer not killed or wounded, so it became his duty to lead what remained of the regiment from the field. He went on to command the regiment in 1864 and was the last colonel of the old Orange Blossoms. After the war, he wrote *The History of the One Hundred and Twenty-Fourth N.Y.S.V.*, published in 1877.

Politics played a big part in the formation of state regiments. The governors preferred to create new regiments rather than reinforce existing ones. Each officer's commission had to be signed by the governor of his state, which made it a political debt requiring repayment. The governor made many political allies each time he created a new regiment. Meanwhile, the existing regiments dwindled in strength and had to send their men home to recruit more members. Later in the war, draftees were sent to fill the ranks, but they were generally regarded with disdain, as were the men who were paid bounties to enlist.

On the eve of the Battle of Chancellorsville, the Army of the Potomac was composed of a mixture of veteran and untried regiments. Corps, division, and brigade commanders were, for the most part, veterans of the battlefield. They were ready and eager for what should have been a decisive victory for the Union. If there was a weakness among them, it was at the top: Joe Hooker, who was in command at Chancellorsville, balked at the telling moments. But the soldiers in the ranks, who were used to defeat and the maligning of their fighting ability, emerged from Chancellorsville with confidence. It was their stoic determination, not the ability of their commanding officers, that would see the army through to final victory.

WEAPONS OF THE CIVIL WAR

In THE YEARS just prior to the American Civil War, there were significant technological advances in weaponry. The new weapons meant that, for the first time in warfare, a man in the ranks could actually hit what he was aiming at with a great degree of certainty. The weapons were accurate and the bullets that they fired were accurate at long range. Accuracy at long range was a deadly advantage against thousands of young men who were led into battle by officers still using tactics from the eighteenth century.

In previous wars, infantrymen carried smooth-bore, muzzle-loading muskets; powder and bullets, usually round lead balls, were rammed down their barrels with ramrods. The balls had to be slightly smaller than the diameter of the bore to fit into the muzzle. When the powder charge exploded, some of the gas that was to propel the ball escaped and was wasted. Furthermore, because it was smaller than the bore, the ball would hit against the sides of the bore, loosing speed and making its path upon leaving the barrel hard to predict. Some smooth-bore weapons lacked sights altogether, since they could not hit what they were aimed at anyway. The effective range of smooth-bore musket fire varied, but it was rarely more than 150 yards. Battling armies before the Civil War would march to within musket range, fire a few volleys, and charge with bayonets. Volley firing insured that, even though the individual soldier might not hit what he aimed at, he might hit something. If several thousand muskets were fired in the general direction of the enemy all at once, some damage at least would be done to the other side.

The nature of the weapons dictated battlefield tactics. Soldiers were trained to move in lock step in compact formations so that their officers could direct their massed volley fire at the enemy. Military manuals of the day contained complex maneuvers so that the firepower of the muskets could be used to the best advantage. Officers were trained to mass their men in order to mass their fire. Of course, massed formations were also inviting targets for the enemy's volley or artillery fire. American manuals recommended a battle line two ranks deep, the men in the rear rank firing over the shoulders of the men in the front rank. The men marched to battle in column, four men abreast, so it was quite a feat to bring a column of four thousand men, for instance, into a line of battle all facing in one direction. Soldiers of this era drilled for hours until they were able to move quickly and with a minimum of confusion; the maneuvers were all designed to compensate for the musket's limited range.

The rifle was different; the inside of the barrel was not smooth but instead was cut with spiraling grooves. Their purpose was to cause the bullet to spin, making it more aerodynamically stable. A cloth patch was wrapped around the ball to make it fit snug as the ball and patch were rammed down the barrel. When the powder charge ignited, the patch helped seal the explosive gasses behind the ball making it travel faster and farther. The patch served a second important purpose: it dug into the rifling grooves and, as the ball and patch traveled out of the barrel, a spin was imparted on the projectile. There was a cost for this increased accuracy; the patch made the loading process more difficult. In some cases, the fit was so tight that the ramrod had to be driven home with a hammer and reloading could take several minutes. Riflemen had been present on many battlefields long before the Civil War, but the advantages of massed, inaccurate musket fire were found to outweigh the disadvantages of slow, accurate rifle fire.

Captain Claude Etienne Minie of the French army changed all that. He developed a cone-shaped lead bullet, later modified to include a hollow base, that was small enough to be rammed easily down a barrel. The bullet was still loaded in the same way, but, when the powder charge ignited, the force of the blast pressed the narrow rim of the lead bullet tightly against the rifling. Explosive gas was trapped tightly behind the bullet, greatly increasing its speed, while the lead gripping the barrel's spiral grooves gave the bullet spin. With this weapon, a bullet could travel much farther and with much greater force.

By the time of the Civil War, flintlocks had been replaced with a percussion cap ignition system. A copper percussion cap fit over a nipple-shaped vent. When the cap was hit with the gun hammer, it exploded, sending a spark through the nipple into the powder charge and causing it to ignite. The cap system was more impervious to the elements than the old flintlock system had been, so the weapon was dependable in wind or rain.

At the start of the Civil War, soldiers on both sides carried a wide variety of weapons, some issued by the states or federal government, some brought from home. The government-issued weapons included War of 1812 flintlocks or whatever else could be found in storage at the arsenals. As the Civil War progressed, the new rifle muskets replaced all others for the infantrymen. While these weapons looked like the tried-and-true muskets, they were, in fact, modern rifles. As domestic production could not keep up with demand, American .58 caliber Springfield rifle muskets were supplemented by .577 caliber Enfield rifle muskets imported from Great Britain in huge numbers by both the North and the South.

The ammunition for the rifle musket was delivered to the soldiers in paper packages of ten cartridges per package. Each cartridge was a paper tube containing the bullet and a powder charge. Soldiers were trained to take the cartridge from the cartridge box, tear the paper with their teeth, pour the powder and bullet down the barrel, and then ram the paper down on top with the ramrod. In some cases, one cartridge in each package contained a special cleaner round designed to scour the fouling from inside the barrel. Black powder, the propellant used during the Civil War, did not burn completely and left a gummy residue that built up quickly inside the barrel. After about twenty rounds were fired, it became more and more difficult to get the bullet rammed down the barrel and sometimes the soldier was left with a weapon that could not be loaded at all. He could either step out of the line to clean his rifle or, more likely, discard it for a less used weapon dropped by a dead or wounded comrade. Fouling caused even greater problems with the Enfield because, while the bore was .577 caliber, .58 caliber ammunition was standard issue.

The effects of the rifle musket on warfare were immediate but not immediately understood. In the early battles of the Civil War, the armies had marched to within a few hundred feet of each other, blazed away for a while, and then charged. With rifle muskets, however, the massed firing became deadly accurate and no one was prepared for the resulting slaughter. Casualties at the First Bull Run were unlike anything seen before in America. Each battle brought the deaths or wounding of thousands; yet two years later, at the Battle of Chancellorsville, battlefield tactics had changed little, if at all, to adapt to the new weaponry.

The rifle musket brought about the shift of advantage in battle from the tactical offensive to the tactical defensive. Bayonet charges against muskets might have succeeded; bayonet charges against massed rifle fire was less often successful and always costly to the attacker. By 1864, it finally became clear that a rifleman behind a log breastwork could hold out against several times his number. The defender, dug in, now held the advantage.

The rifle musket also took its toll on artillery. Gunners working the cannons were now within easy rifle range, as were the horses pulling heavy artillery pieces. At Chancellorsville, on Sunday morning, May 3, 1863, the Confederates could not overrun the Union artillery position by direct assault because there were too many cannons firing canister at them from close range. Some of the Confederate soldiers advanced up the opposite side of Plank Road and, using the road for cover, began picking off Union gunners and horses. Several Federal brigades charged and drove the enemy away before too much damage was done. This exact scenario appears in *The Red Badge of Courage* as the first charge of the 304th New York.

Despite the presence of modern weapons on the battlefield, most generals still relied on tactics of massed attacks. A few understood the impact of modern rifle fire and even suggested ways to minimize its effects. They advocated digging in when on the defense and avoiding massed head-on assults on the offense. They were ridiculed, and their advice was ignored until much later in the war.

CORPS BADGES

IN AN EFFORT to improve morale in the Army of the Potomac, General Hooker regularized corps badges, insignia intended to instill unit identification and pride among the men.

The idea for the badges began with General Phil Kearny, the famous commander of the Third, and later the First, Division of the Third Corps. It was said that Kearny could curse for ten minutes and never use the same expression twice. He once berated some junior officers at great length only to learn afterwards that they were not from his division.

From then on to make sure that he always would be able to recognize his men, he had each of his officers wear a red patch on his hat. The enlisted men liked the idea and also began wearing the red patch. How the patch developed into a diamond is not clear, but soon enough the red diamond was recognized by friend and enemy alike as the mark of elite troops. "Now you are marked men," Kearny told the soldiers of his division. "The enemy will quail when he sees that scarlet patch, and well he may! In the attack you have always driven him; when assailed you have always repulsed him!" Kearny was killed in 1862, but the men of his division kept wearing their red diamonds.

In the winter of 1863, Hooker developed Kearny's idea, ordering his Chief of Staff, Major General Daniel Butterfield, to devise a distinguishing badge for each corps in the Army of the Potomac. On March 21, 1863, Butterfield's circular outlined how the various corps and divisions would be distinguished. In each corps, a red patch designated First Division, a white patch, Second Division, and a blue patch, Third Division. Thus, a white trefoil meant Second Corps, Second Division, and a red crescent meant Eleventh Corps, First Division.

These badges, developed and adopted on the eve of the Battle of Chancellorsville, were the forerunners of the modern army's shoulder patches.

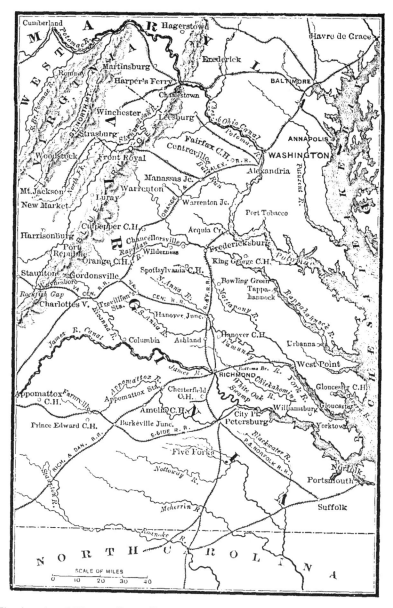

The battle of Chancellorsville took place in an area of Virginia known as the "Wilderness." Located about midway between Washington, D.C., and the Confederate capital at Richmond, the crossroads village of Chancellorsville was about ten miles west of Fredricksburg.

1

The story begins at Falmouth, Virginia, the winter camp of the Army of the Potomac, the major Union army in the east. It is the spring of 1863. Mentioned here is the Rappahannock River; the hostile camp fires across the river mark the camps of General Robert E. Lee's Army of Northern Virginia.

company street: In an encampment, the tents or in this case log huts, were arranged in rows known as company streets which were laid out according to strict military guidelines. At Falmouth where more than 100,000 Union soldiers camped, warmer, more permanent quarters were built. A group of four to six men would work together to built a log foundation and walls; pieces of canvas tent material served as a roof. A fireplace was build with a chimney made of stone and wood plastered with mud to keep it from catching fire.

teamster: Civilian wagon drivers, called teamsters, were hired by the army to drive mules used to pull the supply wagons. While the mules were strong, they were also stubborn and hard to handle. Teamsters were often recent immigrants or blacks who could find no other employment because of the prejudice against them; teamsters were not well thought of by Civil War soldiers.

CHAPTER I.

THE COLD passed reluctantly from the earth, and the retiring fogs revealed an army stretched out on the hills, resting. As the landscape changed from brown to green, the army awakened, and began to tremble with eagerness at the noise of rumors. It cast its eyes upon the roads, which were growing from long troughs of liquid mud to proper thoroughfares. A river, amber-tinted in the shadow of its banks, purled at the army's feet; and at night, when the stream had become of a sorrowful blackness, one could see across it the red, eyelike gleam of hostile campfires set in the low brows of distant hills.

Once a certain tall soldier developed virtues and went resolutely to wash a shirt. He came flying back from a brook waving his garment bannerlike. He was swelled with a tale he had heard from a reliable friend, who had heard it from a truthful cavalryman, who had heard it from his trustworthy brother, one of the orderlies at division headquarters. He adopted the important air of a herald in red and gold.

"We're goin' t' move t' morrah—sure," he said pompously to a group in the company street. "We're goin' 'way up the river, cut across, an' come around in behint 'em."

To his attentive audience he drew a loud and elaborate plan of a very brilliant campaign. When he had finished, the blue-clothed men scattered into small arguing groups between the rows of squat brown huts. A Negro teamster who had been dancing upon a cracker box with the hilarious encouragement of twoscore soldiers was deserted. He sat mournfully down. Smoke drifted lazily from a multitude of quaint chimneys.

"It's a lie! that's all it is—a thunderin' lie!" said another private loudly. His smooth face was flushed, and his hands were thrust sulkily into his trousers' pockets. He took the matter as an affront to him.

3

cracker box: Hardtack, also called hard bread, was a staple food for soldiers in both Union and Confederate armies; it was a flour and water cracker about three inches on a side and one-half inch thick. Hardtack was baked twice to preserve it and packed in large wooden boxes (cracker boxes) for shipment to the armies. Ten crackers was the standard issue for each day. Sometimes the crackers got moldy or became infested with maggots, weevils, or other "critters," as the soldiers called them. If a soldier found critters in his crackers, he had several options to salvage his food. He might hold it over the fire, causing the critters to scamper out, or he might crumble his crackers into boiling coffee—no easy task if the rations were old and rock-hard—so the offending insects would be killed and float to the top, where they could be skimmed off. He then could consume the hardtack and coffee together. Some soldiers simply ate their rations after dark so as not to see what else they might be taking in.

"I don't believe the derned old army's ever going to move. We're set. I've got ready to move eight times in the last two weeks, and we ain't moved yet."

The tall soldier felt called upon to defend the truth of the rumor he himself had introduced. He and the loud one came near to fighting over it.

A corporal began to swear before the assemblage. He had just put a costly board floor in his house, he said. During the early spring he had refrained from adding extensively to the comfort of his environment because he had felt that the army might start on the march at any moment. Of late, however, he had been impressed that they were in a sort of eternal camp.

Many of the men engaged in a spirited debate. One outlined in a peculiarly lucid manner all the plans of the commanding general. He was opposed by men who advocated that there were other plans of campaign. They clamored at each other, numbers making futile bids for the popular attention. Meanwhile, the soldier who had fetched the rumor bustled about with much importance. He was continually assailed by questions.

"What's up, Jim?"

"Th' army's goin' t' move."

"Ah, what yeh talkin' about? How yeh know it is?"

"Well, yeh kin b'lieve me er not, jest as yeh like. I don't care a hang."

There was much food for thought in the manner in which he replied. He came near to convincing them by disdaining to produce proofs. They grew much excited over it.

There was a youthful private who listened with eager ears to the words of the tall soldier and to the varied comments of his comrades. After receiving a fill of discussions concerning marches and attacks, he went to his hut and crawled through an intricate hole that served it as a door. He wished to be alone with some new thoughts that had lately come to him.

He lay down on a wide bank that stretched across the end of the room. In the other end, cracker boxes were made to serve as furniture. They were grouped about the fireplace. A picture from an illustrated weekly was upon the log walls, and three rifles were paralleled on

DIANNE
DREWES

The "Tales of great movements" mentioned here probably recount the early successes of Major General George B. McClellan on the Peninsula of Virginia. In the spring and summer of 1862, McClellan's army came within sight of Richmond before General Robert E. Lee drove them away. The ever cautious McClellan, convinced that he was greatly outnumbered, when in fact he had many more troops than his enemy, withdrew.

This reversal, coupled with defeats by other Union armies north of Richmond, made Northerners despondent, and many began to wonder if the war could be won. It is interesting to note that, just as Henry Fleming read about distant battles in the newspapers, so did the soldiers. Northern newspapers were readily available and very popular among the soldiers. Sometimes they were mailed from home by family members, but often they could be purchased right in camp. Southerners were also eager to get hold of these newspapers because they gave detailed accounts of the Yankee army's conditions and casualties. On occasion, the papers even speculated about where the Union army might strike next.

pegs. Equipments hung on handy projections, and some tin dishes lay upon a small pile of firewood. A folded tent was serving as a roof. The sunlight, without, beating upon it, made it glow a light yellow shade. A small window shot an oblique square of whiter light upon the cluttered floor. The smoke from the fire at times neglected the clay chimney and wreathed into the room, and this flimsy chimney of clay and sticks made endless threats to set ablaze the whole establishment.

The youth was in a little trance of astonishment. So they were at last going to fight. On the morrow, perhaps, there would be a battle, and he would be in it. For a time he was obliged to labor to make himself believe. He could not accept with assurance an omen that he was about to mingle in one of those great affairs of the earth.

He had, of course, dreamed of battles all his life—of vague and bloody conflicts that had thrilled him with their sweep and fire. In visions he had seen himself in many struggles. He had imagined peoples secure in the shadow of his eagle-eyed prowess. But awake he had regarded battles as crimson blotches on the pages of the past. He had put them as things of the bygone with his thought-images of heavy crowns and high castles. There was a portion of the world's history which he had regarded as the time of wars, but it, he thought, had been long gone over the horizon and had disappeared forever.

From his home his youthful eyes had looked upon the war in his own country with distrust. It must be some sort of a play affair. He had long despaired of witnessing a Greeklike struggle. Such would be no more, he had said. Men were better, or more timid. Secular and religious education had effaced the throat-grappling instinct, or else firm finance held in check the passions.

He had burned several times to enlist. Tales of great movements shook the land. They might not be distinctly Homeric, but there seemed to be much glory in them. He had read of marches, sieges, conflicts, and he had longed to see it all. His busy mind had drawn for him large pictures extravagant in color, lurid with breathless deeds.

But his mother had discouraged him. She had affected to look with some contempt upon the quality of his war ardor and patriotism. She could calmly seat herself and with no apparent difficulty give him

By the summer of 1862, it became clear that the war would not be won in one great battle, or even in one great campaign. Early in the war, militia units had been used to defend Washington, D.C., but many state militia regiments could only be called out once a year for service outside of the state and then only for a short period of time. In the first year of war, many volunteer regiments were recruited. Because everyone was optimistic about a quick end to the war, many of these first troops enlisted for short periods of from nine months to two years. As the war ground on into the summer of 1862, President Abraham Lincoln asked the states to provide 300,000 three-year volunteers. However, the reverses suffered by the Union forces made recruitment difficult; few men wanted to enlist in a cause that many felt was already lost. Then, in the late summer of 1862, news came of a planned invasion of the north by the Confederates. Many of the volunteer regiments, like the 124th New York State Volunteers, were quickly filled by men eager to turn back the invaders. Henry Fleming, also eager to enlist despite his mother's objections, appears to be caught up in the patriotic furor.

many hundreds of reasons why he was of vastly more importance on the farm than on the field of battle. She had had certain ways of expression that told him that her statements on the subject came from a deep conviction. Moreover, on her side, was his belief that her ethical motive in the argument was impregnable.

At last, however, he had made firm rebellion against this yellow light thrown upon the color of his ambitions. The newspapers, the gossip of the village, his own picturings, had aroused him to an uncheckable degree. They were in truth fighting finely down there. Almost every day the newspapers printed accounts of a decisive victory.

One night, as he lay in bed, the winds had carried to him the clangoring of the church bell as some enthusiast jerked the rope frantically to tell the twisted news of a great battle. This voice of the people rejoicing in the night had made him shiver in a prolonged ecstasy of excitement. Later, he had gone down to his mother's room and had spoken thus: "Ma, I'm going to enlist."

"Henry, don't you be a fool," his mother had replied. She had then covered her face with the quilt. There was an end to the matter for that night.

Nevertheless, the next morning he had gone to a town that was near his mother's farm and had enlisted in a company that was forming there. When he had returned home his mother was milking the brindle cow. Four others stood waiting. "Ma, I've enlisted," he had said to her diffidently. There was a short silence. "The Lord's will be done, Henry," she had finally replied, and had then continued to milk the brindle cow.

When he had stood in the doorway with his soldier's clothes on his back, and with the light of excitement and expectancy in his eyes almost defeating the glow of regret for the home bonds, he had seen two tears leaving their trails on his mother's scarred cheeks.

Still, she had disappointed him by saying nothing whatever about returning with his shield or on it. He had privately primed himself for a beautiful scene. He had prepared certain sentences which he thought could be used with touching effect. But her words destroyed his plans. She had doggedly peeled potatoes and addressed him as follows: "You watch out, Henry, an' take good care of yerself in this

This departure scene, while it was not to Henry's liking, must have been repeated thousands of times throughout the North that summer of 1862. Henry wears his "soldiers cloths," to which his mother adds socks and shirts. This was typical. In most Civil War units, uniform parts varied according to the strictness of the commanding officers and individual tastes. Soldiers were issued standard clothing, but boots, socks, shirts, vests, gloves, scarfs, and even hats could be purchased or sent from home. The colors and styles were often quite different from government issue. Well-meaning relatives gave the departing men revolvers, portable writing desks, books, preserved food, and a wide variety of other items that were so heavy and burdenson that the men threw them away on the first long march.

This illustration, drawn from an original photograph of the Civil War era, shows soldiers enjoying some of the vices Henry's mother warned him about. Drinking and gambling were popular pastimes in both the Union and Confederate armies. While anti-drinking (temperance) movements were popular at the time, there is no question that alcoholism was a big problem in the armies.

here fighting business—you watch out, an' take good care of yerself. Don't go a-thinkin' you can lick the hull rebel army at the start, because yeh can't. Yer jest one little feller amongst a hull lot of others, and yeh've got to keep quiet an' do what they tell yeh. I know how you are, Henry.

"I've knet yeh eight pair of socks, Henry, and I've put in all yer best shirts, because I want my boy to be jest as warm and comf'able as anybody in the army. Whenever they get holes in 'em, I want yeh to send 'em right-away back to me, so's I kin dern 'em.

"An' allus be careful an' choose yer comp'ny. There's lots of bad men in the army, Henry. The army makes 'em wild, and they like nothing better than the job of leading off a young feller like you, as ain't never been away from home much and has allus had a mother, an' a-learning 'em to drink and swear. Keep clear of them folks, Henry. I don't want yeh to ever do anything, Henry, that yeh would be 'shamed to let me know about. Jest think as if I was a-watchin' yeh. If yeh keep that in yer mind allus, I guess yeh'll come out about right.

"Yeh must allus remember yer father, too, child, an' remember he never drunk a drop of licker in his life, and seldom swore a cross oath.

"I don't know what else to tell yeh, Henry, excepting that yeh must never do no shirking, child, on my account. If so be a time comes when yeh have to be kilt or do a mean thing, why, Henry, don't think of anything 'cept what's right, because there's many a woman has to bear up 'ginst sech things these times, and the Lord 'll take keer of us all.

"Don't forget about the socks and the shirts, child; and I've put a cup of blackberry jam with yer bundle, because I know yeh like it above all things. Good-by, Henry. Watch out, and be a good boy."

He had, of course, been impatient under the ordeal of this speech. It had not been quite what he expected, and he had borne it with an air of irritation. He departed feeling vague relief.

Still, when he had looked back from the gate, he had seen his mother kneeling among the potato parings. Her brown face, upraised, was stained with tears, and her spare form was quivering. He bowed his head and went on, feeling suddenly ashamed of his purposes.

In the late summer and early fall of 1862, thousands of new three-year volunteers departed their homes in the North and headed south toward the battlefields of Virginia. They were cheered and fed by the citizens along the railroad route. In letters home, soldiers frequently mentioned the stopover at the Cooper Shop Volunteer Refreshment Saloon in Philadelphia, where the citizens of that city provided a sumptuous banquet for them. On September 8, 1862, the 124th New York was fed at the Cooper Shop, as were recruits from the 123rd New York, 11th Vermont, 37th Massachusetts, 40th Massachusetts, 3rd New Jersey, and 12th New Jersey. In all, nearly twenty-five hundred soldiers were served free meals there on what was probably a typical day.

From his home he had gone to the seminary to bid adieu to many schoolmates. They had thronged about him with wonder and admiration. He had felt the gulf now between them and had swelled with calm pride. He and some of his fellows who had donned blue were quite overwhelmed with privileges for all of one afternoon, and it had been a very delicious thing. They had strutted.

A certain light-haired girl had made vivacious fun at his martial spirit, but there was another and darker girl whom he had gazed at steadfastly, and he thought she grew demure and sad at sight of his blue and brass. As he had walked down the path between the rows of oaks, he had turned his head and detected her at a window watching his departure. As he perceived her, she had immediately begun to stare up through the high tree branches at the sky. He had seen a good deal of flurry and haste in her movement as she changed her attitude. He often thought of it.

On the way to Washington his spirit had soared. The regiment was fed and caressed at station after station until the youth had believed that he must be a hero. There was a lavish expenditure of bread and cold meats, coffee, and pickles and cheese. As he basked in the smiles of the girls and was patted and complimented by the old men, he had felt growing within him the strength to do mighty deeds of arms.

After complicated journeyings with many pauses, there had come months of monotonous life in a camp. He had had the belief that real war was a series of death struggles with small time in between for sleep and meals; but since his regiment had come to the field the army had done little but sit still and try to keep warm.

He was brought then gradually back to his old ideas. Greeklike struggles would be no more. Men were better, or more timid. Secular and religious education had effaced the throat-grappling instinct, or else firm finance held in check the passions.

He had grown to regard himself merely as a part of a vast blue demonstration. His province was to look out, as far as he could, for his personal comfort. For recreation he could twiddle his thumbs and speculate on the thoughts which must agitate the minds of the generals. Also, he was drilled and drilled and reviewed, and drilled and drilled and reviewed.

Pickets: Both armies used picket lines and forward scouts to keep watch on each other. Picket lines were established several miles from the main camp and the regiments rotated on a regular basis doing picket duty. The duty was more unpleasant in winter because it took the soldiers away from the relative warmth and comfort of the camp. Pickets could be court-martialled and, if found guilty, shot for sleeping on duty. Communication with the enemy was forbidden, but curiosity sometimes got the best of pickets on both sides and led to trading Yankee coffee and newspapers for Rebel tobacco. The officers frowned on such exchanges but the soldiers, bored with picket duty, did it just the same.

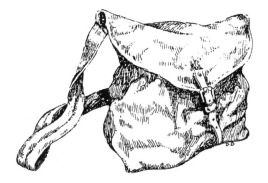

Haversack: a canvas bag, tarred to make it waterproof. The haversack was used to carry food and personal items such as knife and fork, tooth brush, tin plate, needle and thread, etc. The haversack often contained an inner muslin bag that could be removed for cleaning.

"Fresh fish": Soldiers who had been in a battle were veterans; it was said that they had "seen the elephant." Those who had not as yet been in battle were said to be "green," "babies," or "fresh fish," and got no respect from the veterans. Of the 124th New York, very few of the officers or men had been in the army before. Officers studied military manuals to learn commands to use the next day in drills. Henry's whole regiment is green, but the soldiers from other regiments camped nearby have seen the elephant and are not about to let anyone forget it.

The only foes he had seen were some pickets along the river bank. They were a sun-tanned, philosophical lot, who sometimes shot reflectively at the blue pickets. When reproached for this afterward, they usually expressed sorrow, and swore by their gods that the guns had exploded without their permission. The youth, on guard duty one night, conversed across the stream with one of them. He was a slightly ragged man, who spat skillfully between his shoes and possessed a great fund of bland and infantile assurance. The youth liked him personally.

"Yank," the other had informed him, "yer a right dum good feller." This sentiment, floating to him upon the still air, had made him temporarily regret war.

Various veterans had told him tales. Some talked of gray, bewhiskered hordes who were advancing with relentless curses and chewing tobacco with unspeakable valor; tremendous bodies of fierce soldiery who were sweeping along like the Huns. Others spoke of tattered and eternally hungry men who fired despondent powders. "They'll charge through hell's fire an' brimstone t' git a holt on a haversack, an' sech stomachs ain't a-lastin' long," he was told. From the stories, the youth imagined the red, live bones sticking out through slits in the faded uniforms.

Still, he could not put a whole faith in veterans' tales, for recruits were their prey. They talked much of smoke, fire, and blood, but he could not tell how much might be lies. They persistently yelled "Fresh fish!" at him, and were in no wise to be trusted.

However, he perceived now that it did not greatly matter what kind of soldiers he was going to fight, so long as they fought, which fact no one disputed. There was a more serious problem. He lay in his bunk pondering upon it. He tried to mathematically prove to himself that he would not run from a battle.

Previously he had never felt obliged to wrestle too seriously with this question. In his life he had taken certain things for granted, never challenging his belief in ultimate success, and bothering little about means and roads. But here he was confronted with a thing of moment. It had suddenly appeared to him that perhaps in a battle he might run. He was forced to admit that as far as war was concerned he knew nothing of himself.

Knapsack: Many soldiers were issued knapsacks soon after they joined their regiments. Knapsacks were used to carry extra clothing and items that would not fit into haversacks. On top of the knapsack, the soldier would carry his blanket rolled inside a piece of shelter tent. Soldiers on the march quickly learned to lighten their loads as much as possible, often discarding the knapsacks and rolling extra clothing and equipment with their blankets, which were tied at both ends and slung across the shoulders. It was common practice for the troops to drop the knapsacks into a large pile before going into battle. A soldier who was sick or exhausted was left to guard the knapsacks until the regiment returned to claim them. At Chancellorsville, the members of the 124th New York were never able to return to their pile of knapsacks and so lost a great deal of clothing and personal items to the enemy.

A sufficient time before he would have allowed the problem to kick its heels at the outer portals of his mind, but now he felt compelled to give serious attention to it.

A little panic-fear grew in his mind. As his imagination went forward to a fight, he saw hideous possibilities. He contemplated the lurking menaces of the future, and failed in an effort to see himself standing stoutly in the midst of them.

He recalled his visions of broken-bladed glory, but in the shadow of the impending tumult he suspected them to be impossible pictures.

He sprang from the bunk and began to pace nervously to and fro. "Good Lord, what's th' matter with me?" he said aloud.

He felt that in this crisis his laws of life were useless. Whatever he had learned of himself was here of no avail. He was an unknown quantity. He saw that he would again be obliged to experiment as he had in early youth. He must accumulate information of himself, and meanwhile he resolved to remain close upon his guard lest those qualities of which he knew nothing should everlastingly disgrace him. "Good Lord!" he repeated in dismay.

After a time the tall soldier slid dexterously through the hole. The loud private followed. They were wrangling.

"That's all right," said the tall soldier as he entered. He waved his hand expressively. "You can believe me or not, jest as you like. All you got to do is to sit down and wait as quiet as you can. Then pretty soon you'll find out I was right."

His comrade grunted stubbornly. For a moment he seemed to be searching for a formidable reply. Finally he said: "Well, you don't know everything in the world, do you?"

"Didn't say I knew everything in the world," retorted the other sharply. He began to stow various articles snugly into his knapsack.

The youth, pausing in his nervous walk, looked down at the busy figure. "Going to be a battle, sure, is there, Jim?" he asked.

"Of course there is," replied the tall soldier. "Of course there is. You jest wait 'til to-morrow, and you'll see one of the biggest battles ever was. You jest wait."

"Thunder!" said the youth.

This is a reference to the opening move of the Chancellorsville Campaign. Major General Hooker sent the cavalry under General Stoneman on what was to be a sweeping raid behind enemy lines. Stoneman was to cut rail and telegraph lines, burn wagon trains, and generally spread mayhem and panic in the Confederate rear—in short, he was to do what the Rebel cavalry chief, Major General "Jeb" Stuart, did so well. The Union raid was a failure, however, accomplishing little. Furthermore, the loss of his cavalry deprived Hooker of the eyes of his army, for the cavalry screened the movements of the Union army while determining the intentions of the enemy. The terrain and dense woods were hardly ideal conditions for horsemen, but, with the cavalry off raiding, Hooker moved blindly thorough the Wilderness, compounding his disadvantages.

Johnnies: Confederate soldiers.

"Oh, you'll see fighting this time, my boy, what'll be regular out-and-out fighting," added the tall soldier, with the air of a man who is about to exhibit a battle for the benefit of his friends.

"Huh!" said the loud one from a corner.

"Well," remarked the youth, "like as not this story'll turn out jest like them others did."

"Not much it won't," replied the tall soldier, exasperated. "Not much it won't. Didn't the cavalry all start this morning?" He glared about him. No one denied his statement. "The cavalry started this morning," he continued. "They say there ain't hardly any cavalry left in camp. They're going to Richmond, or some place, while we fight all the Johnnies. It's some dodge like that. The regiment's got orders, too. A feller what seen 'em go to headquarters told me a little while ago. And they're raising blazes all over camp—anybody can see that."

"Shucks!" said the loud one.

The youth remained silent for a time. At last he spoke to the tall soldier. "Jim!"

"What?"

"How do you think the reg'ment'll do?"

"Oh, they'll fight all right, I guess, after they once get into it," said the other with cold judgment. He made a fine use of the third person. "There's been heaps of fun poked at 'em because they're new, of course, and all that; but they'll fight all right, I guess."

"Think any of the boys'll run?" persisted the youth.

"Oh, there may be a few of 'em run, but there's them kind in every regiment, 'specially when they first goes under fire," said the other in a tolerant way. "Of course it might happen that the hull kit-and-boodle might start and run, if some big fighting came first-off, and then again they might stay and fight like fun. But you can't bet on nothing. Of course they ain't never been under fire yet, and it ain't likely they'll lick the hull rebel army all-to-oncet the first time; but I think they'll fight better than some, if worse than others. That's the way I figger. They call the reg'ment 'Fresh fish' and everything; but the boys come of good stock, and most of 'em'll fight like sin after they oncet git shootin'," he added, with a mighty emphasis on the last four words.

"Oh, you think you know—" began the loud soldier with scorn.

The other turned savagely upon him. They had a rapid altercation, in which they fastened upon each other various strange epithets.

The youth at last interrupted them. "Did you ever think you might run yourself, Jim?" he asked. On concluding the sentence he laughed as if he had meant to aim a joke. The loud soldier also giggled.

The tall private waved his hand. "Well," said he profoundly, "I've thought it might get too hot for Jim Conklin in some of them scrimmages, and if a whole lot of boys started and run, why, I s'pose I'd start and run. And if I once started to run, I'd run like the devil, and no mistake. But if everybody was a-standing and a-fighting, why, I'd stand and fight. Be jiminey, I would. I'll bet on it."

"Huh!" said the loud one.

The youth of this tale felt gratitude for these words of his comrade. He had feared that all of the untried men possessed a great and correct confidence. He now was in a measure reassured.

Chatfield Corners: There is no town in Orange County by that name, but there were two Chatfields in the 124th New York. Corporal Charles Chatfield stood in the front rank at the left of Company C, almost exactly at the center of the regiment. On his left was the Color Guard, which always drew heavy fire from the enemy. The men standing on either side of him were wounded and Corporal Chatfield himself was killed at Chancellorsville, as was Color Sergeant Thomas Foley, who stood only a few feet from him.

"He is a brave man, he just has cowardly legs," was a common description, even used by President Abraham Lincoln, for Civil War soldiers. Running away from a battle was not unusual during this war, especially among newer units. Some regiments received little training prior to entering battle; the 16th Connecticut infantry fought at Antietam only three weeks after its men had been mustered into service.

CHAPTER II.

THE NEXT MORNING the youth discovered that his tall comrade had been the fast-flying messenger of a mistake. There was much scoffing at the latter by those who had yesterday been firm adherents of his views, and there was even a little sneering by men who had never believed the rumor. The tall one fought with a man from Chatfield Corners and beat him severely.

The youth felt, however, that his problem was in no wise lifted from him. There was, on the contrary, an irritating prolongation. The tale had created in him a great concern for himself. Now, with the newborn question in his mind, he was compelled to sink back into his old place as part of a blue demonstration.

For days he made ceaseless calculations, but they were all wondrously unsatisfactory. He found that he could establish nothing. He finally concluded that the only way to prove himself was to go into the blaze, and then figuratively to watch his legs to discover their merits and faults. He reluctantly admitted that he could not sit still and with a mental slate and pencil derive an answer. To gain it, he must have blaze, blood, and danger, even as a chemist requires this, that, and the other. So he fretted for an opportunity.

Meanwhile he continually tried to measure himself by his comrades. The tall soldier, for one, gave him some assurance. This man's serene unconcern dealt him a measure of confidence, for he had known him since childhood, and from his intimate knowledge he did not see how he could be capable of anything that was beyond him, the youth. Still, he thought that his comrade might be mistaken about himself. Or, on the other hand, he might be a man heretofore doomed to peace and obscurity, but, in reality, made to shine in war.

The "intolerable slowness of the generals" is a reference to General McClellan, who commanded the Army of the Potomac up until the fall of 1862. McClellan was very popular among the rank and file, who referred to him as "Little Mac" or "The Young Napoleon." He had taken command of the army in defeat and rebuilt it into a formidable fighting force. With a genuine interest in the welfare of his men, he saw to it that they were well fed, well clothed, and well drilled. In short, he made them look and feel like soldiers. His fatal flaw, however, was that he was indecisive and slow to act on the battlefield, overcautious in attack and dilatory in pursuit.

An apocryphal story was circulated that President Lincoln came to visit McClellan in the field only to find the General was away. As Lincoln waited for McClellan to return, he heard the noises of hammering and sawing coming from behind the headquarters tent. Upon investigation, he found that a private was building an outhouse for the General. Lincoln inquired if it was to be a one-seater or a two-seater, to which the private replied that it was to be a one seater. "Good," said the President. "If it was a two-seater, McClellan would beshit himself before he could decide which one to use."

Despite Lincoln's exasperation with McClellan, the General remained very popular with the men; but when McClellan ran for President in 1864 against Lincoln, the soldiers voted overwhelmingly for "Father Abraham."

The youth would have liked to have discovered another who suspected himself. A sympathetic comparison of mental notes would have been a joy to him.

He occasionally tried to fathom a comrade with seductive sentences. He looked about to find men in the proper mood. All attempts failed to bring forth any statement which looked in any way like a confession to those doubts which he privately acknowledged in himself. He was afraid to make an open declaration of his concern, because he dreaded to place some unscrupulous confidant upon the high plane of the unconfessed from which elevation he could be derided.

In regard to his companions his mind wavered between two opinions, according to his mood. Sometimes he inclined to believing them all heroes. In fact, he usually admitted in secret the superior development of the higher qualities in others. He could conceive of men going very insignificantly about the world bearing a load of courage unseen, and although he had known many of his comrades through boyhood, he began to fear that his judgment of them had been blind. Then, in other moments, he flouted these theories, and assured himself that his fellows were all privately wondering and quaking.

His emotions made him feel strange in the presence of men who talked excitedly of a prospective battle as of a drama they were about to witness, with nothing but eagerness and curiosity apparent in their faces. It was often that he suspected them to be liars.

He did not pass such thoughts without severe condemnation of himself. He dinned reproaches at times. He was convicted by himself of many shameful crimes against the gods of traditions.

In his great anxiety his heart was continually clamoring at what he considered the intolerable slowness of the generals. They seemed content to perch tranquilly on the river bank, and leave him bowed down by the weight of a great problem. He wanted it settled forthwith. He could not long bear such a load, he said. Sometimes his anger at the commanders reached an acute stage, and he grumbled about the camp like a veteran.

One morning, however, he found himself in the ranks of his prepared regiment. The men were whispering speculations and re-

This is a reference to Colonel Augustus Van Horne Ellis, the stern, profane commander of the 124th New York. He rode a huge grey horse and was feared by his men. He surely would have made an imposing figure on such a morning. Sgt. William Wirt Bailey, later severely wounded at Chancellorsville, wrote of Ellis on September 21, 1862:

> The Colonel sometimes does swear big, that is when he gets mad. I had to laugh the other day Dan was the left guide and was not in his place. The Col. came around and drew his sword as if to strike him and said "I will cut your God damn little hand off and then skedaddle." I did not laugh at what he said but the way Dan looked, his eyes stuck out like pealed onions and he was as white and frightened. We have had a good laugh every time I think of it. The Col. is very flashy but soon gets over it. The only fault I find with him, is he marches us too fast. He is on his horse, and don't seem to think that we are a foot, with our knapsacks and heavy guns. Our guns are heavier than any in Virginia.

Col. Charles Weygant, author of *The History of the One Hundred and Twenty-fourth N.Y.S.V.* and captain of Comapany A at Chancellorsville, described the scene:

> About noon on the 28th, marching orders reached the 124th and at four P. M. we bade adieu to the now roofless log cabins which during the greater part of the time for months past, had been our homes, and marched to General Whipple's head-quarters, where our division was soon assembled, in heavy marching order; decidedly heavy, for each man carried, in addition to his food, blankets, gun, and accoutrements; eighty rounds of ammunition and a change of clothing. About half-past four, the General and his staff rode past, and our division fell in and moved off after them in an easterly direction, passing as it went thousands of deserted log cabins. it soon became evident that the entire army was in motion, and that we had been among the last to break camp. it was very foggy, and we could see but little of what was taking place about us. Just where we were going, or what was to be accomplished or attempted, were matters about which we could but speculate. Gradually, the foggy daylight changed to foggy darkness; but on, on, we pushed, hour after hour until midnight . . . .

The "surly guns" were cannons, which played an important role at Chancellorsville. Veterans of the battle often recalled the large number of guns engaged and the devastating effect of massed artillery fire.

counting the old rumors. In the gloom before the break of the day their uniforms glowed a deep purple hue. From across the river the red eyes were still peering. In the eastern sky there was a yellow patch like a rug laid for the feet of the coming sun; and against it, black and patternlike, loomed the gigantic figure of the colonel on a gigantic horse.

From off in the darkness came the trampling of feet. The youth could occasionally see dark shadows that moved like monsters. The regiment stood at rest for what seemed a long time. The youth grew impatient. It was unendurable the way these affairs were managed. He wondered how long they were to be kept waiting.

As he looked all about him and pondered upon the mystic gloom, he began to believe that at any moment the ominous distance might be aflare, and the rolling crashes of an engagement come to his ears. Staring once at the red eyes across the river, he conceived them to be growing larger, as the orbs of a row of dragons advancing. He turned toward the colonel and saw him lift his gigantic arm and calmly stroke his mustache.

At last he heard from along the road at the foot of the hill the clatter of a horse's galloping hoofs. It must be the coming of orders. He bent forward, scarce breathing. The exciting clickety-click, as it grew louder and louder, seemed to be beating upon his soul. Presently a horseman with jangling equipment drew rein before the colonel of the regiment. The two held a short, sharp-worded conversation. The men in the foremost ranks craned their necks.

As the horseman wheeled his animal and galloped away he turned to shout over his shoulder, "Don't forget that box of cigars!" The colonel mumbled in reply. The youth wondered what a box of cigars had to do with war.

A moment later the regiment went swinging off into the darkness. It was now like one of those moving monsters wending with many feet. The air was heavy, and cold with dew. A mass of wet grass, marched upon, rustled like silk.

There was an occasional flash and glimmer of steel from the backs of all these huge crawling reptiles. From the road came creakings and rumblings as some surly guns were dragged away.

27

In the May 8, 1863, issue of the *Middletown Whig Press*, a letter was reprinted which was probably written by Captain William Jackson, Company K, 124th New York. In part, the letter read:

On the evening of the 27th we received orders to be ready to start at an early hour the next morning, and three days' rations were cooked. Morning came and no orders were received to start and we began to think that it was a false alarm, like many others we had had. In the afternoon, an Orderly riding in at breakneck speed, and the sound of bugles in the neighboring camps blowing "strike tents," announced to us that the Army of the Potomac was really underway.

The Army of the Potomac marched west, up the north bank of the Rappahannock River, and somewhat inland, so as not to be detected by the Rebels on the opposite shore.

The historic 124th had marched east as part of a plan to deceive the Confederates on the other side of the Rappahannock. Once this deception had been accomplished, the regiment, along with the rest of the Third Corps, rapidly countermarched west to cross at the upriver fords and so rejoin the main body of the Army of the Potomac.

This is a reference to the Federal Sixth Corps under General John Sedgwick. This corps remained at Falmouth to deceive Lee. Later in the battle, they crossed the Rappahannock at Fredericksburg and actually broke through Lee's defensive lines near the town. The Sixth Corps was marching to Chancellorsville when it was attacked by Confederate forces at Salem Church.

The men stumbled along still muttering speculations. There was a subdued debate. Once a man fell down, and as he reached for his rifle a comrade, unseeing, trod upon his hand. He of the injured fingers swore bitterly and aloud. A low, tittering laugh went among his fellows.

Presently they passed into a roadway and marched forward with easy strides. A dark regiment moved before them, and from behind also came the tinkle of equipments on the bodies of marching men.

The rushing yellow of the developing day went on behind their backs. When the sunrays at last struck full and mellowingly upon the earth, the youth saw that the landscape was streaked with two long, thin, black columns which disappeared on the brow of a hill in front and rearward vanished in a wood. They were like two serpents crawling from the cavern of the night.

The river was not in view. The tall soldier burst into praises of what he thought to be his powers of perception.

Some of the tall one's companions cried with emphasis that they, too, had evolved the same thing, and they congratulated themselves upon it. But there were others who said that the tall one's plan was not the true one at all. They persisted with other theories. There was a vigorous discussion.

The youth took no part in them. As he walked along in careless line he was engaged with his own eternal debate. He could not hinder himself from dwelling upon it. He was despondent and sullen, and threw shifting glances about him. He looked ahead, often expecting to hear from the advance the rattle of firing.

But the long serpents crawled slowly from hill to hill without bluster of smoke. A dun-colored cloud of dust floated away to the right. The sky overhead was of a fairy blue.

The youth studied the faces of his companions, ever on the watch to detect kindred emotions. He suffered disappointment. Some ardor of the air which was causing the veteran commands to move with glee—almost with song—had infected the new regiment. The men began to speak of victory as of a thing they knew. Also, the tall soldier received his vindication. They were certainly going to come around in behind the enemy. They expressed commiseration for that part of

The veteran soldiers pictured here are typical of those that made Henry Fleming wary. Their status as veterans is evidenced by their "light marching order"; they have learned from experience to lighten their loads and carry only the bare essentials. Each man wears a wool uniform with a New York State-style jacket and is equipped with cartridge box, canteen, haversack, and, of course, a rifle-musket. The soldier in the center wears leggings of canvas. With hat brims turned up in a jaunty manner, these confident veterans look eager to make light of any "fresh fish" who happen by.

the army which had been left upon the river bank, felicitating themselves upon being a part of a blasting host.

The youth, considering himself as separated from the others, was saddened by the blithe and merry speeches that went from rank to rank. The company wags all made their best endeavors. The regiment tramped to the tune of laughter.

The blatant soldier often convulsed whole files by his biting sarcasms aimed at the tall one.

And it was not long before all the men seemed to forget their mission. Whole brigades grinned in unison, and regiments laughed.

A rather fat soldier attempted to pilfer a horse from a dooryard. He planned to load his knapsack upon it. He was escaping with his prize when a young girl rushed from the house and grabbed the animal's mane. There followed a wrangle. The young girl, with pink cheeks and shining eyes, stood like a dauntless statue.

The observant regiment, standing at rest in the roadway, whooped at once, and entered whole-souled upon the side of the maiden. The men became so engrossed in this affair that they entirely ceased to remember their own large war. They jeered the piratical private, and called attention to various defects in his personal appearance; and they were wildly enthusiastic in support of the young girl.

To her, from some distance, came bold advice. "Hit him with a stick."

There were crows and catcalls showered upon him when he retreated without the horse. The regiment rejoiced at his downfall. Loud and vociferous congratulations were showered upon the maiden, who stood panting and regarding the troops with defiance.

At nightfall the column broke into regimental pieces, and the fragments went into the fields to camp. Tents sprang up like strange plants. Camp fires, like red, peculiar blossoms, dotted the night.

The youth kept from intercourse with his companions as much as circumstances would allow him. In the evening he wandered a few paces into the gloom. From this little distance the many fires, with the black forms of men passing to and fro before the crimson rays, made weird and satanic effects.

He lay down in the grass. The blades pressed tenderly against his cheek. The moon had been lighted and was hung in a treetop. The

Cigars were too expensive for enlisted men and cigarettes were considered effeminate, so many soldiers smoked pipes. They either made these themselves from native wood, or purchased clay, meerschaum, or wooden pipes from sutlers, merchants who traveled with the army. Pipes made entirely of clay or with clay bowls and reed stems were by far the most common. These were cheap and could easily be replaced when broken or burned out. During the Civil War era, smoking was thought to have medicinal value. It was supposed that malaria was caused by the damp night air. Clouds of tobacco smoke were thought to counteract the dampness, thus helping to prevent the disease. Tobacco was purchased from the sutler, sent from home, or traded for with Yankee coffee from Rebel pickets.

liquid stillness of the night enveloping him made him feel vast pity for himself. There was a caress in the soft winds; and the whole mood of the darkness, he thought, was one of sympathy for himself in his distress.

He wished, without reserve, that he was at home again making the endless rounds from the house to the barn, from the barn to the fields, from the fields to the barn, from the barn to the house. He remembered he had often cursed the brindle cow and her mates, and had sometimes flung milking stools. But, from his present point of view, there was a halo of happiness about each of their heads, and he would have sacrificed all the brass buttons on the continent to have been enabled to return to them. He told himself that he was not formed for a soldier. And he mused seriously upon the radical differences between himself and those men who were dodging implike around the fires.

As he mused thus he heard the rustle of grass, and, upon turning his head, discovered the loud soldier. He called out, "Oh, Wilson!"

The latter approached and looked down. "Why, hello, Henry; is it you? What you doing here?"

"Oh, thinking," said the youth.

The other sat down and carefully lighted his pipe." You're getting blue, my boy. You're looking thundering peeked. What the dickens is wrong with you?"

"Oh, nothing," said the youth.

The loud soldier launched then into the subject of the anticipated fight. "Oh, we've got 'em now!" As he spoke his boyish face was wreathed in a gleeful smile, and his voice had an exultant ring. "We've got 'em now. At last, by the eternal thunders, we'll lick 'em good!"

"If the truth was known," he added, more soberly, "*they've* licked *us* about every clip up to now; but this time—this time—we'll lick 'em good!"

"I thought you was objecting to this march a little while ago," said the youth coldly.

"Oh, it wasn't that," explained the other. "I don't mind marching, if there's going to be fighting at the end of it. What I hate is this getting moved here and moved there, with no good coming of it, as far as I can see, excepting sore feet and damned short rations."

33

"Skedaddle" means to run away, but it did not carry a connotation of cowardice. Many soldiers "skedaddled" in their first battle, and even veterans ran when the fighting got too heavy. After the Battle of Gettysburg, Captain Benedict of Company D, 124th New York, wrote home that his company had "no skedaddlers this time," implying that members of his company may have run during earlier battles at Fredericksburg, Chancellorsville, or Brandy Station.

Soldiers often paired as sleeping companions. Two men would place one rubber blanket on the ground and then a wool blanket over it to keep out the dampness. They would then cover themselves with a second wool blanket covered by a second rubber blanket to keep the dew from penetrating. Each man also carried half a canvas "dog tent" to button together with another man's and pitch as protection against inclement weather. Thus two soldiers together had all they needed to keep warm and dry.

"Well, Jim Conklin says we'll get a plenty of fighting this time."

"He's right for once, I guess, though I can't see how it come. This time we're in for a big battle, and we've got the best end of it, certain sure. Gee rod! how we will thump 'em!"

He arose and began to pace to and fro excitedly. The thrill of his enthusiasm made him walk with an elastic step. He was sprightly, vigorous, fiery in his belief in success. He looked into the future with clear, proud eye, and he swore with the air of an old soldier.

The youth watched him for a moment in silence. When he finally spoke his voice was as bitter as dregs. "Oh, you're going to do great things, I s'pose!"

The loud soldier blew a thoughtful cloud of smoke from his pipe. "Oh, I don't know," he remarked with dignity; "I don't know. I s'pose I'll do as well as the rest. I'm going to try like thunder." He evidently complimented himself upon the modesty of this statement.

"How do you know you won't run when the time comes?" asked the youth.

"Run?" said the loud one; "run?—of course not!" He laughed.

"Well," continued the youth, "lots of good-a-'nough men have thought they was going to do great things before the fight, but when the time come they skedaddled."

"Oh, that's all true, I s'pose," replied the other; "but I'm not going to skedaddle. The man that bets on my running will lose his money, that's all." He nodded confidently.

"Oh, shucks!" said the youth. "You ain't the bravest man in the world, are you?"

"No, I ain't," exclaimed the loud soldier indignantly; "and I didn't say I was the bravest man in the world, neither. I said I was going to do my share of fighting—that's what I said. And I am, too. Who are you, anyhow? You talk as if you thought you was Napoleon Bonaparte." He glared at the youth for a moment, and then strode away.

The youth called in a savage voice after his comrade: "Well, you needn't git mad about it!" But the other continued on his way and made no reply.

He felt alone in space when his injured comrade had disappeared. His failure to discover any mite of resemblance in their view points

Playing cards, dice, and other gambling matierials were considered "instruments of the Devil," but they were still very popular with soldiers. As they approached a battlefield, however, many men would throw such things away as no man wanted to "meet his Maker" with evidence of evil on his person. Soldiers marching from the rear knew a big battle was underway up ahead by the playing cards and dice strewn along the roadway.

made him more miserable than before. No one seemed to be wrestling with such a terrific personal problem. He was a mental outcast.

He went slowly to his tent and stretched himself on a blanket by the side of the snoring tall soldier. In the darkness he saw visions of a thousand-tongued fear that would babble at his back and cause him to flee, while others were going coolly about their country's business. He admitted that he would not be able to cope with this monster. He felt that every nerve in his body would be an ear to hear the voices, while other men would remain stolid and deaf.

And as he sweated with the pain of these thoughts, he could hear low, serene sentences. "I'll bid five." "Make it six." " Seven." " Seven goes."

He stared at the red, shivering reflection of a fire on the white wall of his tent until, exhausted and ill from the monotony of his suffering, he fell asleep.

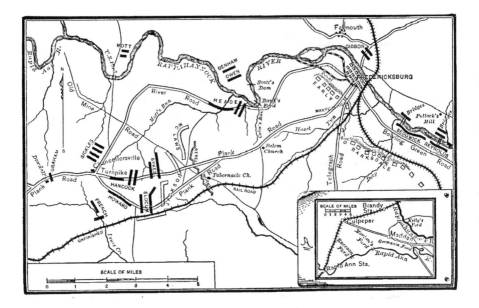

MAP 2: FRIDAY, MAY 1, 1863

Elements of three corps of the Army of the Potomac crossed well upriver at Kelly's Ford. As they advanced in a southeasterly direction, they "uncovered" the lower fords; that is, they outflanked the defenders and forced them to retire. Once United States Ford was uncovered, more Union troops could cross on pontoon bridges. This map shows that Hooker's plan was working perfectly. The troops he sent to flank Lee safely crossed the river and moved out of the Wilderness. The units left behind actually deceived Lee into thinking that Hooker would cross the Rappahannock River at Fredericksburg again. Lee was faced with the real possibility of attack from both front and flank. He was forced to split his army sending Stonewall Jackson west to deal with the Union troops in and around Chancellorsville. Note that by Friday, the Third Corps under Major General Sickles, including the 124th New York, had crossed the river and was near Chancellorsville.

38

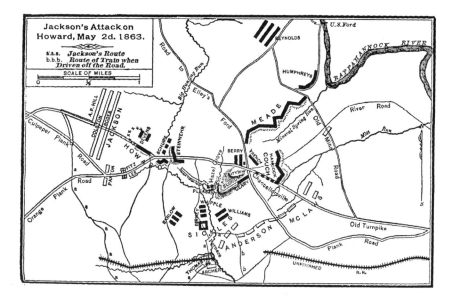

MAP 3: SATURDAY, MAY 2, 1863

Hooker arranged his men in a strong position near Chancellorsville where he expected Lee to attack him head on. Instead, Lee sent Jackson on a flank march on back roads and trails to gain the right flank of the Union army. His approach was detected, but insufficient measures were taken to prevent the planned surprise attack. At about 1 P.M., General Sickles advanced to intercept Jackson's moving column with Birney's Division in the lead and Whipple's Division, including the 124th New York, in support. They captured most of the 23rd Georgia. Sickles wanted to continue the attack, but Hooker remained idle, leaving a huge gap in the Union lines near Hazel Grove. When Jackson fell upon the exposed flank of Major General Howard's Eleventh Corps, Sickles countermarched rapidly to the area of Hazel Grove to aid in halting the Rebel advance.

Letter in the Middletown *Whig Press*, May 8, 1863:

About 11 at night we halted and were ordered to make a cup of coffee (On the march, when tired, there is nothing like this to freshen us up) After a half hour's stop we left our blazing fires and pushed on up the Warrenton road, leaving Berea Church and taking a miserable road to the United States Ford. At 2 am, we halted about two miles from the Ford and lay down for a short nap. At an early hour we started for the Ford, crossing the pontoons at 9 o'clock. . .marching through the woods to the front, distant about four miles.

Col. Weygant wrote:

May 1—Were up at day-break this morning, and after partaking of a hastily prepared breakfast pushed on to, and crossed the Rappahannock at the United States Ford, which we reached about ten A.M. As we stepped off the pontoon bridge on the southern shore, we noticed, running along in front of us, a well constructed line of the enemy's earth-works, behind which a single brigade, it would seem, might have held the ford against any force that could have been brought against it.—

Pontoon bridges were built by laying planking between specially made boats. Two such bridges were built at United States Ford.

CHAPTER III.

WHEN ANOTHER NIGHT came the columns, changed to purple streaks, filed across two pontoon bridges. A glaring fire wine tinted the waters of the river. Its rays, shining upon the moving masses of troops, brought forth here and there sudden gleams of silver or gold. Upon the other shore a dark and mysterious range of hills was curved against the sky. The insect voices of the night sang solemnly.

After this crossing the youth assured himself that at any moment they might be suddenly and fearfully assaulted from the caves of the lowering woods. He kept his eyes watchfully upon the darkness.

But his regiment went unmolested to a camping place, and its soldiers slept the brave sleep of wearied men. In the morning they were routed out with early energy, and hustled along a narrow road that led deep into the forest.

It was during this rapid march that the regiment lost many of the marks of a new command.

The men had begun to count the miles upon their fingers, and they grew tired. "Sore feet an' damned short rations, that's all," said the loud soldier. There was perspiration and grumblings. After a time they began to shed their knapsacks. Some tossed them unconcernedly down; others hid them carefully, asserting their plans to return for them at some convenient time. Men extricated themselves from thick shirts. Presently few carried anything but their necessary clothing, blankets, haversacks, canteens, and arms and ammunition. "You can now eat and shoot," said the tall soldier to the youth. "That's all you want to do."

There was sudden change from the ponderous infantry of theory to the light and speedy infantry of practice. The regiment, relieved of a burden, received a new impetus. But there was much loss of valuable knapsacks, and, on the whole, very good shirts.

41

"Colors" are flags. Union regiments like the 124th New York carried the national flag and sometimes a regimental flag as well. Veteran regiments often painted the names of the battles in which they had fought onto the stripes of the national flag; thus the reference to "letters in faded gold." Since this particular regiment was one of "fresh fish," it had no such battle honors. The flag was carried by the color bearer, usually a sergeant. The color guard was a group of men and one officer designated to protect the flags at all costs. Only the bravest men in the regiment volunteered for the job because the enemy often would direct their fire at the colors. At Chancellorsville, the 124th had two of their color guard killed and two wounded. The flag was the symbol of the regiment and its capture by the enemy was a terrible disgrace. On the other hand, it was the greatest honor to capture the battle flag of the enemy. A Union soldier who accomplished this feat was often rewarded with the Medal of Honor and a promotion.

It was Saturday, May 2, 1863.

This was the turning point in the Battle of Chancellorsville. Up until now, Hooker had Lee in a very tight spot, with large forces on his front at Fredericksburg and on his flank at Chancellorsville. For some reason, however, Hooker halted his advance just as his lead units were entering the cleared ground east of the Wilderness and ordered his puzzled commanders to withdraw from excellent positions back into the woods. He seemed content to allow the enemy to retire or to attack him in his strong position. Lee, of course, had other plans. The firing refered to was from Rebel units left behind to convince Hooker that Lee's whole army was right in front of him, when, in fact Jackson had already started his flank march.

But the regiment was not yet veteranlike in appearance. Veteran regiments in the army were likely to be very small aggregations of men. Once, when the command had first come to the field, some perambulating veterans, noting the length of their column, had accosted them thus: "Hey, fellers, what brigade is that?" And when the men had replied that they formed a regiment and not a brigade, the older soldiers had laughed, and said, "O Gawd!"

Also, there was too great a similarity in the hats. The hats of a regiment should properly represent the history of headgear for a period of years. And, moreover, there were no letters of faded gold speaking from the colors. They were new and beautiful, and the color bearer habitually oiled the pole.

Presently the army again sat down to think. The odor of the peaceful pines was in the men's nostrils. The sound of monotonous axe blows rang through the forest, and the insects, nodding upon their perches, crooned like old women. The youth returned to his theory of a blue demonstration.

One gray dawn, however, he was kicked in the leg by the tall soldier, and then, before he was entirely awake, he found himself running down a wood road in the midst of men who were panting from the first effects of speed. His canteen banged rhythmically upon his thigh, and his haversack bobbed softly. His musket bounced a trifle from his shoulder at each stride and made his cap feel uncertain upon his head.

He could hear the men whisper jerky sentences: "Say—what's all this—about?" "What th' thunder—we—skedaddlin' this way fer?" "Billie—keep off m' feet. Yeh run—like a cow." And the loud soldier's shrill voice could be heard: "What th' devil they in sich a hurry for?"

The youth thought the damp fog of early morning moved from the rush of a great body of troops. From the distance came a sudden spatter of firing.

He was bewildered. As he ran with his comrades he strenuously tried to think, but all he knew was that if he fell down those coming behind would tread upon him. All his faculties seemed to be needed to guide him over and past obstructions. He felt carried along by a mob.

When the army advanced, skirmishers were sent ahead. One company or more might fan out well in front of the main body of troops, usually in a thin double line. Their job was to locate the enemy or to warn of their approach. This skirmisher wears a wool overcoat in addition to his uniform.

A battalion was the left or right half of a regiment when formed in a line of battle.

The sun spread disclosing rays, and, one by one, regiments burst into view like armed men just born of the earth. The youth perceived that the time had come. He was about to be measured. For a moment he felt in the face of his great trial like a babe, and the flesh over his heart seemed very thin. He seized time to look about him calculatingly.

But he instantly saw that it would be impossible for him to escape from the regiment. It inclosed him. And there were iron laws of tradition and law on four sides. He was in a moving box.

As he perceived this fact it occurred to him that he had never wished to come to the war. He had not enlisted of his free will. He had been dragged by the merciless government. And now they were taking him out to be slaughtered.

The regiment slid down a bank and wallowed across a little stream. The mournful current moved slowly on, and from the water, shaded black, some white bubble eyes looked at the men.

As they climbed the hill on the farther side artillery began to boom. Here the youth forgot many things as he felt a sudden impulse of curiosity. He scrambled up the bank with a speed that could not be exceeded by a bloodthirsty man.

He expected a battle scene.

There were some little fields girted and squeezed by a forest. Spread over the grass and in among the tree trunks, he could see knots and waving lines of skirmishers who were running hither and thither and firing at the landscape. A dark battle line lay upon a sunstruck clearing that gleamed orange color. A flag fluttered.

Other regiments floundered up the bank. The brigade was formed in line of battle, and after a pause started slowly through the woods in the rear of the receding skirmishers, who were continually melting into the scene to appear again farther on. They were always busy as bees, deeply absorbed in their little combats.

The youth tried to observe everything. He did not use care to avoid trees and branches, and his forgotten feet were constantly knocking against stones or getting entangled in briers. He was aware that these battalions with their commotions were woven red and startling into the gentle fabric of softened greens and browns. It looked to be a wrong place for a battle field.

"Butternut and brown" were uniform colors often worn by Confederates along with the traditional gray. Rebels also wore battlefield pickups, including the blue pants, shirts, and hats of the enemy, but usually with a gray or brown jacket so as to make their allegiance clear.

"Vista" was a site on the Chancellorsville battlefield, reference to which corroborates the 124th New York/304th New York connection and helps to pinpoint the movement of the 304th New York. At about noon on May 2, Whipple's Division of the Third Corps, including the 124th New York, moved out along the Plank Road and then turned south on Catherine Furnace Road to support Sickles's advance and to attempt to strike Jackson's column. The march took Whipple's men directly through Vista.

The skirmishers in advance fascinated him. Their shots into thickets and at distant and prominent trees spoke to him of trage- dies—hidden, mysterious, solemn.

Once the line encountered the body of a dead soldier. He lay upon his back staring at the sky. He was dressed in an awkward suit of yellowish brown. The youth could see that the soles of his shoes had been worn to the thinness of writing paper, and from a great rent in one the dead foot projected piteously. And it was as if fate had betrayed the soldier. In death it exposed to his enemies that poverty which in life he had perhaps concealed from his friends.

The ranks opened covertly to avoid the corpse. The invulnerable dead man forced a way for himself. The youth looked keenly at the ashen face. The wind raised the tawny beard. It moved as if a hand were stroking it. He vaguely desired to walk around and around the body and stare; the impulse of the living to try to read in dead eyes the answer to the Question.

During the march the ardor which the youth had acquired when out of view of the field rapidly faded to nothing. His curiosity was quite easily satisfied. If an intense scene had caught him with its wild swing as he came to the top of the bank, he might have gone roaring on. This advance upon Nature was too calm. He had opportunity to reflect. He had time in which to wonder about himself and to attempt to probe his sensations.

Absurd ideas took hold upon him. He thought that he did not relish the landscape. It threatened him. A coldness swept over his back, and it is true that his trousers felt to him that they were no fit for his legs at all.

A house standing placidly in distant fields had to him an ominous look. The shadows of the woods were formidable. He was certain that in this vista there lurked fierce-eyed hosts. The swift thought came to him that the generals did not know what they were about. It was all a trap. Suddenly those close forests would bristle with rifle barrels. Ironlike brigades would appear in the rear. They were all going to be sacrificed. The generals were stupids. The enemy would presently swallow the whole command. He glared about him, expect- ing to see the stealthy approach of his death.

A hit with the flat of a sword was a typical reprimand by an officer of a soldier in the Civil War. Keep in mind that this young lieutenant was as inexperienced as the privates.

"Skulking" meant avoiding duty, which could take the form of hanging to the rear as the unit moved toward battle.

This was not typical conduct for a new regiment, especially at Chancellorsville. While many units dug rifle pits or erected earthworks, digging in was more common later in the war. Although the 124th New York helped to dig rifle pits on Monday, May 4, they did most of their fighting at Chancellorsville standing out in the open.

He thought that he must break from the ranks and harangue his comrades. They must not all be killed like pigs; and he was sure it would come to pass unless they were informed of these dangers. The generals were idiots to send them marching into a regular pen. There was but one pair of eyes in the corps. He would step forth and make a speech. Shrill and passionate words came to his lips.

The line, broken into moving fragments by the ground, went calmly on through fields and woods. The youth looked at the men nearest him, and saw, for the most part, expressions of deep interest, as if they were investigating something that had fascinated them. One or two stepped with overvaliant airs as if they were already plunged into war. Others walked as upon thin ice. The greater part of the untested men appeared quiet and absorbed. They were going to look at war, the red animal—war, the blood-swollen god. And they were deeply engrossed in this march.

As he looked the youth gripped his outcry at his throat. He saw that even if the men were tottering with fear they would laugh at his warning. They would jeer him, and, if practicable, pelt him with missiles. Admitting that he might be wrong, a frenzied declamation of the kind would turn him into a worm.

He assumed, then, the demeanor of one who knows that he is doomed alone to unwritten responsibilities. He lagged, with tragic glances at the sky.

He was surprised presently by the young lieutenant of his company, who began heartily to beat him with a sword, calling out in a loud and insolent voice: "Come, young man, get up into ranks there. No skulking'll do here." He mended his pace with suitable haste. And he hated the lieutenant, who had no appreciation of fine minds. He was a mere brute.

After a time the brigade was halted in the cathedral light of a forest. The busy skirmishers were still popping. Through the aisles of the wood could be seen the floating smoke from their rifles. Sometimes it went up in little balls, white and compact.

During this halt many men in the regiment began erecting tiny hills in front of them. They used stones, sticks, earth, and anything they thought might turn a bullet. Some built comparatively large ones, while others seemed content with little ones.   ·

"Veterans on the flanks" refers to the 86th New York and the 122nd Pennsylvania, two experienced regiments that, together with the 124th, comprised the brigade commanded by Col. Emlin Franklin. Sgt. Sprenger of the 122nd Pennsylvania wrote that one reason the 124th New York suffered so many casualties in the battle was because they refused to lie down when the shooting started.

It was then about mid-afternoon. General Sickles was maneuvering two of his divisions in an attempt to attack the Confederates. He moved through an area of thick woods with shallow, sluggish creeks and swamps.

Hardtack—the cracker mentioned here—salt pork, and coffee were the standard marching rations. Alluding to its taste, salt pork was also called "salt horse."

This procedure caused a discussion among the men. Some wished to fight like duelists, believing it to be correct to stand erect and be, from their feet to their foreheads, a mark. They said they scorned the devices of the cautious. But the others scoffed in reply, and pointed to the veterans on the flanks who were digging at the ground like terriers. In a short time there was quite a barricade along the regimental fronts. Directly, however, they were ordered to withdraw from that place.

This astounded the youth. He forgot his stewing over the advance movement. "Well, then, what did they march us out here for?" he demanded of the tall soldier. The latter with calm faith began a heavy explanation, although he had been compelled to leave a little protection of stones and dirt to which he had devoted much care and skill.

When the regiment was aligned in another position each man's regard for his safety caused another line of small intrenchments. They ate their noon meal behind a third one. They were moved from this one also. They were marched from place to place with apparent aimlessness.

The youth had been taught that a man became another thing in a battle. He saw his salvation in such a change. Hence this waiting was an ordeal to him. He was in a fever of impatience. He considered that there was denoted a lack of purpose on the part of the generals. He began to complain to the tall soldier. "I can't stand this much longer," he cried. "I don't see what good it does to make us wear out our legs for nothin'." He wished to return to camp, knowing that this affair was a blue demonstration; or else to go into a battle and discover that he had been a fool in his doubts, and was, in truth, a man of traditional courage. The strain of present circumstances he felt to be intolerable.

The philosophical tall soldier measured a sandwich of cracker and pork and swallowed it in a nonchalant manner. "Oh, I suppose we must go reconnoitering around the country jest to keep 'em from getting too close, or to develop 'em, or something."

"Huh!" said the loud soldier.

"Well," cried the youth, still fidgeting, "I'd rather do anything 'most than go tramping 'round the country all day doing no good to nobody and jest tiring ourselves out."

The 124th New York had been in service for just eight months before going into the Battle of Chancellorsville.

Soldiers were usually issued three days' rations for the march, but many ate all their food in one day with the idea that they might be dead by the next. Just prior to leaving Falmouth, the Union troops were issued eight days' rations, a good indication that they were off on a major campaign.

"So would I," said the loud soldier. "It ain't right. I tell you if anybody with any sense was a-runnin' this army it—"

"Oh, shut up!" roared the tall private. "You little fool. You little damn' cuss. You ain't had that there coat and them pants on for six months, and yet you talk as if—"

"Well, I wanta do some fighting anyway," interrupted the other. "I didn't come here to walk. I could 'ave walked to home—'round an' 'round the barn, if I jest wanted to walk."

The tall one, red-faced, swallowed another sandwich as if taking poison in despair.

But gradually, as he chewed, his face became again quiet and contented. He could not rage in fierce argument in the presence of such sandwiches. During his meals he always wore an air of blissful contemplation of the food he had swallowed. His spirit seemed then to be communing with the viands.

He accepted new environment and circumstance with great coolness, eating from his haversack at every opportunity. On the march he went along with the stride of a hunter, objecting to neither gait nor distance. And he had not raised his voice when he had been ordered away from three little protective piles of earth and stone, each of which had been an engineering feat worthy of being made sacred to the name of his grandmother.

In the afternoon the regiment went out over the same ground it had taken in the morning. The landscape then ceased to threaten the youth. He had been close to it and become familiar with it.

When, however, they began to pass into a new region, his old fears of stupidity and incompetence reassailed him, but this time he doggedly let them babble. He was occupied with his problem, and in his desperation he concluded that the stupidity did not greatly matter.

Once he thought he had concluded that it would be better to get killed directly and end his troubles. Regarding death thus out of the corner of his eye, he conceived it to be nothing but rest, and he was filled with a momentary astonishment that he should have made an extraordinary commotion over the mere matter of getting killed. He would die; he would go to some place where he would be understood. It was useless to expect appreciation of his profound and fine senses

The Federal brigade ahead of Henry's regiment skirmished with the Confederate brigades of Brigadier General A. R. Wright and Brigadier General Carnot Posey. The Confederate soldiers did an effective job of keeping Hooker's attention diverted to his front so he did not discover Jackson marching on his flank.

Captain William Jackson, Company K, 124th New York, wrote home describing the scene:

At 5 heavy firing being heard in front, 1 1/2 miles off, we were ordered to fall in and move up ready to act as support. At dusk the rebels made a charge on a battery but were repulsed with great loss. I stood on some rails and I could see all. How exciting it was. They came on cheering, or yelling rather for they can't give a good honest cheer. How our battery did pour on the grape and canister and cut down the rebs, and just before they reached it, a regiment of ours charged and scattered them. I just felt then as if I wanted some one to hold me to keep me from rushing in.

from such men as the lieutenant. He must look to the grave for comprehension.

The skirmish fire increased to a long clattering sound. With it was mingled far-away cheering. A battery spoke.

Directly the youth would see the skirmishers running. They were pursued by the sound of musketry fire. After a time the hot, dangerous flashes of the rifles were visible. Smoke clouds went slowly and insolently across the fields like observant phantoms. The din became crescendo, like the roar of an oncoming train.

A brigade ahead of them and on the right went into action with a rending roar. It was as if it had exploded. And thereafter it lay stretched in the distance behind a long gray wall, that one was obliged to look twice at to make sure that it was smoke.

The youth, forgetting his neat plan of getting killed, gazed spell bound. His eyes grew wide and busy with the action of the scene. His mouth was a little ways open.

Of a sudden he felt a heavy and sad hand laid upon his shoulder. Awakening from his trance of observation he turned and beheld the loud soldier.

"It's my first and last battle, old boy," said the latter, with intense gloom. He was quite pale and his girlish lip was trembling.

"Eh?" murmured the youth in great astonishment.

"It's my first and last battle, old boy," continued the loud soldier. "Something tells me—"

"What?"

"I'm a gone coon this first time and—and I w-want you to take these here things—to—my—folks." He ended in a quavering sob of pity for himself. He handed the youth a little packet done up in a yellow envelope.

"Why, what the devil—" began the youth again.

But the other gave him a glance as from the depths of a tomb, and raised his limp hand in a prophetic manner and turned away.

States numbered their volunteer regiments sequentially. New York had 196 such infantry regiments. There was no 304th New York, nor was there a 148th Maine. Militia regiments in existence before and after the Civil War were numbered separately. The 20th New York State Militia, from Ulster County, New York, was not the same outfit as the 20th New York State Volunteers. To further confuse matters, when the 20th Militia went into federal service, the regiment was designated the 80th New York State Volunteers, although the men of the regiment never acknowledged that number and always referred to themselves as the 20th Militia or the Ulster Guard. One could suppose Stephen Crane's fictitious "304" to be derived by adding the "1" and "2" of the 124th to get "3." There were no senior officers named Carrott, Perry, or Hannis commanding units on that part of the field, although Brigadier General Hiram Berry commanded the Second Division of the Third Corps. Berry was killed on Sunday, May 3. He had been an able commander; his death was felt by many to be a great loss to the Union cause.

At Chancellorsville, the captain of Company G, Isaac Nicoll, was not present. "That smart lieutenant" may well have been First Lieutenant James O. Denniston, who took over command of Company G for the battle.

batt'ry: This refers to an artillery battery, which, in the Union army, usually consisted of six cannons. At Chancellorsville, a variety of cannons, also called "guns," was used by both sides. The 12-pound Napoleon was a smoothbore, while the 10-pound Parrott was a rifled gun. Cannons fired projectiles ranging from solid iron balls, to hollow exploding shells, to shotgun like ammunition called canister.

The "Turnpike" is not to be confused with the Plank Road. These two roads joined at Chancellorsville to form one road running for about two miles west to Dowdall's Tavern, then split again into two. The Turnpike led northwest to Wilderness Tavern while the Plank Road continued to the southwest. Both roads were major access routes through the thickly wooded terrain. Heavy fighting had taken place earlier along the Turnpike east of Chancellorsville as Rebel forces under Jackson moved to meet Hooker. The man from the 148th Maine no doubt was referring to this engagement.

CHAPTER IV.

THE BRIGADE was halted in the fringe of a grove. The men crouched among the trees and pointed their restless guns out at the fields. They tried to look beyond the smoke.

Out of this haze they could see running men. Some shouted information and gestured as they hurried.

The men of the new regiment watched and listened eagerly, while their tongues ran on in gossip of the battle. They mouthed rumors that had flown like birds out of the unknown.

"They say Perry has been driven in with big loss."

"Yes, Carrott went t' th' hospital. He said he was sick. That smart lieutenant is commanding 'G' Company. Th' boys say they won't be under Carrott no more if they all have t' desert. They allus knew he was a—"

"Hannises' batt'ry is took."

"It ain't either. I saw Hannises' batt'ry off on th' left not more'n fifteen minutes ago."

"Well—"

"Th' general, he ses he is goin' t' take th' hull cammand of th' 304th when we go inteh action, an' then he ses we'll do sech fightin' as never another one reg'ment done."

"They say we're catchin' it over on th' left. They say th' enemy driv' our line inteh a devil of a swamp an' took Hannises' batt'ry."

"No sech thing. Hannises' batt'ry was 'long here 'bout a minute ago."

"That young Hasbrouck, he makes a good off'cer. He ain't afraid 'a nothin'."

"I met one of th' 148th Maine boys an' he ses his brigade fit th' hull rebel army fer four hours over on th' turnpike road an' killed

The following are accounts of this encounter with the enemy.

From *The History of the 122nd Regiment P.V.* by Sgt. George Sprenger:

Saturday, May 2, 1863--We were aroused at an early hour, when we prepared a hasty breakfast, as firing had already commenced on our right and to the northwest. A cavalry skirmish was reported to be in operation, while troops were coming in all directions from the river fordings, as well as from the southeast section along the Rappahannock. It was about 7 o'clock when we were again moved forward, quick pace, to the position we held last night; thence, by a detour, up a road cut through the woods, and past the Chancellor House, a distance of about two miles; thence turned to the left and moved southeast through a pine forest, where we found the advance of our Third Corps (General David B. Birney's Division) had surrounded the 23rd Georgia Regiment and captured it entire—about 500 strong.

The Regiment then proceeded to a clearing, where Companies I and K were deployed as skirmishers, taking a westerly direction along a dense pine forest. In the distance we could plainly see the rebel cavalry moving along from southwest to northeast. We remained on this line but a short time, for the while that a consultation was being held among our Generals, at which it was decided to call us in, when we were formed into brigades and, under proper commands, moved southwesterly, crossed a narrow, winding stream several times. This vicinity was known as Hazel Grove, situate near an ancient furnace, whence we were cautiously moved by flank, with our skirmishers in advance, about one mile, again crossing through a stream bordered by hazel brush; thence into an open bottom spreading out before us. A section of artillery had also been forwarded up the hill to our right; whereupon, just as we had appeared upon the open space and formed our lines, the rebel advance, which had been lying down, concealed in the high grass and beneath the cedar underbrush, fired a volley of balls into us, amidst which a member of Company F had an ear pierced by a bullet. We then again attempted to advance, when the firing became more general and was regularly poured into us upon our flanks as well as from the front. Fortunately, their aim was too high, so that only a few were hit, when Major General Whipple, commanding, immediately ordered us to fall back, which was done, in good order, to higher ground in our rear; after which a few shots from our battery had the effect of driving the rebels out of the underbrush, and the battery retired also in good order.

about five thousand of 'em. He ses one more sech fight as that an' th' war'll be over.''

"Bill wasn't scared either. No, sir! It wasn't that. Bill ain't a-gittin' scared easy. He was jest mad, that's what he was. When that feller trod on his hand, he up an' sed that he was willing t' give his hand t' his country, but he be dumbed if he was goin' t' have every dumb bushwhacker in th' kentry walkin' 'round on it. Se he went t' th' hospital disregardless of th' fight. Three fingers was crunched. Th' dern doctor wanted t' amputate 'm, an' Bill, he raised a heluva row, I hear. He's a funny feller.''

The din in front swelled to a tremendous chorus. The youth and his fellows were frozen to silence. They could see a flag that tossed in the smoke angrily. Near it were the blurred and agitated forms of troops. There came a turbulent stream of men across the fields. A battery changing position at a frantic gallop scattered the stragglers right and left.

A shell screaming like a storm banshee went over the huddled heads of the reserves. It landed in the grove, and exploding redly flung the brown earth. There was a little shower of pine needles.

Bullets began to whistle among the branches and nip at the trees. Twigs and leaves came sailing down. It was as if a thousand axes, wee and invisible, were being wielded. Many of the men were constantly dodging and ducking their heads.

The lieutenant of the youth's company was shot in the hand. He began to swear so wondrously that a nervous laugh went along the regimental line. The officer's profanity sounded conventional. It relieved the tightened senses of the new men. It was as if he had hit his fingers with a tack hammer at home.

He held the wounded member carefully away from his side so that the blood would not drip upon his trousers.

The captain of the company, tucking his sword under his arm, produced a handkerchief and began to bind with it the lieutenant's wound. And they disputed as to how the binding should be done.

The battle flag in the distance jerked about madly. It seemed to be struggling to free itself from an agony. The billowing smoke was filled with horizontal flashes.

From a letter home, dated May 4, 1863, by Corporal William Howell, Company E, 124th New York describing the same encounter:

The 124th then moved to the left the 86th NY and 122 Penn ahead. They come unexpectedly on the enemy and are driven back in disorder. We take a double quick to their support and the rebs fall back in the woods. . .

From a letter to his father by Sgt. Coe Reevs,* Company B, 124th NewYork, which was reprinted in the Goshen, New York, *Democrat*:

We were hurried on at double quick, and the balls began to whistle over our heads. We had orders to throw away our knapsacks. The rebs had planted themselves in the edge of the woods, and we had to cross an open field to get to them, besides a big ditch (the 122nd Pennsylvania were ahead of us, they are nine months men). The rebs fired a volley into them and they broke and ran and put us all in disorder. . . .

From a letter to his parents dated May 29, 1863 by Pvt. Henry Howell, Company E, 124th New York:

That letter in the democrat from Coe Reeves had a misstatement in that does not suit this regiment very well. He says "when the 122nd broke and run back it threw us all in confusion." Now he might have been confused but I did not see anything of the kind near where I was. We were double quicking through the woods, and no regiment that ever fought could keep perfect on account of the trees and bushes. But as soon as we came out in a little opening every man was in his place like a flash. If that was confusion I do not understand the meaning of the word.

---

*Spelling varies, found elsewhere as Reeve and Reeves.

Men running swiftly emerged from it. They grew in numbers until it was seen that the whole command was fleeing. The flag suddenly sank down as if dying. Its motion as it fell was a gesture of despair.

Wild yells came from behind the walls of smoke. A sketch in gray and red dissolved into a moblike body of men who galloped like wild horses.

The veteran regiments on the right and left of the 304th immediately began to jeer. With the passionate song of the bullets and the banshee shrieks of shells were mingled loud catcalls and bits of facetious advice concerning places of safety.

But the new regiment was breathless with horror. "Gawd! Saunders's got crushed!" whispered the man at the youth's elbow. They shrank back and crouched as if compelled to await a flood.

The youth shot a swift glance along the blue ranks of the regiment. The profiles were motionless, carven; and afterward he remembered that the color sergeant was standing with his legs apart, as if he expected to be pushed to the ground.

The following throng went whirling around the flank. Here and there were officers carried along on the stream like exasperated chips. They were striking about them with their swords and with their left fists, punching every head they could reach. They cursed like highwaymen.

A mounted officer displayed the furious anger of a spoiled child. He raged with his head, his arms, and his legs.

Another, the commander of the brigade, was galloping about bawling. His hat was gone and his clothes were awry. He resembled a man who has come from bed to go to a fire. The hoofs of his horse often threatened the heads of the running men, but they scampered with singular fortune. In this rush they were apparently all deaf and blind. They heeded not the largest and longest of the oaths that were thrown at them from all directions.

Frequently over this tumult could be heard the grim jokes of the critical veterans; but the retreating men apparently were not even conscious of the presence of an audience.

The battle reflection that shone for an instant in the faces on the mad current made the youth feel that forceful hands from heaven

From the after-action report on Chancellorsville by Colonel Augustus Van Horne Ellis:

. . . May 2nd about noon when we marched along a plank road & taking a cut in the woods to the right formed a picket line relieving some of Birneys division there posted. At 3 PM we again march toward the left and proceeding about one mile formed line of battle under the directions of Major General Sickels in company with our whole division and many other troops. I was their ordered by Gen. Whipple to support Col. Boormans right which I would find through a wooded hill on our right front and marching thither was halted by an aid from Genl Sickels to know where we were going and ordered to await the arrival of an aid to conduct us but shortly after hearing heavy firing in front I lead the regiment up the Hill and saw the rest of our division engaging a large force of the enemy in the valley below and apparently falling back I instantly ordered an advance & the men cheering lustily charged down a steep hill covered with cedars forming line of Battle at the bottom. But here found that the division were retiring and were ordered by General Whipple to follow the 12th N.H.I. through a marshy thicket back to from whence we had started. In meantime heavy cannonading was going in our rear now our front, and we found that the enemy had turned our position and taken several caisons and prisoners Stampeding our Mules & Nigroes but were driven back by the artillery.

would not have been able to have held him in place if he could have got intelligent control of his legs.

There was an appalling imprint upon these faces. The struggle in the smoke had pictured an exaggeration of itself on the bleached cheeks and in the eyes wild with one desire.

The sight of this stampede exerted a floodlike force that seemed able to drag sticks and stones and men from the ground. They of the reserves had to hold on. They grew pale and firm, and red and quaking.

The youth achieved one little thought in the midst of this chaos. The composite monster which had caused the other troops to flee had not then appeared. He resolved to get a view of it, and then, he thought he might very likely run better than the best of them.

Each man carried in a leather cartridge box forty paper cartridges, optimistically referred to as "40 dead men." Soldiers in the Civil War did not have to make their own ammunition but were issued packages containing ten cartridges and percussion caps. Each cartridge contained a measure of black powder and a .58 caliber cone-shaped "minie ball." Prior to marching to Chancellorsville, each man was issued forty extra rounds, another good indication that they were on the way to a big battle.

DIANNE DREWES

The "rebel yell" was a high-pitched scream intended to relieve tension and to instill fear in the enemy. It was of dubious effectiveness, often referred to by Union men as the "rebel squeal" and likened to the sound made by an animal in distress. The Union battle cry, on the other hand, was a deep-throated, manly "Hurrah!"

CHAPTER V.

THERE WERE MOMENTS OF WAITING. The youth thought of the village street at home before the arrival of the circus parade on a day in the spring. He remembered how he had stood, a small, thrillful boy, prepared to follow the dingy lady upon the white horse, or the band in its faded chariot. He saw the yellow road, the lines of expectant people, and the sober houses. He particularly remembered an old fellow who used to sit upon a cracker box in front of the store and feign to despise such exhibitions. A thousand details of color and form surged in his mind. The old fellow upon the cracker box appeared in middle prominence.

Some one cried, "Here they come!"

There was rustling and muttering among the men. They displayed a feverish desire to have every possible cartridge ready to their hands. The boxes were pulled around into various positions, and adjusted with great care. It was as if seven hundred new bonnets were being tried on.

The tall soldier, having prepared his rifle, produced a red handkerchief of some kind. He was engaged in knitting it about his throat with exquisite attention to its position, when the cry was repeated up and down the line in a muffled roar of sound.

"Here they come! Here they come!" Gun locks clicked.

Across the smoke-infested fields came a brown swarm of running men who were giving shrill yells. They came on, stooping and swinging their rifles at all angles. A flag, tilted forward, sped near the front.

As he caught sight of them the youth was momentarily startled by a thought that perhaps his gun was not loaded. He stood trying to rally his faltering intellect so that he might recollect the moment when he had loaded, but he could not.

A hatless general pulled his dripping horse to a stand near the colonel of the 304th. He shook his fist in the other's face. "You've got to hold 'em back!" he shouted, savagely; "you've got to hold 'em back!"

In his agitation the colonel began to stammer. "A-all r-right, General, all right, by Gawd! We-we'll do our—we- we'll d-d-do—do our best, General." The general made a passionate gesture and galloped away. The colonel, perchance to relieve his feelings, began to scold like a wet parrot. The youth, turning swiftly to make sure that the rear was unmolested, saw the commander regarding his men in a highly resentful manner, as if he regretted above everything his association with them.

The man at the youth's elbow was mumbling, as if to himself: "Oh, we're in for it now! oh, we're in for it now!"

The captain of the company had been pacing excitedly to and fro in the rear. He coaxed in schoolmistress fashion, as to a congregation of boys with primers. His talk was an endless repetition. "Reserve your fire, boys—don't shoot till I tell you—save your fire—wait till they get close up—don't be damned fools—"

Perspiration streamed down the youth's face, which was soiled like that of a weeping urchin. He frequently, with a nervous movement, wiped his eyes with his coat sleeve. His mouth was still a little way open.

He got the one glance at the foe-swarming field in front of him, and instantly ceased to debate the question of his piece being loaded. Before he was ready to begin—before he had announced to himself that he was about to fight—he threw the obedient, well-balanced rifle into position and fired a first wild shot. Directly he was working at his weapon like an automatic affair.

He suddenly lost concern for himself, and forgot to look at a menacing fate. He became not a man but a member. He felt that something of which he was a part—a regiment, an army, a cause, or a country—was in a crisis. He was welded into a common personality which was dominated by a single desire. For some moments he could not flee no more than a little finger can commit a revolution from a hand.

66

If he had thought the regiment was about to be annihilated perhaps he could have amputated himself from it. But its noise gave him assurance. The regiment was like a firework that, once ignited, proceeds superior to circumstances until its blazing vitality fades. It wheezed and banged with a mighty power. He pictured the ground before it as strewn with the discomfited.

There was a consciousness always of the presence of his comrades about him. He felt the subtle battle brotherhood more potent even than the cause for which they were fighting. It was a mysterious fraternity born of the smoke and danger of death.

He was at a task. He was like a carpenter who has made many boxes, making still another box, only there was furious haste in his movements. He, in his thought, was careering off in other places, even as the carpenter who as he works whistles and thinks of his friend or his enemy, his home or a saloon. And these jolted dreams were never perfect to him afterward, but remained a mass of blurred shapes.

Presently he began to feel the effects of the war atmosphere—a blistering sweat, a sensation that his eyeballs were about to crack like hot stones. A burning roar filled his ears.

Following this came a red rage. He developed the acute exasperation of a pestered animal, a well-meaning cow worried by dogs. He had a mad feeling against his rifle, which could only be used against one life at a time. He wished to rush forward and strangle with his fingers. He craved a power that would enable him to make a world-sweeping gesture and brush all back. His impotency appeared to him, and made his rage into that of a driven beast.

Buried in the smoke of many rifles his anger was directed not so much against the men whom he knew were rushing toward him as against the swirling battle phantoms which were choking him, stuffing their smoke robes down his parched throat. He fought frantically for respite for his senses, for air, as a babe being smothered attacks the deadly blankets.

There was a blare of heated rage mingled with a certain expression of intentness on all faces. Many of the men were making low-toned noises with their mouths, and these subdued cheers, snarls, imprecations, prayers, made a wild, barbaric song that went as an undercurrent of sound, strange and chantlike with the resounding chords of the war march. The man at the youth's elbow was babbling. In it there was something soft and tender like the monologue of a babe. The tall soldier was swearing in a loud voice. From his lips came a black procession of curious oaths. Of a sudden another broke out in a querulous way like a man who has mislaid his hat. "Well, why don't they support us? Why don't they send supports? Do they think—"

The youth in his battle sleep heard this as one who dozes hears.

There was a singular absence of heroic poses. The men bending and surging in their haste and rage were in every impossible attitude. The steel ramrods clanked and clanged with incessant din as the men pounded them furiously into the hot rifle barrels. The flaps of the cartridge boxes were all unfastened, and bobbed idiotically with each movement. The rifles, once loaded, were jerked to the shoulder and fired without apparent aim into the smoke or at one of the blurred and shifting forms which upon the field before the regiment had been growing larger and larger like puppets under a magician's hand.

The officers, at their intervals, rearward, neglected to stand in picturesque attitudes. They were bobbing to and fro roaring directions and encouragements. The dimensions of their howls were extraordinary. They expended their lungs with prodigal wills. And often they nearly stood upon their heads in their anxiety to observe the enemy on the other side of the tumbling smoke.

The lieutenant of the youth's company had encountered a soldier who had fled screaming at the first volley of his comrades. Behind the lines these two were acting a little isolated scene. The man was blubbering and staring with sheeplike eyes at the lieutenant, who had seized him by the collar and was pommeling him. He drove him back into the ranks with many blows. The soldier went mechanically, dully, with his animal-like eyes upon the officer. Perhaps there was to him a divinity expressed in the voice of the other—stern, hard, with no reflection of fear in it. He tried to reload his gun, but his shaking hands prevented. The lieutenant was obliged to assist him.

The men dropped here and there like bundles. The captain of the youth's company had been killed in an early part of the action. His body lay stretched out in the position of a tired man resting, but upon his face there was an astonished and sorrowful look, as if he thought some friend had done him an ill turn. The babbling man was grazed by a shot that made the blood stream widely down his face. He clapped both hands to his head. "Oh!" he said, and ran. Another grunted suddenly as if he had been struck by a club in the stomach. He sat down and gazed ruefully. In his eyes there was mute, indefinite reproach. Farther up the line a man, standing behind a tree, had had his knee joint splintered by a ball. Immediately he had dropped his rifle and gripped the tree with both arms. And there he remained, clinging desperately and crying for assistance that he might withdraw his hold upon the tree.

At last an exultant yell went along the quivering line. The firing dwindled from an uproar to a last vindictive popping. As the smoke slowly eddied away, the youth saw that the charge had been repulsed. The enemy were scattered into reluctant groups. He saw a man climb to the top of the fence, straddle the rail, and fire a parting shot. The waves had receded, leaving bits of dark *débris* upon the ground.

Some in the regiment began to whoop frenziedly. Many were silent. Apparently they were trying to contemplate themselves.

After the fever had left his veins, the youth thought that at last he was going to suffocate. He became aware of the foul atmosphere in which he had been struggling. He was grimy and dripping like a laborer in a foundry. He grasped his canteen and took a long swallow of the warmed water.

A sentence with variations went up and down the line. "Well, we've helt 'em back. We've helt 'em back; derned if we haven't." The men said it blissfully, leering at each other with dirty smiles.

The youth turned to look behind him and off to the right and off to the left. He experienced the joy of a man who at last finds leisure in which to look about him.

Under foot there were a few ghastly forms motionless. They lay twisted in fantastic contortions. Arms were bent and heads were turned in incredible ways. It seemed that the dead men must have fallen from some great height to get into such positions. They looked to be dumped out upon the ground from the sky.

From a position in the rear of the grove a battery was throwing shells over it. The flash of the guns startled the youth at first. He thought they were aimed directly at him. Through the trees he watched the black figures of the gunners as they worked swiftly and

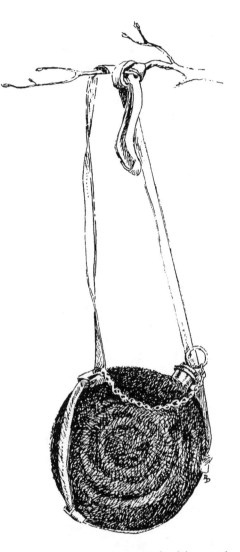

A Civil War-issue canteen was metal with a cork stopper. It was often covered with wool that could be soaked in water. As the dampness of the wool evaporated, the water in the canteen was cooled. Soldiers might have better canteens sent from home. Some were made of wood, while others were glass flasks or bottles, which, while not as durable, did not rust like the issue canteens.

intently. Their labor seemed a complicated thing. He wondered how they could remember its formula in the midst of confusion.

The guns squatted in a row like savage chiefs. They argued with abrupt violence. It was a grim pow-wow. Their busy servants ran hither and thither.

A small procession of wounded men were going drearily toward the rear. It was a flow of blood from the torn body of the brigade.

To the right and to the left were the dark lines of other troops. Far in front he thought he could see lighter masses protruding in points from the forest. They were suggestive of unnumbered thousands.

Once he saw a tiny battery go dashing along the line of the horizon. The tiny riders were beating the tiny horses.

From a sloping hill came the sound of cheerings and clashes. Smoke welled slowly through the leaves.

Batteries were speaking with thunderous oratorical effort. Here and there were flags, the red in the stripes dominating. They splashed bits of warm color upon the dark lines of troops.

The youth felt the old thrill at the sight of the emblem. They were like beautiful birds strangely undaunted in a storm.

As he listened to the din from the hillside, to a deep pulsating thunder that came from afar to the left, and to the lesser clamors which came from many directions, it occurred to him that they were fighting, too, over there, and over there, and over there. Heretofore he had supposed that all the battle was directly under his nose.

As he gazed around him the youth felt a flash of astonishment at the blue, pure sky and the sun gleamings on the trees and fields. It was surprising that Nature had gone tranquilly on with her golden process in the midst of so much devilment.

CHAPTER VI.

THE YOUTH awakened slowly. He came gradually back to a position from which he could regard himself. For moments he had been scrutinizing his person in a dazed way as if he had never before seen himself. Then he picked up his cap from the ground. He wriggled in his jacket to make a more comfortable fit, and kneeling relaced his shoe. He thoughtfully mopped his reeking features.

So it was all over at last! The supreme trial had been passed. The red, formidable difficulties of war had been vanquished.

He went into an ecstasy of self-satisfaction. He had the most delightful sensations of his life. Standing as if apart from himself, he viewed that last scene. He perceived that the man who had fought thus was magnificent.

He felt that he was a fine fellow. He saw himself even with those ideals which he had considered as far beyond him. He smiled in deep gratification.

Upon his fellows he beamed tenderness and good will. "Gee! ain't it hot, hey?" he said affably to a man who was polishing his streaming face with his coat sleeves.

"You bet!" said the other, grinning sociably. "I never seen sech dumb hotness." He sprawled out luxuriously on the ground. "Gee, yes! An' I hope we don't have no more fightin' till a week from Monday."

There were some handshakings and deep speeches with men whose features were familiar, but with whom the youth now felt the bonds of tied hearts. He helped a cursing comrade to bind up a wound of the shin.

But, of a sudden, cries of amazement broke out along the ranks of the new regiment. "Here they come ag'in! Here they come ag'in!"

The man who had sprawled upon the ground started up and said, "Gosh!"

The youth turned quick eyes upon the field. He discerned forms begin to swell in masses out of a distant wood. He again saw the tilted flag speeding forward.

The shells, which had ceased to trouble the regiment for a time, came swirling again, and exploded in the grass or among the leaves of the trees. They looked to be strange war flowers bursting into fierce bloom.

The men groaned. The luster faded from their eyes. Their smudged countenances now expressed a profound dejection. They moved their stiffened bodies slowly, and watched in sullen mood the frantic approach of the enemy. The slaves toiling in the temple of this god began to feel rebellion at his harsh tasks.

They fretted and complained each to each. "Oh, say, this is too much of a good thing! Why can't somebody send us supports?"

"We ain't never goin' to stand this second banging. I didn't come here to fight the hull damn' rebel army."

There was one who raised a doleful cry. "I wish Bill Smithers had trod on my hand, insteader me treddin' on his'n." The sore joints of the regiment creaked as it painfully floundered into position to repulse.

The youth stared. Surely, he thought, this impossible thing was not about to happen. He waited as if he expected the enemy to suddenly stop, apologize, and retire bowing. It was all a mistake.

But the firing began somewhere on the regimental line and ripped along in both directions. The level sheets of flame developed great clouds of smoke that tumbled and tossed in the mild wind near the ground for a moment, and then rolled through the ranks as through a gate. The clouds were tinged an earthlike yellow in the sunrays and in the shadow were a sorry blue. The flag was sometimes eaten and lost in this mass of vapor, but more often it projected, suntouched, resplendent.

Into the youth's eyes there came a look that one can see in the orbs of a jaded horse. His neck was quivering with nervous weakness and the muscles of his arms felt numb and bloodless. His hands, too, seemed large and awkward as if he was wearing invisible mittens. And there was a great uncertainty about his knee joints.

The words that comrades had uttered previous to the firing began to recur to him. "Oh, say, this is too much of a good thing! What do they take us for—why don't they send supports? I didn't come here to fight the hull damned rebel army."

He began to exaggerate the endurance, the skill, and the valor of those who were coming. Himself reeling from exhaustion, he was astonished beyond measure at such persistency. They must be machines of steel. It was very gloomy struggling against such affairs, wound up perhaps to fight until sundown.

He slowly lifted his rifle and catching a glimpse of the thickspread field he blazed at a cantering cluster. He stopped then and began to peer as best he could through the smoke. He caught changing views of the ground covered with men who were all running like pursued imps, and yelling.

To the youth it was an onslaught of redoubtable dragons. He became like the man who lost his legs at the approach of the red and green monster. He waited in a sort of a horrified, listening attitude. He seemed to shut his eyes and wait to be gobbled.

A man near him who up to this time had been working feverishly at his rifle suddenly stopped and ran with howls. A lad whose face had borne an expression of exalted courage, the majesty of he who dares give his life, was, at an instant, smitten abject. He blanched like one who has come to the edge of a cliff at midnight and is suddenly made aware. There was a revelation. He, too, threw down his gun and fled. There was no shame in his face. He ran like a rabbit.

Others began to scamper away through the smoke. The youth turned his head, shaken from his trance by this movement as if the regiment was leaving him behind. He saw the few fleeting forms.

He yelled then with fright and swung about. For a moment, in the great clamor, he was like a proverbial chicken. He lost the direction of safety. Destruction threatened him from all points.

Directly he began to speed toward the rear in great leaps. His rifle and cap were gone. His unbuttoned coat bulged in the wind. The flap of his cartridge box bobbed wildly, and his canteen, by its slender cord, swung out behind. On his face was all the horror of those things which he imagined.

The lieutenant sprang forward bawling. The youth saw his features wrathfully red, and saw him make a dab with his sword. His one thought of the incident was that the lieutenant was a peculiar creature to feel interested in such matters upon this occasion.

He ran like a blind man. Two or three times he fell down. Once he knocked his shoulder so heavily against a tree that he went headlong.

Since he had turned his back upon the fight his fears had been wondrously magnified. Death about to thrust him between the shoulder blades was far more dreadful than death about to smite him between the eyes. When he thought of it later, he conceived the impression that it is better to view the appalling than to be merely within hearing. The noises of the battle were like stones; he believed himself liable to be crushed.

As he ran on he mingled with others. He dimly saw men on his right and on his left, and he heard footsteps behind him. He thought that all the regiment was fleeing, pursued by these ominous crashes.

In his flight the sound of these following footsteps gave him his one meager relief. He felt vaguely that death must make a first choice of the men who were nearest; the initial morsels for the dragons would be then those who were following him. So he displayed the zeal of an insane sprinter in his purpose to keep them in the rear. There was a race.

As he, leading, went across a little field, he found himself in a region of shells. They hurtled over his head with long wild screams. As he listened he imagined them to have rows of cruel teeth that grinned at him. Once one lit before him and the livid lightning of the explosion effectually barred the way in his chosen direction. He groveled on the ground and then springing up went careering off through some bushes.

He experienced a thrill of amazement when he came within view of a battery in action. The men there seemed to be in conventional moods altogether unaware of the impending annihilation. The battery was disputing with a distant antagonist and the gunners were wrapped in admiration of their shooting. They were continually

     This refers either to Brigadier General Whipple, who commanded the Third Division of the Third Corps, or to Major General Sickles, the Third Corp commander. Such high ranking officers typically had staffs, including aides, that would carry orders to the various brigades and regiments of their commands. Both Sickles and Whipple enjoyed great reputations among their men.

bending in coaxing postures over the guns. They seemed to be patting them on the back and encouraging them with words. The guns, stolid and undaunted, spoke with dogged valor.

The precise gunners were coolly enthusiastic. They lifted their eyes every chance to the smokewreathed hillock from whence the hostile battery addressed them. The youth pitied them as he ran. Methodical idiots! Machine-like fools! The refined joy of planting shells in the midst of the other battery's formation would appear a little thing when the infantry came swooping out of the woods.

The face of a youthful rider, who was jerking his frantic horse with an abandon of temper he might display in a placid barn yard, was impressed deeply upon his mind. He knew that he looked upon a man who would presently be dead.

Too, he felt a pity for the guns, standing, six good comrades, in a bold row.

He saw a brigade going to the relief of its pestered fellows. He scrambled upon a wee hill and watched it sweeping finely, keeping formation in difficult places. The blue of the line was crusted with steel color, and the brilliant flags projected. Officers were shouting.

This sight also filled him with wonder. The brigade was hurrying briskly to be gulped into the infernal mouths of the war god. What manner of men were they, anyhow? Ah, it was some wondrous breed! Or else they didn't comprehend—the fools.

A furious order caused commotion in the artillery. An officer on a bounding horse made maniacal motions with his arms. The teams went swinging up from the rear, the guns were whirled about, and the battery scampered away. The cannon with their noses poked slantingly at the ground grunted and grumbled like stout men, brave but with objections to hurry.

The youth went on, moderating his pace since he had left the place of noises.

Later he came upon a general of division seated upon a horse that pricked its ears in an interested way at the battle. There was a great gleaming of yellow and patent leather about the saddle and bridle. The quiet man astride looked mouse-colored upon such a splendid charger.

A jingling staff was galloping hither and thither. Sometimes the general was surrounded by horsemen and at other times he was quite alone. He looked to be much harassed. He had the appearance of a business man whose market is swinging up and down.

The youth went slinking around this spot. He went as near as he dared trying to overhear words. Perhaps the general, unable to comprehend chaos, might call upon him for information. And he could tell him. He knew all concerning it. Of a surety the force was in a fix, and any fool could see that if they did not retreat while they had opportunity— why—

He felt that he would like to thrash the general, or at least approach and tell him in plain words exactly what he thought him to be. It was criminal to stay calmly in one spot and make no effort to stay destruction. He loitered in a fever of eagerness for the division commander to apply to him.

As he warily moved about, he heard the general call out irritably: "Tompkins, go over an' see Taylor, an' tell him not t' be in such an all fired hurry; tell him t' halt his brigade in th' edge of th' woods; tell him t' detach a reg'ment—say I think th' center 'll break if we don't help it out some; tell him t' hurry up."

A slim youth on a fine chestnut horse caught these swift words from the mouth of his superior. He made his horse bound into a gallop almost from a walk in his haste to go upon his mission. There was a cloud of dust.

A moment later the youth saw the general bounce excitedly in his saddle.

"Yes, by heavens, they have!" The officer leaned forward. His face was aflame with excitement. "Yes, by heavens, they've held 'im! They've held 'im !"

He began to blithely roar at his staff: "We'll wallop 'im now. We'll wallop 'im now. We've got 'em sure." He turned suddenly upon an aid: "Here—you—Jones—quick—ride after Tompkins— see Taylor—tell him t' go in—everlastingly—like blazes—anything."

As another officer sped his horse after the first messenger, the general beamed upon the earth like a sun. In his eyes was a desire to chant a paean. He kept repeating, "They've held 'em, by heavens!"

His excitement made his horse plunge, and he merrily kicked and swore at it. He held a little carnival of joy on horseback.

CHAPTER VII.

THE YOUTH cringed as if discovered in a crime. By heavens, they had won after all! The imbecile line had remained and become victors. He could hear cheering.

He lifted himself upon his toes and looked in the direction of the fight. A yellow fog lay wallowing on the treetops. From beneath it came the clatter of musketry. Hoarse cries told of an advance.

He turned away amazed and angry. He felt that he had been wronged.

He had fled, he told himself, because annihilation approached. He had done a good part in saving himself, who was a little piece of the army. He had considered the time, he said, to be one in which it was the duty of every little piece to rescue itself if possible. Later the officers could fit the little pieces together again, and make a battle front. If none of the little pieces were wise enough to save themselves from the flurry of death at such a time, why, then, where would be the army? It was all plain that he had proceeded according to very correct and commendable rules. His actions had been sagacious things. They had been full of strategy. They were the work of a master's legs.

Thoughts of his comrades came to him. The brittle blue line had withstood the blows and won. He grew bitter over it. It seemed that the blind ignorance and stupidity of those little pieces had betrayed him. He had been overturned and crushed by their lack of sense in holding the position, when intelligent deliberation would have convinced them that it was impossible. He, the enlightened man who looks afar in the dark, had fled because of his superior perceptions and knowledge. He felt a great anger against his comrades. He knew it could be proved that they had been fools.

He wondered what they would remark when later he appeared in camp. His mind heard howls of derision. Their density would not enable them to understand his sharper point of view.

He began to pity himself acutely. He was ill used. He was trodden beneath the feet of an iron injustice. He had proceeded with wisdom and from the most righteous motives under heaven's blue only to be frustrated by hateful circumstances.

A dull, animal-like rebellion against his fellows, war in the abstract, and fate grew within him. He shambled along with bowed head, his brain in a tumult of agony and despair. When he looked loweringly up, quivering at each sound, his eyes had the expression of those of a criminal who thinks his guilt and his punishment great, and knows that he can find no words.

He went from the fields into a thick wood, as if resolved to bury himself. He wished to get out of hearing of the crackling shots which were to him like voices.

The ground was cluttered with vines and bushes, and the trees grew close and spread out like bouquets. He was obliged to force his way with much noise. The creepers, catching against his legs, cried out harshly as their sprays were torn from the barks of trees. The swishing saplings tried to make known his presence to the world. He could not conciliate the forest. As he made his way, it was always calling out protestations. When he separated embraces of trees and vines the disturbed foliages waved their arms and turned their face leaves toward him. He dreaded lest these noisy motions and cries should bring men to look at him. So he went far, seeking dark and intricate places.

After a time the sound of musketry grew faint and the cannon boomed in the distance. The sun, suddenly apparent, blazed among the trees. The insects were making rhythmical noises. They seemed to be grinding their teeth in unison. A woodpecker stuck his impudent head around the side of a tree. A bird flew on lighthearted wing.

Off was the rumble of death. It seemed now that Nature had no ears.

This landscape gave him assurance. A fair field holding life. It was the religion of peace. It would die if its timid eyes were compelled to see blood. He conceived Nature to be a woman with a deep aversion to tragedy.

He threw a pine cone at a jovial squirrel, and he ran with chattering fear. High in a treetop he stopped, and, poking his head cautiously from behind a branch, looked down with a air of trepidation.

The youth felt triumphant at this exhibition. There was the law, he said. Nature had given him a sign. The squirrel, immediately upon recognizing danger, had taken to his legs without ado. He did not stand stolidly baring his furry belly to the missile, and die with an upward glance at the sympathetic heavens. On the contrary, he had fled as fast as his legs could carry him; and he was but an ordinary squirrel, too—doubtless no philosopher of his race. The youth wended, feeling that Nature was of his mind. She re-enforced his argument with proofs that lived where the sun shone.

Once he found himself almost into a swamp. He was obliged to walk upon bog tufts and watch his feet to keep from the oily mire. Pausing at one time to look about him he saw, out at some black water, a small animal pounce in and emerge directly with a gleaming fish.

The youth went again into the deep thickets. The brushed branches made a noise that drowned the sounds of cannon. He walked on, going from obscurity into promises of a greater obscurity.

At length he reached a place where the high, arching boughs made a chapel. He softly pushed the green doors aside and entered. Pine needles were a gentle brown carpet. There was a religious half light.

Near the threshold he stopped, horror-stricken at the sight of a thing.

He was being looked at by a dead man who was seated with his back against a columnlike tree. The corpse was dressed in a uniform that once had been blue, but was now faded to a melancholy shade of green. The eyes, staring at the youth, had changed to the dull hue to be seen on the side of a dead fish. The mouth was open. Its red had changed to an appalling yellow. Over the gray skin of the face ran little ants. One was trundling some sort of a bundle along the upper lip.

The youth gave a shriek as he confronted the thing. He was for moments turned to stone before it. He remained staring into the liquid-looking eyes. The dead man and the living man exchanged a long look. Then the youth cautiously put one hand behind him and brought it against a tree. Leaning upon this he retreated, step by step, with his face still toward the thing. He feared that if he turned his back the body might spring up and stealthily pursue him.

The branches, pushing against him, threatened to throw him over upon it. His unguided feet, too, caught aggravatingly in brambles; and with it all he received a subtle suggestion to touch the corpse. As he thought of his hand upon it he shuddered profoundly.

At last he burst the bonds which had fastened him to the spot and fled, unheeding the underbrush. He was pursued by a sight of the black ants swarming greedily upon the gray face and venturing horribly near to the eyes.

After a time he paused, and, breathless and panting, listened. He imagined some strange voice would come from the dead throat and squawk after him in horrible menaces.

The trees about the portal of the chapel moved soughingly in a soft wind. A sad silence was upon the little guarding edifice.

DIANNE DREWES

It was six in the evening. The roar that was heard was Stonewall Jackson's men striking the Union Eleventh Corps of by Major General Oliver O. Howard, at the extreme right of the line. While many of the Eleventh Corps fought well, they were in a very bad spot. In the end, they were routed. Both Howard and Hooker had been warned repeatedly that a lot of Rebel soldiers were moving up on the flank; but both generals and many of their subordinates refused to believe it. Couriers carrying the warnings to headquarters were mocked and ignored, even as Jackson was deploying thousands of his veteran soldiers into position. The unfortunate loss at Chancellorsville, coupled with a similar loss at Gettysburg, tarnished the reputation of both the Eleventh Corps and its commander.

Many of the soldiers in the Eleventh Corps were recent German immigrants who spoke little or no English. In the mid-nineteenth century, Germans were called Dutchmen by some Americans, erroneously believing that Deutsch, as the Germans called their language, was also the name of their homeland. The Eleventh Corps became known as the "Flying Dutchmen."

CHAPTER VIII.

THE TREES began softly to sing a hymn of twilight. The sun sank until slanted bronze rays struck the forest. There was a lull in the noises of insects as if they had bowed their beaks and were making a devotional pause. There was silence save for the chanted chorus of the trees.

Then, upon this stillness, there suddenly broke a tremendous clangor of sounds. A crimson roar came from the distance.

The youth stopped. He was transfixed by this terrific medley of all noises. It was as if worlds were being rended. There was the ripping sound of musketry and the breaking crash of the artillery.

His mind flew in all directions. He conceived the two armies to be at each other panther fashion. He listened for a time. Then he began to run in the direction of the battle. He saw that it was an ironical thing for him to be running thus toward that which he had been at such pains to avoid. But he said, in substance, to himself that if the earth and the moon were about to clash, many persons would doubtless plan to get upon the roofs to witness the collision.

As he ran, he became aware that the forest had stopped its music, as if at last becoming capable of hearing the foreign sounds. The trees hushed and stood motionless. Everything seemed to be listening to the crackle and clatter and earshaking thunder. The chorus pealed over the still earth.

It suddenly occurred to the youth that the fight in which he had been was, after all, but perfunctory popping. In the hearing of this present din he was doubtful if he had seen real battle scenes. This uproar explained a celestial battle; it was tumbling hordes a-struggle in the air.

Reflecting, he saw a sort of a humor in the point of view of himself and his fellows during the late encounter. They had taken themselves

A "forlorn hope" was a small group of soldiers sent on a mission from which they were not expected to return. Such groups were sent forward as shock troops or to break a hole in the enemy position through which their comrades could advance.

and the enemy very seriously and had imagined that they were deciding the war. Individuals must have supposed that they were cutting the letters of their names deep into everlasting tablets of brass, or enshrining their reputations forever in the hearts of their country-men, while, as to fact, the affair would appear in printed reports under a meek and immaterial title. But he saw that it was good, else, he said, in battle every one would surely run save forlorn hopes and their ilk.

He went rapidly on. He wished to come to the edge of the forest that he might peer out.

As he hastened, there passed through his mind pictures of stupen-dous conflicts. His accumulated thought upon such subjects was used to form scenes. The noise was as the voice of an eloquent being, describing.

Sometimes the brambles formed chains and tried to hold him back. Trees, confronting him, stretched out their arms and forbade him to pass. After its previous hostility this new resistance of the forest filled him with a fine bitterness. It seemed that Nature could not be quite ready to kill him.

But he obstinately took roundabout ways, and presently he was where he could see long gray walls of vapor where lay battle lines. The voices of cannon shook him. The musketry sounded in long irregular surges that played havoc with his ears. He stood retardant for a moment. His eyes had an awestruck expression. He gawked in the direction of the fight.

Presently he proceeded again on his forward way. The battle was like the grinding of an immense and terrible machine to him. Its complexities and powers, its grim processes, fascinated him. He must go close and see it produce corpses.

He came to a fence and clambered over it. On the far side, the ground was littered with clothes and guns. A newspaper, folded up, lay in the dirt. A dead soldier was stretched with his face hidden in his arm. Farther off there was a group of four or five corpses keeping mournful company. A hot sun had blazed upon the spot.

In this place the youth felt that he was an invader. This forgotten part of the battle ground was owned by the dead men, and he hurried, in the vague apprehension that one of the swollen forms would rise and tell him to begone.

Some of these men were wounded soldiers making their way to the rear. Hospitals were places to be avoided, so they likely would have relied on their friends and comrades to care for them. The soldiers, including some of Sickles' Third Corps who were casualties in the brush with Jackson's men, had been wounded earlier in the day. Others were wounded in the fighting staged by Lee to keep Hooker in place and focused on the front while Jackson marched to gain the flank.

He came finally to a road from which he could see in the distance dark and agitated bodies of troops, smoke-fringed. In the lane was a blood-stained crowd streaming to the rear. The wounded men were cursing, groaning, and wailing. In the air, always, was a mighty swell of sound that it seemed could sway the earth. With the courageous words of the artillery and the spiteful sentences of the musketry mingled red cheers. And from this region of noises came the steady current of the maimed.

One of the wounded men had a shoeful of blood. He hopped like a schoolboy in a game. He was laughing hysterically.

One was swearing that he had been shot in the arm through the commanding general's mismanagement of the army. One was marching with an air imitative of some sublime drum major. Upon his features was an unholy mixture of merriment and agony. As he marched he sang a bit of doggerel in a high and quavering voice:

"Sing a song 'a vic'try,
A pocketful 'a bullets,
Five an' twenty dead men
Baked in a—pie."

Parts of the procession limped and staggered to this tune.

Another had the gray seal of death already upon his face. His lips were curled in hard lines and his teeth were clinched. His hands were bloody from where he had pressed them upon his wound. He seemed to be awaiting the moment when he should pitch headlong. He stalked like the specter of a soldier, his eyes burning with the power of a stare into the unknown.

There were some who proceeded sullenly, full of anger at their wounds, and ready to turn upon anything as an obscure cause.

An officer was carried along by two privates. He was peevish. "Don't joggle so, Johnson, yeh fool," he cried. "Think m' leg is made of iron? If yeh can't carry me decent, put me down an' let some one else do it."

He bellowed at the tottering crowd who blocked the quick march of his bearers. "Say, make way there, can't yeh? Make way, dickens take it all."

89

They sulkily parted and went to the roadsides. As he was carried past they made pert remarks to him. When he raged in reply and threatened them, they told him to be damned.

The shoulder of one of the tramping bearers knocked heavily against the spectral soldier who was staring into the unknown.

The youth joined this crowd and marched along with it. The torn bodies expressed the awful machinery in which the men had been entangled.

Orderlies and couriers occasionally broke through the throng in the roadway, scattering wounded men right and left, galloping on followed by howls. The melancholy march was continually disturbed by the messengers, and sometimes by bustling batteries that came swinging and thumping down upon them, the officers shouting orders to clear the way.

There was a tattered man, fouled with dust, blood and powder stain from hair to shoes, who trudged quietly at the youth's side. He was listening with eagerness and much humility to the lurid descriptions of a bearded sergeant. His lean features wore an expression of awe and admiration. He was like a listener in a country store to wondrous tales told among the sugar barrels. He eyed the story-teller with unspeakable wonder. His mouth was agape in yokel fashion.

The sergeant, taking note of this, gave pause to his elaborate history while he administered a sardonic comment. "Be keerful, honey, you'll be a-ketchin' flies," he said.

The tattered man shrank back abashed.

After a time he began to sidle near to the youth, and in a different way try to make him a friend. His voice was gentle as a girl's voice and his eyes were pleading. The youth saw with surprise that the soldier had two wounds, one in the head, bound with a blood-soaked rag, and the other in the arm, making that member dangle like a broken bough.

After they had walked together for some time the tattered man mustered sufficient courage to speak. "Was pretty good fight, wa'n't it?" he timidly said. The youth, deep in thought, glanced up at the bloody and grim figure with its lamblike eyes. "What?"

"Was pretty good fight, wa'n't it?"

"Yes," said the youth shortly. He quickened his pace.

But the other hobbled industriously after him. There was an air of apology in his manner, but he evidently thought that he needed only to talk for a time, and the youth would perceive that he was a good fellow.

"Was pretty good fight, wa'n't it?" he began in a small voice, and then he achieved the fortitude to continue. "Dern me if I ever see fellers fight so. Laws, how they did fight! I knowed th' boys'd like when they onct got square at it. Th' boys ain't had no fair chanct up t' now, but this time they showed what they was. I knowed it'd turn out this way. Yeh can't lick them boys. No, sir! They're fighters, they be."

He breathed a deep breath of humble admiration. He had looked at the youth for encouragement several times. He received none, but gradually he seemed to get absorbed in his subject.

"I was talkin' 'cross pickets with a boy from Georgie, onct, an' that boy, he ses, 'Your fellers 'll all run like hell when they onct hearn a gun,' he ses. 'Mebbe they will,' I ses, 'but I don't b'lieve none of it,' I ses; ' an' b'jiminey,' I ses back t' 'um, 'mebbe your fellers 'll all run like hell when they onct hearn a gun,' I ses. He larfed. Well, they didn't run t' day, did they, hey? No, sir! They fit, an' fit, an' fit."

His homely face was suffused with a light of love for the army which was to him all things beautiful and powerful.

After a time he turned to the youth. "Where yeh hit, ol' boy?" he asked in a brotherly tone.

The youth felt instant panic at this question, although at first its full import was not borne in upon him.

"What?" he asked.

"Where yeh hit?" repeated the tattered man.

"Why," began the youth, "I—I—that is—why—I—"

He turned away suddenly and slid through the crowd. His brow was heavily flushed, and his fingers were picking nervously at one of his buttons. He bent his head and fastened his eyes studiously upon the button as if it were a little problem.

The tattered man looked after him in astonishment.

CHAPTER IX.

THE YOUTH fell back in the procession until the tattered soldier was not in sight. Then he started to walk on with the others.

But he was amid wounds. The mob of men was bleeding. Because of the tattered soldier's question he now felt that his shame could be viewed. He was continually casting sidelong glances to see if the men were contemplating the letters of guilt he felt burned into his brow.

At times he regarded the wounded soldiers in an envious way. He conceived persons with torn bodies to be peculiarly happy. He wished that he, too, had a wound, a red badge of courage.

The spectral soldier was at his side like a stalking reproach. The man's eyes were still fixed in a stare into the unknown. His gray, appalling face had attracted attention in the crowd, and men, slowing to his dreary pace, were walking with him. They were discussing his plight, questioning him and giving him advice. In a dogged way he repelled them, signing to them to go on and leave him alone. The shadows of his face were deepening and his tight lips seemed holding in check the moan of great despair. There could be seen a certain stiffness in the movements of his body, as if he were taking infinite care not to arouse the passion of his wounds. As he went on, he seemed always looking for a place, like one who goes to choose a grave.

Something in the gesture of the man as he waved the bloody and pitying soldiers away made the youth start as if bitten. He yelled in horror. Tottering forward he laid a quivering hand upon the man's arm. As the latter slowly turned his waxlike features toward him, the youth screamed:

"Gawd! Jim Conklin!"

The tall soldier made a little commonplace smile. "Hello, Henry," he said.

The youth swayed on his legs and glared strangely. He stuttered and stammered. "Oh, Jim—oh, Jim—oh, Jim—"

The tall soldier held out his gory hand. There was a curious red and black combination of new blood and old blood upon it. "Where yeh been, Henry?" he asked. He continued in a monotonous voice, "I thought mebbe yeh got keeled over. There's been thunder t' pay t'-day. I was worryin' about it a good deal."

The youth still lamented. "Oh, Jim—oh, Jim—oh, Jim—"

"Yeh know," said the tall soldier, "I was out there." He made a careful gesture. "An', Lord, what a circus! An', b'jiminey, I got shot—I got shot. Yes, b'jiminey, I got shot." He reiterated this fact in a bewildered way, as if he did not know how it came about.

The youth put forth anxious arms to assist him, but the tall soldier went firmly on as if propelled. Since the youth's arrival as a guardian for his friend, the other wounded men had ceased to display much interest. They occupied themselves again in dragging their own tragedies toward the rear.

Suddenly, as the two friends marched on, the tall soldier seemed to be overcome by a terror. His face turned to a semblance of gray paste. He clutched the youth's arm and looked all about him, as if dreading to be overheard. Then he began to speak in a shaking whisper:

"I tell yeh what I'm 'fraid of, Henry—I'll tell yeh what I'm 'fraid of. I'm 'fraid I'll fall down—an' then yeh know— them damned artillery wagons—they like as not'll run over me. That's what I'm 'fraid of—"

The youth cried out to him hysterically: "I'll take care of yeh, Jim! I'll take care of yeh! I swear t' Gawd I will!"

"Sure—will yeh, Henry?" the tall soldier beseeched.

"Yes—yes—I tell yeh—I'll take care of yeh, Jim!" protested the youth. He could not speak accurately because of the gulpings in his throat.

But the tall soldier continued to beg in a lowly way. He now hung babelike to the youth's arm. His eyes rolled in the wildness of his terror. "I was allus a good friend t' yeh, wa'n't I, Henry? I've allus been a pretty good feller, ain't I? An' it ain't much t' ask, is it? Jest t' pull me along outer th' road? I'd do it fer you, wouldn't I, Henry?"

Caissons, two-wheeled vehicles, were used as artillery wagons to haul ammunition for the guns. Limbers were similar vehicles to which artillery pieces were hooked. The gun, limber, and caisson usually were drawn by a team of six horses.

He paused in piteous anxiety to await his friend's reply.

The youth had reached an anguish where the sobs scorched him. He strove to express his loyalty, but he could only make fantastic gestures.

However, the tall soldier seemed suddenly to forget all those fears. He became again the grim, stalking specter of a soldier. He went stonily forward. The youth wished his friend to lean upon him, but the other always shook his head and strangely protested. "No—no—no—leave me be—leave me be—"

His look was fixed again upon the unknown. He moved with mysterious purpose, and all of the youth's offers he brushed aside. "No—no—leave me be—leave me be—"

The youth had to follow.

Presently the latter heard a voice talking softly near his shoulders. Turning he saw that it belonged to the tattered soldier. "Ye'd better take 'im outa th' road, pardner. There's a batt'ry comin' helitywhoop down th' road an' he'll git runned over. He's a goner anyhow in about five minutes— yeh kin see that. Ye 'd better take 'im outa th' road. Where th' blazes does he git his stren'th from?"

"Lord knows!" cried the youth. He was shaking his hands helplessly.

He ran forward presently and grasped the tall soldier by the arm. "Jim! Jim!" he coaxed "come with me."

The tall soldier weakly tried to wrench himself free. "Huh," he said vacantly. He stared at the youth for a moment. At last he spoke as if dimly comprehending. "Oh! Inteh th' fields? Oh!"

He started blindly through the grass.

The youth turned once to look at the lashing riders and jouncing guns of the battery. He was startled from this view by a shrill outcry from the tattered man.

"Gawd! He's runnin'!"

Turning his head swiftly, the youth saw his friend running in a staggering and stumbling way toward a little clump of bushes. His heart seemed to wrench itself almost free from his body at this sight. He made a noise of pain. He and the tattered man began a pursuit. There was a singular race.

When he overtook the tall soldier he began to plead with all the words he could find. "Jim—Jim—what are you doing—what makes you do this way—you'll hurt yerself."

The same purpose was in the tall soldier's face. He protested in a dulled way, keeping his eyes fastened on the mystic place of his intentions. "No—no—don't tech me—leave me be—leave me be—"

The youth, aghast and filled with wonder at the tall soldier, began quaveringly to question him. "Where yeh goin', Jim? What you thinking about? Where you going? Tell me, won't you, Jim?"

The tall soldier faced about as upon relentless pursuers. In his eyes there was a great appeal. "Leave me be, can't yeh? Leave me be fer a minnit."

The youth recoiled. "Why, Jim," he said, in a dazed way, "what's the matter with you?"

The tall soldier turned and, lurching dangerously, went on. The youth and the tattered soldier followed, sneaking as if whipped, feeling unable to face the stricken man if he should again confront them. They began to have thoughts of a solemn ceremony. There was something rite-like in these movements of the doomed soldier. And there was a resemblance in him to a devotee of a mad religion, blood-sucking, muscle-wrenching, bone-crushing. They were awed and afraid. They hung back lest he have at command a dreadful weapon.

At last, they saw him stop and stand motionless. Hastening up, they perceived that his face wore an expression telling that he had at last found the place for which he had struggled. His spare figure was erect; his bloody hands were quietly at his side. He was waiting with patience for something that he had come to meet. He was at the rendezvous. They paused and stood, expectant.

There was a silence.

Finally, the chest of the doomed soldier began to heave with a strained motion. It increased in violence until it was as if an animal was within and was kicking and tumbling furiously to be free.

This spectacle of gradual strangulation made the youth writhe, and once as his friend rolled his eyes, he saw something in them that made him sink wailing to the ground. He raised his voice in a last supreme call.

"Jim—Jim—Jim—"

The tall soldier opened his lips and spoke. He made a gesture. "Leave me be—don't tech me—leave me be—"

There was another silence while he waited.

Suddenly, his form stiffened and straightened. Then it was shaken by a prolonged ague. He stared into space. To the two watchers there was a curious and profound dignity in the firm lines of his awful face.

He was invaded by a creeping strangeness that slowly enveloped him. For a moment the tremor of his legs caused him to dance a sort of hideous hornpipe. His arms beat wildly about his head in expression of implike enthusiasm.

His tall figure stretched itself to its full height. There was a slight rending sound. Then it began to swing forward, slow and straight, in the manner of a falling tree. A swift muscular contortion made the left shoulder strike the ground first.

The body seemed to bounce a little way from the earth. "God!" said the tattered soldier.

The youth had watched, spellbound, this ceremony at the place of meeting. His face had been twisted into an expression of every agony he had imagined for his friend.

He now sprang to his feet and, going closer, gazed upon the pastelike face. The mouth was open and the teeth showed in a laugh.

As the flap of the blue jacket fell away from the body, he could see that the side looked as if it had been chewed by wolves.

The youth turned, with sudden, livid rage, toward the battlefield. He shook his fist. He seemed about to deliver a philippic.

"Hell—"

The red sun was pasted in the sky like a wafer.

CHAPTER X.

THE TATTERED MAN stood musing.

"Well, he was reg'lar jim-dandy fer nerve, wa'n't he,' said he finally in a little awestruck voice. "A reg'lar jim- dandy." He thoughtfully poked one of the docile hands with his foot. "I wonner where he got 'is stren'th from? I never seen a man do like that before. It was a funny thing. Well, he was a reg'lar jim-dandy."

The youth desired to screech out his grief. He was stabbed, but his tongue lay dead in the tomb of his mouth. He threw himself again upon the ground and began to brood.

The tattered man stood musing.

"Look-a-here, pardner," he said, after a time. He regarded the corpse as he spoke. "He's up an' gone, ain't 'e, an' we might as well begin t' look out fer ol' number one. This here thing is all over. He's up an' gone, ain't 'e ? An' he's all right here. Nobody won't bother 'im. An' I must say I ain't enjoying any great health m'self these days."

The youth, awakened by the tattered soldier's tone, looked quickly up. He saw that he was swinging uncertainly on his legs and that his face had turned to a shade of blue.

"Good Lord!" he cried, "you ain't goin' t'--not you, too."

The tattered man waved his hand. "Nary die," he said. "All I want is some pea soup an' a good bed. Some pea soup," he repeated dreamfully.

The youth arose from the ground. "I wonder where he came from. I left him over there." He pointed. "And now I find 'im here. And he was coming from over there, too." He indicated a new direction. They both turned toward the body as if to ask of it a question.

"Well," at length spoke the tattered man, "there ain't no use in our staying here an' tryin' t' ask him anything."

The youth nodded an assent wearily. They both turned to gaze for a moment at the corpse.

The youth murmured something.

"Well, he was a jim-dandy, wa'n't 'e?" said the tattered man as if in response.

They turned their backs upon it and started away. For a time they stole softly, treading with their toes. It remained laughing there in the grass.

"I'm commencin' t' feel pretty bad," said the tattered man, suddenly breaking one of his little silences. "I'm commencin' t' feel pretty damn' bad."

The youth groaned. "O Lord!" He wondered if he was to be the tortured witness of another grim encounter.

But his companion waved his hand reassuringly. "Oh, I'm not goin' t' die yit! There too much dependin' on me fer me t' die yit. No, sir! Nary die! I *can't!* Ye'd oughta see th' swad a' chil'ren I've got, an' all like that."

The youth glancing at his companion could see by the shadow of a smile that he was making some kind of fun.

As they plodded on the tattered soldier continued to talk. "Besides, if I died, I wouldn't die th' way that feller did. That was th' funniest thing. I'd jest flop down, I would. I never seen a feller die th' way that feller did.

"Yeh know Tom Jamison, he lives next door t' me up home. He's a nice feller, he is, an' we was allus good friends. Smart, too. Smart as a steel trap. Well, when we was a- fightin' this afternoon, all-of-a-sudden he begin t' rip up an' cuss an' beller at me. 'Yer shot, yeh blamed infernal!'—he swear horrible—he ses t' me. I put up m' hand t' m' head an' when I looked at m' fingers, I seen, sure 'nough, I was shot. I give a holler an' begin t' run, but b'fore I could git away another one hit me in th' arm an' whirl' me clean 'round. I got skeared when they was all a-shootin' b'hind me an' I run t' beat all, but I cotch it pretty bad. I've an idee I'd a' been fightin' yit, if t'was n't fer Tom Jamison."

Then he made a calm announcement: "There's two of 'em-- little ones--but they're beginnin' t' have fun with me now. I don't b'lieve I kin walk much furder."

They went slowly on in silence. "Yeh look pretty peek-ed yerself," said the tattered man at last. "I bet yeh've got a worser one than yeh think. Ye'd better take keer of yer hurt. It don't do t' let sech things go. It might be inside mostly, an' them plays thunder. Where is it located?" But he continued his harangue without waiting for a reply. "I see 'a feller git hit plum in th' head when my reg'ment was a- standin' at ease onct. An' everybody yelled out to 'im: Hurt, John? Are yeh hurt much? 'No,' ses he. He looked kinder surprised, an' he went on tellin' 'em how he felt. He sed he didn't feel nothin'. But, by dad, th' first thing that feller knowed he was dead. Yes, he was dead--stone dead. So, yeh wanta watch out. Yeh might have some queer kind 'a hurt yerself. Yeh can't never tell. Where is your'n located?"

The youth had been wriggling since the introduction of this topic. He now gave a cry of exasperation and made a furious motion with his hand. "Oh, don't bother me!" he said. He was enraged against the tattered man, and could have strangled him. His companions seemed ever to play intolerable parts. They were ever upraising the ghost of shame on the stick of their curiosity. He turned toward the tattered man as one at bay. "Now, don't bother me," he repeated with desperate menace.

"Well, Lord knows I don't wanta bother anybody," said the other. There was a little accent of despair in his voice as he replied, "Lord knows I 've gota 'nough m' own t' tend to."

The youth, who had been holding a bitter debate with himself and casting glances of hatred and contempt at the tattered man, here spoke in a hard voice. "Good-by," he said.

The tattered man looked at him in gaping amazement. "Why-- why, pardner, where yeh goin'?" he asked unsteadily. The youth looking at him, could see that he, too, like that other one, was beginning to act dumb and animal-like. His thoughts seemed to be floundering about in his head. "Now--now--look-a--here, you Tom Jamison--now--I won't have this--this here won't do. Where--where yeh goin'?"

The youth pointed vaguely. "Over there," he replied.

"Well, now look-a--here--now," said the tattered man, rambling on in idiot fashion. His head was hanging forward and his words were slurred. "This thing won't do, now, Tom Jamison. It won't do. I know yeh, yeh pig-headed devil. Yeh wanta go trompin' off with a bad hurt. It ain't right--now-- Tom Jamison--it ain't. Yeh wanta leave me take keer of yeh, Tom Jamison. It ain't--right--it ain't--fer yeh t' go-- trompin' off--with a bad hurt--it ain't--ain't--ain't right-- it ain't."

In reply the youth climbed a fence and started away. He could hear the tattered man bleating plaintively.

Once he faced about angrily. "What?"

"Look—a—here, now, Tom Jamison—now—it ain't—"

The youth went on. Turning at a distance he saw the tattered man wandering about helplessly in the field.

He now thought that he wished he was dead. He believed that he envied those men whose bodies lay strewn over the grass of the fields and on the fallen leaves of the forest.

The simple questions of the tattered man had been knife thrusts to him. They asserted a society that probes pitilessly at secrets until all is apparent. His late companion's chance persistency made him feel that he could not keep his crime concealed in his bosom. It was sure to be brought plain by one of those arrows which cloud the air and are constantly pricking, discovering, proclaiming those things which are willed to be forever hidden. He admitted that he could not defend himself against this agency. It was not within the power of vigilance.

The men of Howard's Eleventh Corps were retreating before the Jackson's assault. Some of Howard's men did stand and fight for a time, but Jackson had skillfully concentrated his men in an overwhelming onslaught against a weak point in the Union line. Many Union soldiers ran back down the Plank Road in the general direction of Chancellorsville right through Union lines and into the waiting arms of Lee's men on the other side of the village.

This illustration (from *Battles and Leaders*) shows the Confederates overrunning a Union breastworks, taking many prisoners in the process.

Reinforcements were coming. If Henry Fleming was somewhere between Hazel Grove and the Plank Road, he might have been watching Sickles' divisions rapidly retracing their march earlier in the day to halt Jackson's advance. Other troops rushing to the front were units of the Second Corps and Twelfth Corps.

CHAPTER XI.

HE BECAME AWARE that the furnace roar of the battle was growing louder. Great brown clouds had floated to the still heights of air before him. The noise, too, was approaching. The woods filtered men and the fields became dotted.

As he rounded a hillock, he perceived that the roadway was now a crying mass of wagons, teams, and men. From the heaving tangle issued exhortations, commands, imprecations. Fear was sweeping it all along. The cracking whips bit and horses plunged and tugged. The whitetopped wagons strained and stumbled in their exertions like fat sheep.

The youth felt comforted in a measure by this sight. They were all retreating. Perhaps, then, he was not so bad after all. He seated himself and watched the terror-stricken wagons. They fled like soft, ungainly animals. All the roarers and lashers served to help him to magnify the dangers and horrors of the engagement that he might try to prove to himself that the thing with which men could charge him was in truth a symmetrical act. There was an amount of pleasure to him in watching the wild march of this vindication.

Presently the calm head of a forward-going column of infantry appeared in the road. It came swiftly on. Avoiding the obstructions gave it the sinuous movement of a serpent. The men at the head butted mules with their musket stocks. They prodded teamsters indifferent to all howls. The men forced their way through parts of the dense mass by strength. The blunt head of the column pushed. The raving teamsters swore many strange oaths.

The commands to make way had the ring of a great importance in them. The men were going forward to the heart of the din. They were to confront the eager rush of the enemy. They felt the pride of their onward movement when the remainder of the army seemed trying to dribble down this road. They tumbled teams about with a fine feeling that it was no matter so long as their column got to the front in time. This importance made their faces grave and stern. And the backs of the officers were very rigid.

As the youth looked at them the black weight of his woe returned to him. He felt that he was regarding a procession of chosen beings. The separation was as great to him as if they had marched with weapons of flame and banners of sunlight. He could never be like them. He could have wept in his longings.

He searched about in his mind for an adequate malediction for the indefinite cause, the thing upon which men turn the words of final blame. It—whatever it was—was responsible for him, he said. There lay the fault.

The haste of the column to reach the battle seemed to the forlorn young man to be something much finer than stout fighting. Heroes, he thought, could find excuses in that long seething lane. They could retire with perfect self-respect and make excuses to the stars.

He wondered what those men had eaten that they could be in such haste to force their way to grim chances of death. As he watched his envy grew until he thought that he wished to change lives with one of them. He would have liked to have used a tremendous force, he said, throw off himself and become a better. Swift pictures of himself, apart, yet in himself, came to him—a blue desperate figure leading lurid charges with one knee forward and a broken blade high—a blue, determined figure standing before a crimson and steel assault, getting calmly killed on a high place before the eyes of all. He thought of the magnificent pathos of his dead body.

These thoughts uplifted him. He felt the quiver of war desire. In his ears, he heard the ring of victory. He knew the frenzy of a rapid successful charge. The music of the trampling feet, the sharp voices, the clanking arms of the column near him made him soar on the red wings of war. For a few moments he was sublime.

He thought that he was about to start for the front. Indeed, he saw a picture of himself, dust-stained, haggard, panting, flying to the front at the proper moment to seize and throttle the dark, leering witch of calamity.

Then the difficulties of the thing began to drag at him. He hesitated, balancing awkwardly on one foot.

He had no rifle; he could not fight with his hands, said he resentfully to his plan. Well, rifles could be had for the picking. They were extraordinarily profuse.

Also, he continued, it would be a miracle if he found his regiment. Well, he could fight with any regiment.

He started forward slowly. He stepped as if he expected to tread upon some explosive thing. Doubts and he were struggling.

He would truly be a worm if any of his comrades should see him returning thus, the marks of his flight upon him. There was a reply that the intent fighters did not care for what happened rearward saving that no hostile bayonets appeared there. In the battle-blur his face would, in a way be hidden, like the face of a cowled man.

But then he said that his tireless fate would bring forth, when the strife lulled for a moment, a man to ask of him an explanation. In imagination he felt the scrutiny of his companions as he painfully labored through some lies.

Eventually, his courage expended itself upon these objections. The debates drained him of his fire.

He was not cast down by this defeat of his plan, for, upon studying the affair carefully, he could not but admit that the objections were very formidable.

Furthermore, various ailments had begun to cry out. In their presence he could not persist in flying high with the wings of war; they rendered it almost impossible for him to see himself in a heroic light. He tumbled headlong.

He discovered that he had a scorching thirst. His face was so dry and grimy that he thought he could feel his skin crackle. Each bone of his body had an ache in it, and seemingly threatened to break with each movement. His feet were like two sores. Also, his body was calling for food. It was more powerful than a direct hunger. There was a dull, weight like feeling in his stomach, and, when he tried to walk, his head swayed and he tottered. He could not see with distinctness. Small patches of green mist floated before his vision.

While he had been tossed by many emotions, he had not been aware of ailments. Now they beset him and made clamor. As he was

One of the great strengths of the Army of the Potomac throughout the war was its ability to come back time and again after repeated defeats. Following a major defeat, the commanding general would be fired to be replaced by a rising officer still able to inspire high hopes. After Chancellorville, when Hooker's resignation was accepted, command of the army was offered to Major General John Reynolds, the much respected commander of the First Corps. Reynolds wanted no part of the political meddling of the Washington politician/generals and refused the promotion. Next, Major General George G. Meade, Commander of the Fifth Corps, was chosen; but in Meade's case, he was ordered to assume command of the army without even being given the chance to refuse. Through it all, the soldiers in the ranks maintained a confidence in their own fighting ability and the belief that once a competent commanding general were found, they were sure to win in the end.

The general "chosen for barbs" in this case would have been Major General Hooker, the Union commander.

at last compelled to pay attention to them, his capacity for self-hate was multiplied. In despair, he declared that he was not like those others. He now conceded it to be impossible that he should ever become a hero. He was a craven loon. Those pictures of glory were piteous things. He groaned from his heart and went staggering off.

A certain mothlike quality within him kept him in the vicinity of the battle. He had a great desire to see, and to get news. He wished to know who was winning.

He told himself that, despite his unprecedented suffering, he had never lost his greed for a victory, yet, he said, in a half-apologetic manner to his conscience, he could not but know that a defeat for the army this time might mean many favorable things for him. The blows of the enemy would splinter regiments into fragments. Thus, many men of courage, he considered, would be obliged to desert the colors and scurry like chickens. He would appear as one of them. They would be sullen brothers in distress, and he could then easily believe he had not run any farther or faster than they. And if he himself could believe in his virtuous perfection, he conceived that there would be small trouble in convincing all others.

He said, as if in excuse for this hope, that previously the army had encountered great defeats and in a few months had shaken off all blood and tradition of them, emerging as bright and valiant as a new one; thrusting out of sight the memory of disaster, and appearing with the valor and confidence of unconquered legions. The shrilling voices of the people at home would pipe dismally for a time, but various generals were usually compelled to listen to these ditties. He of course felt no compunctions for proposing a general as a sacrifice. He could not tell who the chosen for the barbs might be, so he could center no direct sympathy upon him. The people were afar and he did not conceive public opinion to be accurate at long range. It was quite probable they would hit the wrong man who, after he had recovered from his amazement would perhaps spend the rest of his days in writing replies to the songs of his alleged failure. It would be very unfortunate, no doubt, but in this case a general was of no consequence to the youth.

In a defeat there would be a roundabout vindication of himself. He thought it would prove, in a manner, that he had fled early because of his superior powers of perception. A serious prophet upon predicting a flood should be the first man to climb a tree. This would demonstrate that he was indeed a seer.

A moral vindication was regarded by the youth as a very important thing. Without salve, he could not, he thought, wear the sore badge of his dishonor through life. With his heart continually assuring him that he was despicable, he could not exist without making it, through his actions, apparent to all men.

If the army had gone gloriously on he would be lost. If the din meant that now his army's flags were tilted forward he was a condemned wretch. He would be compelled to doom himself to isolation. If the men were advancing, their indifferent feet were trampling upon his chances for a successful life.

As these thoughts went rapidly through his mind, he turned upon them and tried to thrust them away. He denounced himself as a villain. He said that he was the most unutterably selfish man in existence. His mind pictured the soldiers who would place their defiant bodies before the spear of the yelling battle fiend, and as he saw their dripping corpses on an imagined field, he said that he was their murderer.

Again he thought that he wished he was dead. He believed that he envied a corpse. Thinking of the slain, he achieved a great contempt for some of them, as if they were guilty for thus becoming lifeless. They might have been killed by lucky chances, he said, before they had had opportunities to flee or before they had been really tested. Yet they would receive laurels from tradition. He cried out bitterly that their crowns were stolen and their robes of glorious memories were shams. However, he still said that it was a great pity he was not as they.

A defeat of the army had suggested itself to him as a means of escape from the consequences of his fall. He considered, now, however, that it was useless to think of such a possibility. His education had been that success for that mighty blue machine was certain; that it would make victories as a contrivance turns out buttons. He presently discarded all his speculations in the other direction. He returned to the creed of soldiers.

When he perceived again that it was not possible for the army to be defeated, he tried to bethink him of a fine tale which he could take back to his regiment, and with it turn the expected shafts of derision.

But, as he mortally feared these shafts, it became impossible for him to invent a tale he felt he could trust. He experimented with many schemes, but threw them aside one by one as flimsy. He was quick to see vulnerable places in them all.

Furthermore, he was much afraid that some arrow of scorn might lay him mentally low before he could raise his protecting tale.

He imagined the whole regiment saying: "Where's Henry Fleming? He run, didn't 'e? Oh, my!" He recalled various persons who would be quite sure to leave him no peace about it. They would doubtless question him with sneers, and laugh at his stammering hesitation. In the next engagement they would try to keep watch of him to discover when he would run.

Wherever he went in camp, he would encounter insolent and lingeringly cruel stares. As he imagined himself passing near a crowd of comrades, he could hear some one say, "There he goes!"

Then, as if the heads were moved by one muscle, all the faces were turned toward him with wide, derisive grins. He seemed to hear some one make a humorous remark in a low tone. At it the others all crowed and cackled. He was a slang phrase.

These "burly men" were from Howard's Eleventh Corps. Here
they are depicted as fleeing in panic. Crane wrote his novel in the
early 1890s when the stereotype of the dumb German or Swede
was the butt of ethnic jokes.

CHAPTER XII.

THE COLUMN that had butted stoutly at the obstacles in the roadway was barely out of the youth's sight before he saw dark waves of men come sweeping out of the woods and down through the fields. He knew at once that the steel fibers had been washed from their hearts. They were bursting from their coats and their equipments as from entanglements. They charged down upon him like terrified buffaloes.

Behind them blue smoke curled and clouded above the treetops, and through the thickets he could sometimes see a distant pink glare. The voices of the cannon were clamoring in interminable chorus.

The youth was horrorstricken. He stared in agony and amazement. He forgot that he was engaged in combating the universe. He threw aside his mental pamphlets on the philosophy of the retreated and rules for the guidance of the damned.

The fight was lost. The dragons were coming with invincible strides. The army, helpless in the matted thickets and blinded by the overhanging night, was going to be swallowed. War, the red animal, war, the blood-swollen god, would have bloated fill.

Within him something bade to cry out. He had the impulse to make a rallying speech, to sing a battle hymn, but he could only get his tongue to call into the air: "Why—why—what—what's th' matter?"

Soon he was in the midst of them. They were leaping and scampering all about him. Their blanched faces shone in the dusk. They seemed, for the most part, to be very burly men. The youth turned from one to another of them as they galloped along. His incoherent questions were lost. They were heedless of his appeals. They did not seem to see him.

An officer of the Third Corps described the scene: ''The officers of the other corps made themselves speechless by striving to rally the 'flying Dutchman,' who was no longer an illusion, but a despicable reality. . .''

They sometimes gabbled insanely. One huge man was asking of the sky: "Say, where de plank road? Where de plank road!" It was as if he had lost a child. He wept in his pain and dismay.

Presently, men were running hither and thither in all ways. The artillery booming, forward, rearward, and on the flanks made jumble of ideas of direction. Landmarks had vanished into the gathered gloom. The youth began to imagine that he had got into the center of the tremendous quarrel, and he could perceive no way out of it. From the mouths of the fleeing men came a thousand wild questions, but no one made answers.

The youth, after rushing about and throwing interrogations at the heedless bands of retreating infantry, finally clutched a man by the arm. They swung around face to face.

"Why—why—" stammered the youth struggling with his balking tongue.

The man screamed: "Let go me! Let go me!" His face was livid and his eyes were rolling uncontrolled. He was heaving and panting. He still grasped his rifle, perhaps having forgotten to release his hold upon it. He tugged frantically, and the youth being compelled to lean forward was dragged several paces.

"Let go me! Let go me!"

"Why—why—" stuttered the youth.

"Well, then!" bawled the man in a lurid rage. He adroitly and fiercely swung his rifle. It crushed upon the youth's head. The man ran on.

The youth's fingers had turned to paste upon the other's arm. The energy was smitten from his muscles. He saw the flaming wings of lighting flash before his vision. There was a deafening rumble of thunder within his head.

Suddenly his legs seemed to die. He sank writhing to the ground. He tried to arise. In his efforts against the numbing pain he was like a man wrestling with a creature of the air.

There was a sinister struggle.

Sometimes he would achieve a position half erect, battle with the air for a moment, and then fall again, grabbing at the grass. His face was of a clammy pallor. Deep groans were wrenched from him.

Gauntlets were heavy leather gloves worn by cavalrymen and officers to protect their hands while on horseback.

As this battle was almost entirely devoid of cavalry action, this description pinpoints Fleming's location. He was a witness to the charge of Major Pennock Huey's 8th Pennsylvania Cavalry. These men were called upon to charge the massed Rebel infantry and stall their advance long enough for another defensive line of artillery to deploy closer to Chancellorsville. Cavalrymen's uniforms were trimmed in yellow, hence the reference to yellow facings.

At last, with a twisting movement, he got upon his hands and knees, and from thence, like a babe trying to walk, to his feet. Pressing his hands to his temples he went lurching over the grass.

He fought an intense battle with his body. His dulled senses wished him to swoon and he opposed them stubbornly, his mind portraying unknown dangers and mutilations if he should fall upon the field. He went tall soldier fashion. He imagined secluded spots where he could fall and be unmolested. To search for one he strove against the tide of his pain.

Once he put his hand to the top of his head and timidly touched the wound. The scratching pain of the contact made him draw a long breath through his clinched teeth. His fingers were dabbled with blood. He regarded them with a fixed stare.

Around him he could hear the grumble of jolted cannon as the scurrying horses were lashed toward the front. Once, a young officer on a besplashed charger nearly ran him down. He turned and watched the mass of guns, men, and horses sweeping in a wide curve toward a gap in a fence. The officer was making excited motions with a gauntleted hand. The guns followed the teams with an air of unwillingness, of being dragged by the heels.

Some officers of the scattered infantry were cursing and railing like fishwives. Their scolding voices could be heard above the din. Into the unspeakable jumble in the roadway rode a squadron of cavalry. The faded yellow of their facings shone bravely. There was a mighty altercation.

The artillery were assembling as if for a conference.

The blue haze of evening was upon the field. The lines of forest were long purple shadows. One cloud lay along the western sky partly smothering the red.

As the youth left the scene behind him, he heard the guns suddenly roar out. He imagined them shaking in black rage. They belched and howled like brass devils guarding a gate. The soft air was filled with the tremendous remonstrance. With it came the shattering peal of opposing infantry. Turning to look behind him, he could see sheets of orange light illumine the shadowy distance. There were subtle and sudden lightnings in the far air. At times he thought he could see heaving masses of men.

At this point, the devastating Confederate attack ground to a halt. Jackson's flank attack was stalled by the approach of darkness, the stiffening of resistance by his enemy, and the vigorous counterattack of the Third Corps and other Federal units. He halted his troops' advance and ordered his front units, which had become disorganized during the attack, to the rear. Fresh units were moved up with the intention of renewing the attack in the darkness. While this switch took place, Jackson rode out between the lines to reconnoiter and was fired upon by Federal troops near the Plank Road. As he rode back toward his own lines with his staff, the group was mistaken in the darkness for Union cavalry and fired upon. Jackson was mortally wounded by this gunfire.

He hurried on in the dusk. The day had faded until he could barely distinguish place for his feet. The purple darkness was filled with men who lectured and jabbered. Sometimes he could see them gesticulating against the blue and somber sky. There seemed to be a great ruck of men and munitions spread about in the forest and in the fields.

The little narrow roadway now lay lifeless. There were overturned wagons like sun-dried bowlders. The bed of the former torrent was choked with the bodies of horses and splintered parts of war machines.

It had come to pass that his wound pained him but little. He was afraid to move rapidly, however, for a dread of disturbing it. He held his head very still and took many precautions against stumbling. He was filled with anxiety, and his face was pinched and drawn in anticipation of the pain of any sudden mistake of his feet in the gloom.

His thoughts, as he walked, fixed intently upon his hurt. There was a cool, liquid feeling about it and he imagined blood moving slowly down under his hair. His head seemed swollen to a size that made him think his neck to be inadequate.

The new silence of his wound made much worriment. The little blistering voices of pain that had called out from his scalp were, he thought, definite in their expression of danger. By them he believed that he could measure his plight. But when they remained ominously silent he became frightened and imagined terrible fingers that clutched into his brain.

Amid it he began to reflect upon various incidents and conditions of the past. He bethought him of certain meals his mother had cooked at home, in which those dishes of which he was particularly fond had occupied prominent positions. He saw the spread table. The pine walls of the kitchen were glowing in the warm light from the stove. Too, he remembered how he and his companions used to go from the schoolhouse to the bank of a shaded pool. He saw his clothes in disorderly array upon the grass of the bank. He felt the swash of the fragrant water upon his body. The leaves of the overhanging maple rustled with melody in the wind of youthful summer.

He was overcome presently by a dragging weariness. His head hung forward and his shoulders were stooped as if he were bearing a great bundle. His feet shuffled along the ground.

He held continuous arguments as to whether he should lie down and sleep at some near spot, or force himself on until he reached a certain haven. He often tried to dismiss the question, but his body persisted in rebellion and his senses nagged at him like pampered babies.

At last he heard a cheery voice near his shoulder: "Yeh seem t' be in a pretty bad way, boy?"

The youth did not look up, but he assented with thick tongue. "Uh!"

The owner of the cheery voice took him firmly by the arm. "Well,"he said, with a round laugh, "I'm goin' your way. Th' hull gang is goin' your way. An' I guess I kin give yeh a lift." They began to walk like a drunken man and his friend.

As they went along, the man questioned the youth and assisted him with the replies like one manipulating the mind of a child. Sometimes he interjected anecdotes. "What reg'ment do yeh b'long teh? Eh? What's that? Th' 304th N' York? Why, what corps is that in? Oh, it is? Why, I thought they wasn't engaged t'-day—they're 'way over in th' center. Oh, they was, eh? Well, pretty nearly everybody got their share 'a fightin' t'-day. By dad, I give myself up fer dead any number 'a times. There was shootin' here an' shootin' there, an' hollerin' here an' hollerin' there, in th' damn' darkness, until I couldn't tell t' save m' soul which side I was on. Sometimes I thought I was sure 'nough from Ohier, an' other times I could 'a swore I was from th' bitter end of Florida. It was th' most mixed up dern thing I ever see. An' these here hull woods is a reg'lar mess. It'll be a miracle if we find our reg'ments t'-night. Pretty soon, though, we'll meet a-plenty of guards an' provost-guards, an' one thing an' another. Ho! there they go with an off'cer, I guess. Look at his hand a-draggin'. He's got all th' war he wants, I bet. He won't be talkin' so big about his reputation an' all when they go t' sawin' off his leg. Poor feller! My brother's got whiskers jest like that. How did yeh git 'way over here, anyhow? Your reg'ment is a long way from here, ain't it? Well, I guess we can find it. Yeh know there was a boy killed in my comp'ny t'-day that I thought th' world an' all of. Jack was a nice feller. By ginger, it hurt like thunder t' see ol' Jack jest git knocked flat. We was a-standin' purty peaceable fer a spell, 'though there was men runnin' ev'ry way all 'round us, an' while we was a-standin' like that,'long come a big fat feller. He began t' peck at Jack's elbow, an' he ses: 'Say, where's th' road t' th' river?' An' Jack, he never paid no attention, an' th' feller kept on a- peckin' at his elbow an' saying 'Say, where's th' road t' th' river?' Jack was a-lookin' ahead all th' time tryin' t' see th' Johnnies comin' through th' woods, an' he never paid no attention t' this big fat feller fer a long time, but at last he turned 'round an' he ses: 'Ah, go t' hell an' find th' road t' th' river!' An' jest then a shot slapped him bang on th' side th' head. He was a sergeant, too. Them was his last words. Thunder, I wish we was sure 'a findin' our reg'ments t'-night. It's goin' t' be long huntin'. But I guess we kin do it."

In the search which followed, the man of the cheery voice seemed to the youth to possess a wand of a magic kind. He threaded the mazes of the tangled forest with a strange fortune. In encounters with guards and patrols he displayed the keenness of a detective and the valor of a gamin. Obstacles fell before him and became of assistance. The youth, with his chin still on his breast, stood woodenly by while his companion beat ways and means out of sullen things.

The forest seemed a vast hive of men buzzing about in frantic circles, but the cheery man conducted the youth without mistakes, until at last he began to chuckle with glee and self-satisfaction. "Ah, there yeh are! See that fire?"

The youth nodded stupidly.

"Well, there's where your reg'ment is. An' now, good-by, ol' boy, good luck t' yeh."

A warm and strong hand clasped the youth's languid fingers for an instant, and then he heard a cheerful and audacious whistling as the man strode away. As he who had so befriended him was thus passing out of his life, it suddenly occurred to the youth that he had not once seen his face.

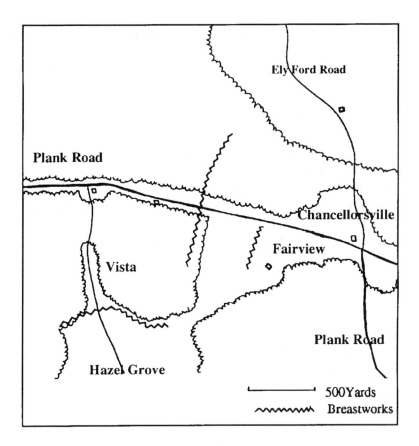

Plank Road

Ely Ford Road

Chancellorsville

Fairview

Vista

Plank Road

Hazel Grove

500 Yards

Breastworks

MAP 4: THE HAZEL GROVE-FAIRVIEW AREA

On Sunday, May 3, 1863, the area west of Chancellorsville saw some of the most desparate fighting of the Civil War. In reality, the village of Chancellorsville consisted of only a few structures at the junction of the Plank Road, the Turnpike, and Ely's Ford Road. Fairview, a piece of cleared high ground, contained a farm house and graveyard. Hazel Grove, lower in elevation, was not a grove at all but another cleared area. Hazel Grove was important because it separated the wings of Lee's army and could be used as a staging area for a counter attack. Aside from the roads and a few cleared places, this area was a heavily wooded part of the Wilderness. In some places the breastworks built by Union troops were substantial barricades.

120

CHAPTER XIII.

THE YOUTH went slowly toward the fire indicated by his departed friend. As he reeled, he bethought him of the welcome his comrades would give him. He had a conviction that he would soon feel in his sore heart the barbed missiles of ridicule. He had no strength to invent a tale; he would be a soft target.

He made vague plans to go off into the deeper darkness and hide, but they were all destroyed by the voices of exhaustion and pain from his body. His ailments, clamoring, forced him to seek the place of food and rest, at whatever cost.

He swung unsteadily toward the fire. He could see the forms of men throwing black shadows in the red light, and as he went nearer it became known to him in some way that the ground was strewn with sleeping men.

Of a sudden he confronted a black and monstrous figure. A rifle barrel caught some glinting beams. "Halt! halt!" He was dismayed for a moment, but he presently thought that he recognized the nervous voice. As he stood tottering before the rifle barrel, he called out: "Why, hello, Wilson, you—you here?"

The rifle was lowered to a position of caution and the loud soldier came slowly forward. He peered into the youth's face. "That you, Henry?"

"Yes, it's–it's me."

"Well, well, ol' boy," said the other, "by ginger, I'm glad t' see yeh! I give yeh up fer a goner. I thought yeh was dead sure enough." There was husky emotion in his voice.

The youth found that now he could barely stand upon his feet. There was a sudden sinking of his forces. He thought he must hasten to produce his tale to protect him from the missiles already at the lips of his redoubtable comrades. So, staggering before the loud soldier,

"Way over on th' right" would have had Henry among the fleeing soldiers of the Eleventh Corps, where the earlier battle had taken place.

A corporal wore two stripes and carried some authority.

he began: "Yes, yes. I've—I've had an awful time. I've been all over. Way over on th' right. Ter'ble fightin' over there. I had an awful time. I got separated from th' reg'ment. Over on th' right, I got shot. In th' head. I never see sech fightin.' Awful time. I don't see how I could a' got separated from th' reg'ment. I got shot, too."

His friend had stepped forward quickly. "What? Got shot? Why didn't yeh say so first? Poor ol' boy, we must—hol' on a minnit; what am I doin'. I'll call Simpson."

Another figure at that moment loomed in the gloom. They could see that it was the corporal. "Who yeh talkin' to, Wilson?" he demanded. His voice was anger-toned. " Who yeh talkin' to? Yeh th' derndest sentinel—why—hello, Henry, you here? Why, I thought you was dead four hours ago! Great Jerusalem, they keep turnin' up every ten minutes or so! We thought we'd lost forty-two men by straight count, but if they keep on a-comin' this way, we'll git th' comp'ny all back by mornin' yit. Where was yeh?"

"Over on th' right. I got separated"—began the youth with considerable glibness.

But his friend had interrupted hastily. "Yes, an' he got shot in th' head an' he's in a fix, an' we must see t' him right away." He rested his rifle in the hollow of his left arm and his right around the youth's shoulder.

"Gee, it must hurt like thunder!" he said.

The youth leaned heavily upon his friend. "Yes, it hurts—hurts a good deal," he replied. There was a faltering in his voice.

"Oh," said the corporal. He linked his arm in the youth's and drew him forward. "Come on, Henry. I'll take keer 'a yeh."

As they went on together the loud private called out after them: "Put 'im t' sleep in my blanket, Simpson. An'—hol' on a minnit—here's my canteen. It's full a' coffee. Look at his head by th' fire an' see how it looks. Maybe it's a pretty bad un. When I git relieved in a couple 'a minnits, I'll be over an' see t' him."

The youth's senses were so deadened that his friend's voice sounded from afar and he could scarcely feel the pressure of the corporal's arm. He submitted passively to the latter's directing strength. His head was in the old manner hanging forward upon his breast. His knees wobbled.

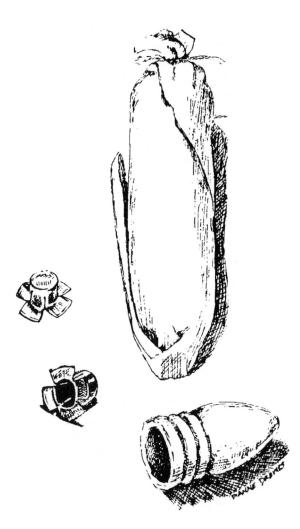

The ball referred to was the cone-shaped bullet fired from a Civil War rifle. The soldiers called it a "minie ball," mispronouncing the name of the bullet's inventor, Captain Etienne Minee.

The corporal led him into the glare of the fire. "Now, Henry," he said, "let's have look at yer ol' head."

The youth sat down obediently and the corporal, laying aside his rifle, began to fumble in the bushy hair of his comrade. He was obliged to turn the other's head so that the full flush of the fire light would beam upon it. He puckered his mouth with a critical air. He draw back his lips and whistled through his teeth when his fingers came in contact with the splashed blood and the rare wound.

"Ah, here we are!" he said. He awkwardly made further investigations. "Jest as I thought," he added, presently. "Yeh've been grazed by a ball. It's raised a queer lump jest as if some feller had lammed yeh on th' head with a club. It stopped a-bleedin' long time ago. Th' most about it is that in th' mornin' yeh'll feel that a number ten hat wouldn't fit yeh. An' your head'll be all het up an' feel as dry as burnt pork. An' yeh may git a lot 'a other sicknesses, too, by mornin'. Yeh can't never tell. Still, I don't much think so. It's jest a damn' good belt on th' head, an' nothing more. Now, you jest sit here an' don't move, while I go rout out th' relief. Then I'll send Wilson t' take keer 'a yeh."

The corporal went away. The youth remained on the ground like a parcel. He stared with a vacant look into the fire.

After a time he aroused, for some part, and the things about him began to take form. He saw that the ground in the deep shadows was cluttered with men, sprawling in every conceivable posture. Glancing narrowly into the more distant darkness, he caught occasional glimpses of visages that loomed pallid and ghostly, lit with a phosphorescent glow. These faces expressed in their lines the deep stupor of the tired soldiers. They made them appear like men drunk with wine. This bit of forest might have appeared to an ethereal wanderer as a scene of the result of some frightful debauch.

On the other side of the fire the youth observed an officer asleep, seated bolt upright, with his back against a tree. There was something perilous in his position. Badgered by dreams, perhaps, he swayed with little bounces and starts, like an old, toddy-stricken grandfather in a chimney corner. Dust and stains were upon his face. His lower jaw hung down as if lacking strength to assume its normal position. He was the picture of an exhausted soldier after a feast of war.

He had evidently gone to sleep with his sword in his arms. These two had slumbered in an embrace, but the weapon had been allowed in time to fall unheeded to the ground. The brass-mounted hilt lay in contact with some parts of the fire.

Within the gleam of rose and orange light from the burning sticks were other soldiers, snoring and heaving, or lying deathlike in slumber. A few pairs of legs were stuck forth, rigid and straight. The shoes displayed the mud or dust of marches and bits of rounded trousers, protruding from the blankets, showed rents and tears from hurried pitchings through the dense brambles.

The fire crackled musically. From it swelled light smoke. Overhead the foliage moved softly. The leaves, with their faces turned toward the blaze, were colored shifting hues of silver, often edged with red. Far off to the right, through a window in the forest could be seen a handful of stars lying, like glittering pebbles, on the black level of the night.

Occasionally, in this low-arched hall, a soldier would arouse and turn his body to a new position, the experience of his sleep having taught him of uneven and objectionable places upon the ground under him. Or, perhaps, he would lift himself to a sitting posture, blink at the fire for an unintelligent moment, throw a swift glance at his prostrate companion, and then cuddle down again with a grunt of sleepy content.

The youth sat in a forlorn heap until his friend the loud young soldier came, swinging two canteens by their light strings. "Well, now, Henry, ol' boy," said the latter, "we'll have yeh fixed up in jest about a minnit."

He had the bustling ways of an amateur nurse. He fussed around the fire and stirred the sticks to brilliant exertions. He made his patient drink largely from the canteen that contained the coffee. It was to the youth a delicious draught. He tilted his head afar back and held the canteen long to his lips. The cool mixture went caressingly down his blistered throat. Having finished, he sighed with comfortable delight.

The loud young soldier watched his comrade with an air of satisfaction. He later produced an extensive handkerchief from his pocket. He folded it into a manner of bandage and soused water from the other canteen upon the middle of it. This crude arrangement he bound over the youth's head, tying the ends in a queer knot at the back of the neck.

"There," he said, moving off and surveying his deed, "yeh look like th' devil, but I bet yeh feel better."

The youth contemplated his friend with grateful eyes. Upon his aching and swelling head the cold cloth was like a tender woman's hand.

"Yeh don't holler ner say nothin'," remarked his friend approvingly. "I know I'm a blacksmith at taken' keer 'a sick folks, an' yeh never squeaked. Yer a good un, Henry. Most 'a men would a' been in th' hospital long ago. A shot in th' head ain't fooling business."

The youth made no reply, but began to fumble with the buttons of his jacket.

"Well, come, now," continued his friend, "come on. I must put yeh t' bed an' see that yeh git a good night's rest."

The other got carefully erect, and the loud young soldier led him among the sleeping forms lying in groups and rows. Presently he stooped and picked up his blankets. He spread the rubber one upon the ground and placed the woolen one about the youth's shoulders.

"There now," he said, "lie down an' git some sleep."

The youth, with his manner of doglike obedience, got carefully down like a crone stooping. He stretched out with a murmur of relief and comfort. The ground felt like the softest couch.

But of a sudden he ejaculated: "Hol' on a minnit! Where you goin' t' sleep?"

His friend waved his hand impatiently. "Right down there by yeh."

"Well, but hol' on a minnit," continued the youth. "What yeh goin' t' sleep in? I've got your—"

The loud young soldier snarled: "Shet up an' go on t' sleep. Don't be makin' a damn' fool 'a yerself," he said severely.

After the reproof the youth said no more. An exquisite drowsiness had spread through him. The warm comfort of the blanket enveloped him and made a gentle languor. His head fell forward on his crooked arm and his weighted lids went softly down over his eyes. Hearing a splatter of musketry from the distance, he wondered indifferently if those men sometimes slept. He gave a long sigh, snuggled down into his blanket, and in a moment was like his comrades.

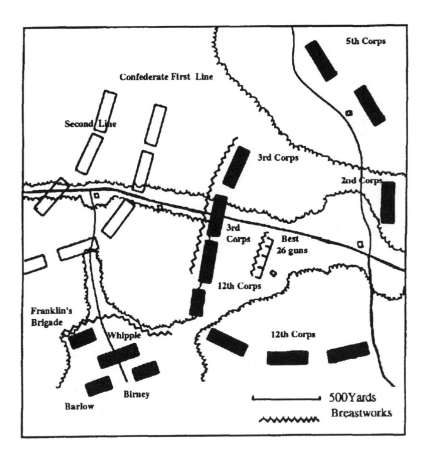

MAP 5: SUNDAY, MAY 3, 1863

Though driven back during Saturday's fighting, the Union still held a very strong position on Sunday morning. The key was Hazel Grove because Lee's forces could not be reunited while Union infantry and artillery crowned this piece of cleared high ground. At dawn, Hooker ordered Sickles to abandon Hazel Grove and march to Fairview. Whipple's Division and the 124th New York made that march and were posted to the rear of the Union line of guns at Fairview.

CHAPTER XIV.

WHEN THE YOUTH awoke it seemed to him that he had been asleep for a thousand years, and he felt sure that he opened his eyes upon an unexpected world. Gray mists were slowly shifting before the first efforts of the sun rays. An impending splendor could be seen in the eastern sky. An icy dew had chilled his face, and immediately upon arousing he curled farther down into his blanket. He stared for a while at the leaves overhead, moving in a heraldic wind of the day.

The distance was splintering and blaring with the noise of fighting. There was in the sound an expression of a deadly persistency, as if it had not begun and was not to cease.

About him were the rows and groups of men that he had dimly seen the previous night. They were getting a last draught of sleep before the awakening. The gaunt, careworn features and dusty figures were made plain by this quaint light at the dawning, but it dressed the skin of the men in corpselike hues and made the tangled limbs appear pulseless and dead. The youth started up with a little cry when his eyes first swept over this motionless mass of men, thickspread upon the ground, pallid, and in strange postures. His disordered mind interpreted the hall of the forest as a charnel place. He believed for an instant that he was in the house of the dead, and he did not dare to move lest these corpses start up, squalling and squawking. In a second, however, he achieved his proper mind. He swore a complicated oath at himself. He saw that this somber picture was not a fact of the present, but a mere prophecy.

He heard then the noise of a fire crackling briskly in the cold air, and, turning his head, he saw his friend pottering busily about a small blaze. A few other figures moved in the fog, and he heard the hard cracking of axe blows.

The iron colored mixture is coffee. To increase profits, unscrupulous contractors mixed sawdust with the ground coffee they sold to the army. The US government later bought coffee beans whole to make adulteration easier to detect. On the march, soldiers were issued coffee and sugar and were responsible for brewing their own. It was no easy task to grind whole coffee beans in the field. The beans might be placed in a small cloth bag and beaten with a rock or rifle butt; a handful of ground coffee and some sugar were thrown into a pail or tin cup with water and boiled until the coffee attained the desired strength. In theory, the grounds would settle to the bottom, but soldiers often drank coffee with grounds and bits of ash from the fire still floating in the brew.

John Billings, a Civil War veteran, wrote:

The coffee ration was most heartily appreciated by the soldier. . .One of the most interesting scenes presented in army life took place at night when the army was on the point of bivouacking. As soon as this fact became known along the column, each man would seize a rail from the nearest fence, and with this additional arm on the shoulder would enter the proposed camping-ground. In no more time than it takes to tell the story, the little camp-fires, rapidly increasing to hundreds in number, would shoot up along the hills and plains, and as if by magic acres of territory would be luminous with them. Soon they would be surrounded by the soldiers, who made it an almost invariable rule to cook their coffee first. . . .

It was coffee *at* meals and *between* meals; and men going on a guard or coming off guard drank it at all hours of the night, and to-day the old soldiers who can stand it are the hardest coffee-drinkers in the community. . . .

Suddenly there was a hollow rumble of drums. A distant bugle sang faintly. Similar sounds, varying in strength, came from near and far over the forest. The bugles called to each other like brazen gamecocks. The near thunder of the regimental drums rolled.

The body of men in the woods rustled. There was a general uplifting of heads. A murmuring of voices broke upon the air. In it there was much bass of grumbling oaths. Strange gods were addressed in condemnation of the early hours necessary to correct war. An officer's peremptory tenor rang out and quickened the stiffened movement of the men. The tangled limbs unraveled. The corpse-hued faces were hidden behind fists that twisted slowly in the eye sockets.

The youth sat up and gave vent to an enormous yawn. "Thunder!" he remarked petulantly. He rubbed his eyes, and then putting up his hand felt carefully of the bandage over his wound. His friend, perceiving him to be awake, came from the fire. "Well, Henry, ol' man, how do yeh feel this mornin'?" he demanded.

The youth yawned again. Then he puckered his mouth to a little pucker. His head, in truth, felt precisely like a melon, and there was an unpleasant sensation at his stomach.

"Oh, Lord, I feel pretty bad," he said.

"Thunder!" exclaimed the other. "I hoped ye'd feel all right this morning. Let's see th' bandage— I guess it's slipped." He began to tinker at the wound in rather a clumsy way until the youth exploded.

"Gosh-dern it!" he said in sharp irritation; "you're the hangdest man I ever saw! You wear muffs on your hands. Why in good thunderation can't you be more easy? I'd rather you'd stand off an' throw guns at it. Now, go slow, an' don't act as if you was nailing down carpet."

He glared with insolent command at his friend, but the latter answered soothingly. "Well, well, come now, an' git some grub," he said. "Then, maybe, yeh'll feel better."

At the fireside the loud young soldier watched over his comrade's wants with tenderness and care. He was very busy marshaling the little black vagabonds of tin cups and pouring into them the streaming, iron colored mixture from a small and sooty tin pail. He had some fresh meat, which he roasted hurriedly upon a stick. He sat down then and contemplated the youth's appetite with glee.

133

The youth took note of a remarkable change in his comrade since those days of camp life upon the river bank. He seemed no more to be continually regarding the proportions of his personal prowess. He was not furious at small words that pricked his conceits. He was no more a loud young soldier. There was about him now a fine reliance. He showed a quiet belief in his purposes and his abilities. And this inward confidence evidently enabled him to be indifferent to little words of other men aimed at him.

The youth reflected. He had been used to regarding his comrade as a blatant child with an audacity grown from his inexperience, thoughtless, headstrong, jealous, and filled with a tinsel courage. A swaggering babe accustomed to strut in his own dooryard. The youth wondered where had been born these new eyes; when his comrade had made the great discovery that there were many men who would refuse to be subjected by him. Apparently, the other had now climbed a peak of wisdom from which he could perceive himself as a very wee thing. And the youth saw that ever after it would be easier to live in his friend's neighborhood.

His comrade balanced his ebony coffee-cup on his knee. "Well, Henry," he said, "what d'yeh think th' chances are? D'yeh think we'll wallop 'em?"

The youth considered for a moment. "Day-b'fore-yesterday," he finally replied, with boldness, "you would 'a' bet you'd lick the hull kit-an'-boodle all by yourself."

His friend looked a trifle amazed. "Would I?" he asked. He pondered. "Well, perhaps I would," he decided at last. He stared humbly at the fire.

The youth was quite disconcerted at this surprising reception of his remarks. "Oh, no, you wouldn't either," he said, hastily trying to retrace.

But the other made a deprecating gesture. "Oh, yeh needn't mind, Henry," he said. "I believe I was a pretty big fool in those days." He spoke as after a lapse of years.

There was a little pause.

"All th' officers say we've got th' rebs in a pretty tight box," said the friend, clearing his throat in a commonplace way. "They all seem t' think we've got 'em jest where we want 'em."

"I don't know about that," the youth replied. "What I seen over on th' right makes me think it was th' other way about. From where I was, it looked as if we was gettin' a good poundin' yestirday."

"D'yeh think so?" inquired the friend. "I thought we handled 'em pretty rough yestirday."

"Not a bit," said the youth. "Why, lord, man, you didn't see nothing of the fight. Why!" Then a sudden thought came to him. "Oh! Jim Conklin's dead."

His friend started. "What? Is he? Jim Conklin?"

The youth spoke slowly. "Yes. He's dead. Shot in th' side." "Yeh don't say so. Jim Conklin. . . .poor cuss!"

All about them were other small fires surrounded by men with their little black utensils. From one of these near came sudden sharp voices in a row. It appeared that two lightfooted soldiers had been teasing a huge, bearded man, causing him to spill coffee upon his blue knees. The man had gone into a rage and had sworn comprehensively. Stung by his language, his tormentors had immediately bristled at him with a great show of resenting unjust oaths. Possibly there was going to be a fight.

The friend arose and went over to them, making pacific motions with his arms. "Oh, here, now, boys, what's th' use?" he said. "We'll be at th' rebs in less'n an hour. What's th' good fightin' 'mong ourselves?"

One of the light-footed soldiers turned upon him red-faced and violent. "Yeh needn't come around here with yer preachin'. I s'pose yeh don't approve 'a fighting since Charley Morgan licked yeh; but I don't see what business this here is 'a yours or anybody else."

"Well, it ain't," said the friend mildly. "Still I hate t' see— "

There was a tangled argument.

"Well, he— ," said the two, indicating their opponent with accusative forefingers.

The huge soldier was quite purple with rage. He pointed at the two soldiers with his great hand, extended clawlike. "Well, they— "

But during this argumentative time the desire to deal blows seemed to pass, although they said much to each other. Finally the friend returned to his old seat. In a short while the three antagonists could be seen together in an amiable bunch.

DIANNE DREWES

Irish soldiers had a reputation as great brawlers in the Army of the Potomac. It was said that when there were no Confederates to fight, the Irishmen fought each other. In fact, large numbers of recent immigrants from Ireland enlisted in the Southern army as well. This reference is important because Brigadier General Thomas Francis Meagher's Irish Brigade, one of the most colorful units in the Army of the Potomac, fought near Franklin's Brigade on May 3, 1863.

Here the soldiers have been discussing the military situation with great perception. It was mentioned earlier that some felt they had the Rebels in a "pretty tight box." This was a very accurate assessment of Lee's precarious condition. His army was divided before a more numerous enemy, his men were exhausted, and they had suffered terrible losses. His most able subordinate, General Jackson, had been carried from the field and many junior officers— company, regimental, and brigade commanders—had been killed or wounded. All that was needed for a Union victory was a coordinated attack by Hooker. His men knew it, his officers knew it—only Hooker refused to believe it.

"Jimmie Rogers ses I'll have t' fight him after th' battle t'-day," announced the friend as he again seated himself. "He ses he don't allow no interferin' in his business. I hate t' see th' boys fightin' 'mong themselves."

The youth laughed. "Yer changed a good bit. Yeh ain't at all like yeh was. I remember when you an' that Irish feller— " He stopped and laughed again.

"No, I didn't use t' be that way," said his friend thoughtfully. "That's true 'nough."

"Well, I didn't mean— " began the youth.

The friend made another deprecatory gesture. "Oh, yeh needn't mind, Henry."

There was another little pause.

"Th' reg'ment lost over half th' men yestirday," remarked the friend eventually. "I thought a course they was all dead, but, laws, they kep' a-comin' back last night until it seems, after all, we didn't lose but a few. They'd been scattered all over, wanderin' around in th' woods, fightin' with other reg'ments, an' everything. Jest like you done."

"So?" said the youth.

CHAPTER XV.

THE REGIMENT was standing at order arms at the side of a lane, waiting for the command to march, when suddenly the youth remembered the little packet enwrapped in a faded yellow envelope which the loud young soldier with lugubrious words had intrusted to him. It made him start. He uttered an exclamation and turned toward his comrade.

"Wilson!"

"What?"

His friend, at his side in the ranks, was thoughtfully staring down the road. From some cause his expression was at that moment very meek. The youth, regarding him with sidelong glances, felt impelled to change his purpose. "Oh, nothing," he said.

His friend turned his head in some surprise, "Why, what was yeh goin' t' say?"

"Oh, nothing," repeated the youth.

He resolved not to deal the little blow. It was sufficient that the fact made him glad. It was not necessary to knock his friend on the head with the misguided packet.

He had been possessed of much fear of his friend, for he saw how easily questionings could make holes in his feelings. Lately, he had assured himself that the altered comrade would not tantalize him with a persistent curiosity, but he felt certain that during the first period of leisure his friend would ask him to relate his adventures of the previous day.

He now rejoiced in the possession of a small weapon with which he could prostrate his comrade at the first signs of a cross-examination. He was master. It would now be he who could laugh and shoot the shafts of derision.

The friend had, in a weak hour, spoken with sobs of his own death. He had delivered a melancholy oration previous to his funeral, and had doubtless in the packet of letters, presented various keepsakes to relatives. But he had not died, and thus he had delivered himself into the hands of the youth.

The latter felt immensely superior to his friend, but he inclined to condescension. He adopted toward him an air of patronizing good humor.

His self-pride was now entirely restored. In the shade of its flourishing growth he stood with braced and self-confident legs, and since nothing could now be discovered he did not shrink from an encounter with the eyes of judges, and allowed no thoughts of his own to keep him from an attitude of manfulness. He had performed his mistakes in the dark, so he was still a man.

Indeed, when he remembered his fortunes of yesterday, and looked at them from a distance he began to see something fine there. He had license to be pompous and veteranlike.

His panting agonies of the past he put out of his sight.

In the present, he declared to himself that it was only the doomed and the damned who roared with sincerity at circumstance. Few but they ever did it. A man with a full stomach and the respect of his fellows had no business to scold about anything that he might think to be wrong in the ways of the universe, or even with the ways of society. Let the unfortunates rail; the others may play marbles.

He did not give a great deal of thought to these battles that lay directly before him. It was not essential that he should plan his ways in regard to them. He had been taught that many obligations of a life were easily avoided. The lessons of yesterday had been that retribution was a laggard and blind. With these facts before him he did not deem it necessary that he should become feverish over the possibilities of the ensuing twenty-four hours. He could leave much to chance. Besides, a faith in himself had secretly blossomed. There was a little flower of confidence growing within him. He was now a man of experience. He had been out among the dragons, he said, and he assured himself that they were not so hideous as he had imagined them. Also, they were inaccurate; they did not sting with precision. A stout heart often defied, and defying, escaped.

And, furthermore, how could they kill him who was the chosen of gods and doomed to greatness?

He remembered how some of the men had run from the battle. As he recalled their terror-struck faces he felt a scorn for them. They had surely been more fleet and more wild than was absolutely necessary. They were weak mortals. As for himself, he had fled with discretion and dignity.

He was aroused from this reverie by his friend, who, having hitched about nervously and blinked at the trees for a time, suddenly coughed in an introductory way, and spoke.

"Fleming!"

"What?"

The friend put his hand up to his mouth and coughed again. He fidgeted in his jacket.

"Well," he gulped, at last, "I guess yeh might as well give me back them letters." Dark, prickling blood had flushed into his checks and brow.

"All right, Wilson," said the youth. He loosened two buttons of his coat, thrust in his hand, and brought forth the packet. As he extended it to his friend the latter's face was turned from him.

He had been slow in the act of producing the packet because during it he had been trying to invent a remarkable comment upon the affair. He could conjure nothing of sufficient point. He was compelled to allow his friend to escape unmolested with his packet. And for this he took unto himself considerable credit. It was a generous thing.

His friend at his side seemed suffering great shame. As he contemplated him, the youth felt his heart grow more strong and stout. He had never been compelled to blush in such a manner for his acts; he was an individual of extraordinary virtues.

He reflected, with condescending pity: "Too bad! Too bad! The poor devil, it makes him feel tough!"

After this incident, and as he reviewed the battle pictures he had seen, he felt quite competent to return home and make the hearts of the people glow with stories of war. He could see himself in a room of warm tints telling tales to listeners. He could exhibit laurels. They were insignificant; still, in a district where laurels were infrequent, they might shine.

He saw his gaping audience picturing him as the central figure in blazing scenes. And he imagined the consternation and the ejaculations of his mother and the young lady at the seminary as they drank his recitals. Their vague feminine formula for beloved ones doing brave deeds on the field of battle without risk of life would be destroyed.

This description fits the rifle pits that were at the edge of Hazel Grove. The 122nd Pennsylvania had manned the front line, but was relieved by the 124th New York at about eleven o'clock on the night of May 2. The 124th remained all night at the edge of the dense woods, just as Crane described it. The "terrific fracas" on the right was the start of Stuart's attack.

The roaring guns were part of the Union line of artillery positioned about a half-mile away at Fairview. Artillery was also at Hazel Grove, but there Hooker made the serious blunder of ordering his men to leave this important piece of high ground and march to Fairview.

CHAPTER XVI.

A SPUTTERING of musketry was always to be heard. Later, the cannon had entered the dispute. In the fog-filled air their voices made a thudding sound. The reverberations were continued. This part of the world led a strange, battleful existence.

The youth's regiment was marched to relieve a command that had lain long in some damp trenches. The men took positions behind a curving line of rifle pits that had been turned up, like a large furrow, along the line of woods. Before them was a level stretch, peopled with short, deformed stumps. From the woods beyond came the dull popping of the skirmishers and pickets, firing in the fog. From the right came the noise of a terrific fracas.

The men cuddled behind the small embankment and sat in easy attitudes awaiting their turn. Many had their backs to the firing. The youth's friend lay down, buried his face in his arms, and almost instantly, it seemed, he was in a deep sleep.

The youth leaned his breast against the brown dirt and peered over at the woods and up and down the line. Curtains of trees interfered with his ways of vision. He could see the low line of trenches but for a short distance. A few idle flags were perched on the dirt hills. Behind them were rows of dark bodies with a few heads sticking curiously over the top.

Always the noise of skirmishers came from the woods on the front and left, and the din on the right had grown to frightful proportions. The guns were roaring without an instant's pause for breath. It seemed that the cannon had come from all parts and were engaged in a stupendous wrangle. It became impossible to make a sentence heard.

The youth wished to launch a joke—a quotation from newspapers. He desired to say, "All quiet on the Rappahannock," but the

The march to Fairview was underway. The Rebels had expected to suffer heavy casualties in the attack on Hazel Grove, but Hooker surrendered it without a struggle. The Rebels yelled as they could not believe their good fortune.

Sgt. Sprenger of the 122nd Pennsylvania describes this scene:

> At times we were almost intermingled with Major-General Anderson's troops of the rebel army, as their calls to us were distinctly heard, such as "Never mind, boys, we will give it to you yet, to-day;" "We shall not forget Stonewall Jackson," etc—all correctly indicating the circumstance that we were certainly occupying close quarters with the enemy.

Pvt. Fleming's description of the generals as "lunkheads" is mirrored in a conversation among "Orange Blossoms" about General Hooker. Col. Weygant wrote:

> . . .our leading star, which had mounted so high and shone with such dazzling brightness, suddenly grew dim. "Our giant has become a pigmy," says one. "Fighting Joe Hooker has lost his head for once," says another. "Was he drunk?" whispers a third.

guns refused to permit even a comment upon their uproar. He never successfully concluded the sentence. But at last the guns stopped, and among the men in the rifle pits rumors again flew, like birds, but they were now for the most part black creatures who flapped their wings drearily near to the ground and refused to rise on any wings of hope. The men's faces grew doleful from the interpreting of omens. Tales of hesitation and uncertainty on the part of those high in place and responsibility came to their ears. Stories of disaster were borne into their minds with many proofs. This din of musketry on the right, growing like a released genie of sound, expressed and emphasized the army's plight.

The men were disheartened and began to mutter. They made gestures expressive of the sentence: "Ah, what more can we do?" And it could always be seen that they were bewildered by the alleged news and could not fully comprehend a defeat.

Before the gray mists had been totally obliterated by the sun rays, the regiment was marching in a spread column that was retiring carefully through the woods. The disordered, hurrying lines of the enemy could sometimes be seen down through the groves and little fields. They were yelling, shrill and exultant.

At this sight the youth forgot many personal matters and became greatly enraged. He exploded in loud sentences. "B'jiminey, we're generaled by a lot 'a lunkheads."

"More than one feller has said that t'-day," observed a man.

His friend, recently aroused, was still very drowsy. He looked behind him until his mind took in the meaning of the movement. Then he sighed. "Oh, well, I s'pose we got licked," he remarked sadly.

The youth had a thought that it would not be handsome for him to freely condemn other men. He made an attempt to restrain himself, but the words upon his tongue were too bitter. He presently began a long and intricate denunciation of the commander of the forces.

"Mebbe, it wa'n't all his fault—not all together. He did th' best he knowed. It's our luck t' git licked often," said his friend in a weary tone. He was trudging along with stooped shoulders and shifting eyes like a man who has been caned and kicked.

"Well, don't we fight like the devil? Don't we do all that men can?" demanded the youth loudly.

145

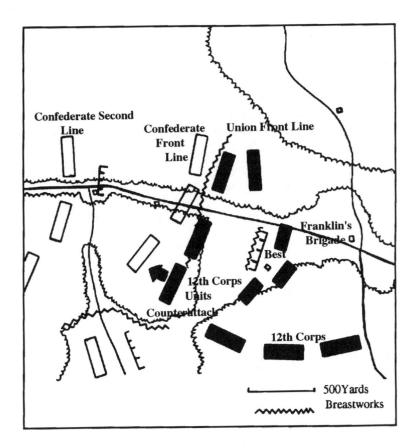

Confederate Second Line

Confederate Front Line

Union Front Line

Franklin's Brigade

Best

12th Corps Units Counterattack

12th Corps

500 Yards

Breastworks

MAP 6: SUNDAY, MAY 3, 1863, 7:00 AM

As Hooker had ordered, Hazel Grove was abandoned and the Union move to Fairview was completed. Captain Clermont Best held the position at Fairview with a reinforced line of nearly forty artillery pieces. The Confederates, quick to take advantage of Hooker's blunder, massed thirty-one guns at Hazel Grove with infantry support. Confederate artillery at Hazel Grove, along with guns on the Plank Road, engaged Best in a fierce artillery duel. The Confederate first line attacked the Union position but was repulsed with great loss. At the same time, Franklin's brigade was on the Plank Road supporting Union artillery batteries.

146

He was secretly dumbfounded at this sentiment when it came from his lips. For a moment his face lost its valor and he looked guiltily about him. But no one questioned his right to deal in such words, and presently he recovered his air of courage. He went on to repeat a statement he had heard going from group to group at camp that morning. "The brigadier said never saw a new reg'ment fight the way we fought yestirday, didn't he? And we didn't do better than many another reg'ment, did we? Well, then, you can't say it's th' army's fault, can you?"

In his reply, the friend's voice was stern. "'A course not," he said. "No man dare say we don't fight like th' devil. No man will ever dare say it. Th' boys fight like hell-roosters. But still—still, we don't have no luck."

"Well, then, if we fight like the devil an' don't ever whip, it must be the general's fault," said the youth grandly and decisively. "And I don't see any sense in fighting and fighting and fighting, yet always losing through some derned old lunkhead of a general."

A sarcastic man who was tramping at the youth's side, then spoke lazily. "Mebbe yeh think yeh fit th' hull battle yestirday, Fleming," he remarked.

The speech pierced the youth. Inwardly he was reduced to an abject pulp by these chance words. His legs quaked privately. He cast a frightened glance at the sarcastic man.

"Why, no," he hastened to say in a conciliating voice, "I don't think I fought the whole battle yesterday."

But the other seemed innocent of any deeper meaning. Apparently, he had no information. It was merely his habit. "Oh!" he replied in the same tone of calm derision.

The youth, nevertheless, felt a threat. His mind shrank from going near to the danger, and thereafter he was silent. The significance of the sarcastic man's words took from him all loud moods that would make him appear prominent. He became suddenly a modest person.

There was low-toned talk among the troops. The officers were impatient and snappy, their countenances clouded with the tales of misfortune. The troops, sifting through the forest, were sullen. In the youth's company once a man's laugh rang out. A dozen soldiers

The regiment had reached Fairview and taken up a position to the rear of Captain Clermont Best's powerful line of cannons.

A member of the 124th New York, who signed his letters "Felix," wrote home to the *Newburgh Telegraph* on May 7, 1863:

> on Sabbath morning at day-light all hands fell at the work with a will. Our regiment lay supporting our battery for a good while till the enemy were driving our forces and getting rather near us, then, we were ordered to the front and formed our battle line in the woods a little to the right. . .

Sgt. Peter P. Hazen, also of the 124th New York, wrote on the same day:

> About daylight Sunday morning, the 3d instant, we were ordered up and again on the move. We were cold and tired, sleepy and hungry, and we thought that we were going to be relieved and allowed to get us something to eat and to rest awhile; but alas! alas! it was for the battle field we were traveling. Oh, the bursting shells and booming cannons, and noise of musketry. Oh! I cannot describe it; and would not if I could. The noise of the roaring cannon I can compare to nothing but a continuous roar of thunder.

turned their faces quickly toward him and frowned with vague displeasure.

The noise of firing dogged their footsteps. Sometimes, it seemed to be driven a little way, but it always returned again with increased insolence. The men muttered and cursed, throwing black looks in its direction.

In a clear space the troops were at last halted. Regiments and brigades, broken and detached through their encounters with thickets, grew together again and lines were faced toward the pursuing bark of the enemy's infantry.

This noise, following like the yellings of eager, metallic hounds, increased to a loud and joyous burst, and then, as the sun went serenely up the sky, throwing illuminating rays into the gloomy thickets, it broke forth into prolonged pealings. The woods began to crackle as if afire.

"Whoop-a-dadee," said a man, "here we are! Everybody fightin'. Blood an' destruction."

"I was willin' t' bet they'd attack as soon as th' sun got fairly up," savagely asserted the lieutenant who commanded the youth's company. He jerked without mercy at his little mustache. He strode to and fro with dark dignity in the rear of his men, who were lying down behind whatever protection they had collected.

A battery had trundled into position in the rear and was thoughtfully shelling the distance. The regiment, unmolested as yet, awaited the moment when the gray shadows of the woods before them should be slashed by the lines of flame. There was much growling and swearing.

"Good Gawd," the youth grumbled, "we're always being chased around like rats! It makes me sick. Nobody seems to know where we go or why we go. We just get fired around from pillar to post and get licked here and get licked there, and nobody knows what it's done for. It makes a man feel like a damn' kitten in a bag. Now, I'd like to know what the eternal thunders we was marched into these woods for anyhow, unless it was to give the rebs a regular pot shot at us. We came in here and got our legs all tangled up in these cussed briars, and then we begin to fight and the rebs had an easy time of it. Don't tell me its just luck! I know better. It's this derned old— "

The Rebels assaulted Best's line vigorously in the hours after dawn but were thrown back with great losses. The massed Union guns, firing over the heads of their own troops in front, kept the enemy from advancing. As the morning wore on, the Rebel artillery at Hazel Grove, firing into the flank of the Union guns, together with Rebel guns on the Plank Road firing directly at them, took a fearful toll. Unsuccessful with frontal infantry assaults, the Rebels next tried to flank Best's line on the Plank Road side.

The *Middletown Whig Press* published a soldier's letter about the battle:

> . . .as I told you in another letter not a man of the regiment turned his back to the foe, or gave the slightest indication that he was pigeonlivered. The chief of the battery we were supporting cautioned his men to look out as he was supported by a "green regiment," as he was pleased to call us. We had not fired many rounds when things took a turn, as the pig said on the spit, and he told his men to blaze away, for there was no danger of them as long as the "Orange Blossoms" lasted.

The friend seemed jaded, but he interrupted his comrade with a voice of calm confidence "It'll turn out all right in th' end," he said.

"Oh, the devil it will! You always talk like a dog-hanged parson. Don't tell me! I know—"

At this time there was an interposition by the savage-minded lieutenant, who was obliged to vent some of his inward dissatisfaction upon his men. "You boys shut right up! There no need 'a your wastin' your breath in long-winded arguments about this an' that an' th' other. You've been jawin' like a lot 'a old hens. All you've got t' do is to fight, an' you'll get plenty 'a that t' do in about ten minutes. Less talking an' more fightin' is what's best for you boys. I never saw sech gabbling jackasses."

He paused, ready to pounce upon any man who might have the temerity to reply. No words being said, he resumed his dignified pacing.

"There's too much chin music an' too little fightin' in this war, anyhow," he said to them, turning his head for a final remark.

The day had grown more white, until the sun shed his full radiance upon the thronged forest. A sort of a gust of battle came sweeping toward that part of the line where lay the youth's regiment. The front shifted a trifle to meet it squarely. There was a wait. In this part of the field there passed slowly the intense moments that precede the tempest.

A single rifle flashed in a thicket before the regiment. In an instant it was joined by many others. There was a mighty song of clashes and crashes that went sweeping through the woods. The guns in the rear, aroused and enraged by shells that had been thrown burr-like at them, suddenly involved themselves in a hideous altercation with another band of guns. The battle roar settled to a rolling thunder, which was a single, long explosion.

In the regiment there was a peculiar kind of hesitation denoted in the attitudes of the men. They were worn, exhausted, having slept but little and labored much. They rolled their eyes toward the advancing battle as they stood awaiting the shock. Some shrank and flinched. They stood as men tied to stakes.

At about 7:30 A.M., the leading brigades of the Confederate army attacked near Fairview. Their objective was to overrun the Union artillery position there and either drive the Union troops into the Rappahannock River or cut them off from the river crossings. The Confederate advance was blocked by Franklin's Brigade and by Union General William French's powerful counterattack against their left flank.

CHAPTER XVII.

THIS ADVANCE of the enemy had seemed to the youth like a ruthless hunting. He began to fume with rage and exasperation. He beat his foot upon the ground, and scowled with hate at the swirling smoke that was approaching like a phantom flood. There was a maddening quality in this seeming resolution of the foe to give him no rest, to give him no time to sit down and think. Yesterday he had fought and had fled rapidly. There had been many adventures. For to-day he felt that he had earned opportunities for contemplative repose. He could have enjoyed portraying to uninitiated listeners various scenes at which he had been a witness or ably discussing the processes of war with other proved men. Too it was important that he should have time for physical recuperation. He was sore and stiff from his experiences. He had received his fill of all exertions, and he wished to rest.

But those other men seemed never to grow weary; they were fighting with their old speed. He had a wild hate for the relentless foe. Yesterday, when he had imagined the universe to be against him, he had hated it, little gods and big gods; to-day he hated the army of the foe with the same great hatred. He was not going to be badgered of his life, like a kitten chased by boys, he said. It was not well to drive men into final corners; at those moments they could all develop teeth and claws.

He leaned and spoke into his friend's ear. He menaced the woods with a gesture. "If they keep on chasing us, by Gawd, they'd better watch out. Can't stand *too* much."

The friend twisted his head and made a calm reply. "If they keep on a-chasin' us they'll drive us all inteh th' river."

The youth cried out savagely at this statement. He crouched behind a little tree, with his eyes burning hatefully and his teeth set

153

in a cur-like snarl. The awkward bandage was still about his head, and upon it, over his wound, there was a spot of dry blood. His hair was wondrously tousled, and some straggling, moving locks hung over the cloth of the bandage down toward his forehead. His jacket and shirt were open at the throat, and exposed his young bronzed neck. There could be seen spasmodic gulpings at his throat.

His fingers twined nervously about his rifle. He wished that it was an engine of annihilating power. He felt that he and his companions were being taunted and derided from sincere convictions that they were poor and puny. His knowledge of his inability to take vengeance for it made his rage into a dark and stormy specter, that possessed him and made him dream of abominable cruelties. The tormentors were flies sucking insolently at his blood, and he thought that he would have given his life for a revenge of seeing their faces in pitiful plights.

The winds of battle had swept all about the regiment, until the one rifle, instantly followed by others, flashed in its front. A moment later the regiment roared forth its sudden and valiant retort. A dense wall of smoke settled slowly down. It was furiously slit and slashed by the knifelike fire from the rifles.

To the youth the fighters resembled animals tossed for a death struggle into a dark pit. There was a sensation that he and his fellows, at bay, were pushing back, always pushing fierce onslaughts of creatures who were slippery. Their beams of crimson seemed to get no purchase upon the bodies of their foes; the latter seemed to evade them with ease, and come through, between, around, and about with unopposed skill.

When, in a dream, it occurred to the youth that his rifle was an impotent stick, he lost sense of everything but his hate, his desire to smash into pulp the glittering smile of victory which he could feel upon the faces of his enemies.

The blue smoke-swallowed line curled and writhed like a snake stepped upon. It swung its ends to and fro in an agony of fear and rage.

The youth was not conscious that he was erect upon his feet. He did not know the direction of the ground. Indeed, once he even lost the habit of balance and fell heavily. He was up again immediately.

One thought went through the chaos of his brain at the time. He wondered if he had fallen because he had been shot. But the suspicion flew away at once. He did not think more of it.

He had taken up a first position behind the little tree, with a direct determination to hold it against the world. He had not deemed it possible that his army could that day succeed, and from this he felt the ability to fight harder. But the throng had surged in all ways, until he lost directions and locations, save that he knew where lay the enemy.

The flames bit him, and the hot smoke broiled his skin. His rifle barrel grew so hot that ordinarily he could not have borne it upon his palms; but he kept on stuffing cartridges into it, and pounding them with his clanking, bending ramrod. If he aimed at some changing form through the smoke, he pulled his trigger with a fierce grunt, as if he were dealing a blow of the fist with all his strength.

When the enemy seemed falling back before him and his fellows, he went instantly forward, like a dog who, seeing his foes lagging, turns and insists upon being pursued. And when he was compelled to retire again, he did it slowly, sullenly, taking steps of wrathful despair.

Once he, in his intent hate, was almost alone, and was firing, when all those near him had ceased. He was so engrossed in his occupation that he was not aware of a lull.

He was recalled by a hoarse laugh and a sentence that came to his ears in a voice of contempt and amazement. "Yeh infernal fool, don't yeh know enough t' quit when there ain't anything t' shoot at? Good Gawd!"

He turned then and, pausing with his rifle thrown half into position, looked at the blue line of his comrades. During this moment of leisure they seemed all to be engaged in staring with astonishment at him. They had become spectators. Turning to the front again he saw, under the lifted smoke, a deserted ground.

He looked bewildered for a moment. Then there appeared upon the glazed vacancy of his eyes a diamond point of intelligence. "Oh," he said, comprehending.

He returned to his comrades and threw himself upon the ground. He sprawled like a man who had been thrashed. His flesh seemed strangely on fire, and the sounds of the battle continued in his ears. He groped blindly for his canteen.

The lieutenant was crowing. He seemed drunk with fighting. He called out to the youth: "By heavens, if I had ten thousand wild cats like you I could tear th' stomach outa this war in less'n a week!" He puffed out his chest with large dignity as he said it.

Some of the men muttered and looked at the youth in awe-struck ways. It was plain that as he had gone on loading and firing and cursing without the proper intermission, they had found time to regard him. And they now looked upon him as a war devil.

The friend came staggering to him. There was some fright and dismay in his voice. "Are yeh all right, Fleming? Do yeh feel all right? There ain't nothing th' matter with yeh, Henry, is there?"

"No," said the youth with difficulty. His throat seemed full of knobs and burs.

These incidents made the youth ponder. It was revealed to him that he had been a barbarian, a beast. He had fought like a pagan who defends his religion. Regarding it, he saw that it was fine, wild, and, in some ways, easy. He had been a tremendous figure, no doubt. By this struggle he had overcome obstacles which he had admitted to be mountains. They had fallen like paper peaks, and he was now what he called a hero. And he had not been aware of the process. He had slept and, awakening, found him self a knight.

He lay and basked in the occasional stares of his comrades. Their faces were varied in degrees of blackness from the burned powder. Some were utterly smudged. They were reeking with perspiration, and their breaths came hard and wheezing. And from these soiled expanses they peered at him.

"Hot work! Hot work!" cried the lieutenant deliriously. He walked up and down, restless and eager. Sometimes his voice could be heard in a wild, incomprehensible laugh.

When he had a particularly profound thought upon the science of war he always unconsciously addressed himself to the youth.

There was some grim rejoicing by the men. "By thunder, I bet this army'll never see another new reg'ment like us!"

"You bet!"

"A dog, a woman, an' a walnut tree,
Th' more yeh beat 'em, th' better they be!

That's like us."

"Lost a piler men, they did. If an' ol' woman swep' up th' woods she'd git a dustpanful."

"Yes, an' if she'll come around ag'in in 'bout an' hour she'll git a pile more."

The forest still bore its burden of clamor. From off under the trees came the rolling clatter of the musketry. Each distant thicket seemed a strange porcupine with quills of flame. A cloud of dark smoke, as from smoldering ruins, went up toward the sun now bright and gay in the blue, enameled sky.

CHAPTER XVIII.

THE RAGGED LINE had respite for some minutes, but during its pause the struggle in the forest became magnified until the trees seemed to quiver from the firing and the ground to shake from the rushing of the men. The voices of the cannon were mingled in a long and interminable row. It seemed difficult to live in such an atmosphere. The chests of the men strained for a bit of freshness, and their throats craved water.

There was one shot through the body, who raised a cry of bitter lamentation when came this lull. Perhaps he had been calling out during the fighting also, but at that time no one had heard him. But now the men turned at the woeful complaints of him upon the ground.

"Who is it? Who is it?"

"It's Jimmie Rogers. Jimmie Rogers."

When their eyes first encountered him there was a sudden halt, as if they feared to go near. He was thrashing about in the grass, twisting his shuddering body into many strange postures. He was screaming loudly. This instant's hesitation seemed to fill him with a tremendous, fantastic contempt, and he damned them in shrieked sentences.

The youth's friend had a geographical illusion concerning a stream, and he obtained permission to go for some water. Immediately canteens were showered upon him. "Fill mine, will yeh?" "Bring me some, too." "And me, too." He departed, ladened. The youth went with his friend, feeling a desire to throw his heated body onto the stream and, soaking there, drink quarts.

They made a hurried search for the supposed stream, but did not find it. "No water here," said the youth. They turned without delay and began to retrace their steps.

159

At this point in the battle, the Confederates were launching attacks up and down the Union line seeking a weak spot where they could break through.

From their position, Fleming and Wilson could see the Union artillery at Fairview and the Chancellor House, which was set on fire by bursting artillery shells during the battle. The commander of their division that they see with his staff is Brigadier General Amiel Whipple.

From their position as they again faced toward the place of the fighting, they could of course comprehend a greater amount of the battle than when their visions had been blurred by the hurling smoke of the line. They could see dark stretches winding along the land, and on one cleared space there was a row of guns making gray clouds, which were filled with large flashes of orange-colored flame. Over some foliage they could see the roof of a house. One window, glowing a deep murder red, shone squarely through the leaves. From the edifice a tall leaning tower of smoke went far into the sky.

Looking over their own troops, they saw mixed masses slowly getting into regular form. The sunlight made twinkling points of the bright steel. To the rear there was a glimpse of a distant roadway as it curved over a slope. It was crowded with retreating infantry. From all the interwoven forest arose the smoke and bluster of the battle. The air was always occupied by a blaring.

Near where they stood shells were flip-flapping and hooting. Occasional bullets buzzed in the air and spanged into tree trunks. Wounded men and other stragglers were slinking through the woods.

Looking down an aisle of the grove, the youth and his companion saw a jangling general and his staff almost ride upon a wounded man, who was crawling on his hands and knees. The general reined strongly at his charger's opened and foamy mouth and guided it with dexterous horsemanship past the man. The latter scrambled in wild and torturing haste. His strength evidently failed him as he reached a place of safety. One of his arms suddenly weakened, and he fell, sliding over upon his back. He lay stretched out, breathing gently.

A moment later the small, creaking cavalcade was directly in front of the two soldiers. Another officer, riding with the skillful abandon of a cowboy, galloped his horse to a position directly before the general. The two unnoticed foot soldiers made a little show of going on, but they lingered near in the desire to overhear the conversation. Perhaps, they thought, some great inner historical things would be said.

The general, whom the boys knew as the commander of their division, looked at the other officer and spoke coolly, as if he were criticizing his clothes. "Th' enemy's formin' over there for another

162

charge," he said. "It'll be directed against Whiterside, an' I fear they'll break through there unless we work like thunder t' stop them."

The other swore at his restive horse, and then cleared his throat. He made a gesture toward his cap. "It'll be hell t' pay stoppin' them," he said shortly.

"I presume so," remarked the general. Then he began to talk rapidly and in a lower tone. He frequently illustrated his words with a pointing finger. The two infantrymen could hear nothing until finally he asked: "What troops can you spare?"

The officer who rode like a cowboy reflected for an instant. "Well," he said, "I had to order in th' 12th to help th' 76th, an' I haven't really got any. But there's th' 304th. They fight like a lot 'a mule drivers. I can spare them best of any."

The youth and his friend exchanged glances of astonishment.

The general spoke sharply. "Get 'em ready, then. I'll watch developments from here, an' send you word when t' start them. It'll happen in five minutes."

As the other officer tossed his fingers toward his cap and wheeling his horse, started away, the general called out to him in a sober voice: "I don't believe many of your mule drivers will get back."

The other shouted something in reply. He smiled.

With scared faces, the youth and his companion hurried back to the line.

These happenings had occupied an incredibly short time, yet the youth felt that in them he had been made aged. New eyes were given to him. And the most startling thing was to learn suddenly that he was very insignificant. The officer spoke of the regiment as if he referred to a broom. Some part of the woods needed sweeping, perhaps, and he merely indicated a broom in a tone properly indifferent to its fate. It was war, no doubt, but it appeared strange.

As the two boys approached the line, the lieutenant perceived them and swelled with wrath. "Fleming—Wilson—how long does it take yeh to git water, anyhow—where yeh been to."

But his oration ceased as he saw their eyes, which were large with great tales. "We're goin' t' charge—we're goin' t' charge!" cried the youth's friend, hastening with his news.

"Charge?" said the lieutenant. "Charge? Well, b'Gawd! Now, this is real fightin'." Over his soiled countenance there went a boastful smile. "Charge? Well, b'Gawd!"

A little group of soldiers surrounded the two youths. "Are we, sure 'nough? Well, I'll be derned! Charge? What fer? What at? Wilson, you're lyin'."

"I hope to die," said the youth, pitching his tones to the key of angry remonstrance. "Sure as shooting, I tell you."

And his friend spoke in re-enforcement. "Not by a blame sight, he ain't lyin'. We heard 'em talkin'."

They caught sight of two mounted figures a short distance from them. One was the colonel of the regiment and the other was the officer who had received orders from the commander of the division. They were gesticulating at each other. The soldier, pointing at them, interpreted the scene.

One man had a final objection: "How could yeh hear 'em talkin'?" But the men, for a large part, nodded, admitting that previously the two friends had spoken truth.

They settled back into reposeful attitudes with airs of having accepted the matter. And they mused upon it, with a hundred varieties of expression. It was an engrossing thing to think about. Many tightened their belts carefully and hitched at their trousers.

A moment later the officers began to bustle among the men, pushing them into a more compact mass and into a better alignment. They chased those that straggled and fumed at a few men who seemed to show by their attitudes that they had decided to remain at that spot. They were like critical shepherds struggling with sheep.

Presently, the regiment seemed to draw itself up and heave a deep breath. None of the men's faces were mirrors of large thoughts. The soldiers were bended and stooped like sprinters before a signal. Many pairs of glinting eyes peered from the grimy faces toward the curtains of the deeper woods. They seemed to be engaged in deep calculations of time and distance.

They were surrounded by the noises of the monstrous altercation between the two armies. The world was fully interested in other matters. Apparently, the regiment had its small affair to itself.

The youth, turning, shot a quick, inquiring glance at his friend. The latter returned to him the same manner of look. They were the only ones who possessed an inner knowledge. "Mule drivers—hell t' pay—don't believe many will get back." It was an ironical secret. Still, they saw no hesitation in each other's faces, and they nodded a mute and unprotesting assent when a shaggy man near them said in a meek voice: "We'll git swallowed."

This was the first charge of Franklin's Brigade. They had to blunt the Confederate advance and push back those attempting to outflank Best's line of artillery.

Accouterments: Cartridge box, cap pouch, waist belt, and other gear typically carried by the soldiers.

CHAPTER XIX.

THE YOUTH stared at the land in front of him. Its foliages now seemed to veil powers and horrors. He was unaware of the machinery of orders that started the charge, although from the corners of his eyes he saw an officer, who looked like a boy a-horseback, come galloping, waving his hat. Suddenly he felt a straining and heaving among the men. The line fell slowly forward like a toppling wall, and, with a convulsive gasp that was intended for a cheer, the regiment began its journey. The youth was pushed and jostled for a moment before he understood the movement at all, but directly he lunged ahead and began to run.

He fixed his eye upon a distant and prominent clump of trees where he had concluded the enemy were to be met, and he ran toward it as toward a goal. He had believed throughout that it was a mere question of getting over an unpleasant matter as quickly as possible, and he ran desperately, as if pursued for a murder. His face was drawn hard and tight with the stress of his endeavor. His eyes were fixed in a lurid glare. And with his soiled and disordered dress, his red and inflamed features surmounted by the dingy rag with its spot of blood, his wildly swinging rifle and banging accouterments, he looked to be an insane soldier.

As the regiment swung from its position out into a cleared space the woods and thickets before it awakened. Yellow flames leaped toward it from many directions. The forest made a tremendous objection.

The line lurched straight for a moment. Then the right wing swung forward; it in turn was surpassed by the left. Afterward the center careered to the front until the regiment was a wedge-shaped mass, but an instant later the opposition of the bushes, trees, and

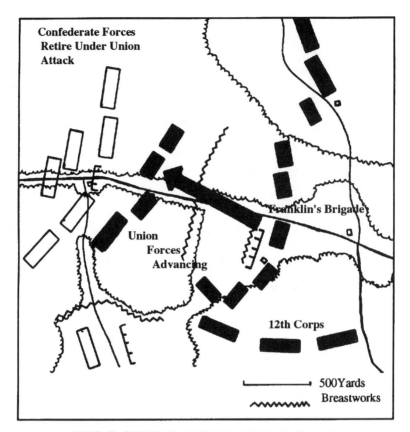

Confederate Forces
Retire Under Union
Attack

Franklin's Brigade

Union
Forces
Advancing

12th Corps

500 Yards
Breastworks

MAP 7: SUNDAY, MAY 3, 1863, 7:45 A.M.
THE FIRST CHARGE OF FRANKLIN'S BRIGADE

Union forces on the left advanced, but on the right, the situation deteriorated rapidly. Stuart's men broke the Union line in places and were on the verge of sweeping into the flank and rear of Best's guns. At his crucial juncture, Franklin's men came into line "with orders to repulse any attack and cover the artillery at all hazards." They advanced into the dense woods in line of battle just as Hooker ordered an attack by General French against the Confederate left flank. Col. Ellis of the 124th wrote in his official report ". . .a severe engagement of about an hour's duration ensued, the enemy, in force, trying to drive us and capture our battery. Our men fought like tigers, cheering loudly and falling fast, the officers, without exception, standing up to their duty and encouraging their commands. Three color-bearers were shot down in succession, but the colors never touched the ground."

168

uneven places on the ground split the command and scattered it into detached clusters.

The youth, light-footed, was unconsciously in advance. His eyes still kept note of the clump of trees. From all places near it the clannish yell of the enemy could be heard. The little flames of rifles leaped from it. The song of the bullets was in the air and shells snarled among the tree tops. One tumbled directly into the middle of a hurrying group and exploded in crimson fury. There was an instant's spectacle of a man, almost over it, throwing up his hands to shield his eyes.

Other men, punched by bullets, fell in grotesque agonies. The regiment left a coherent trail of bodies.

They had passed into a clearer atmosphere. There was an effect like a revelation in the new appearance of the landscape. Some men working madly at a battery were plain to them, and the opposing infantry's lines were defined by the gray walls and fringes of smoke.

It seemed to the youth that he saw everything. Each blade of the green grass was bold and clear. He thought that he was aware of every change in the thin, transparent vapor that floated idly in sheets. The brown or gray trunks of the trees showed each roughness of their surfaces. And the men of the regiment, with their starting eyes and sweating faces, running madly, or falling, as if thrown headlong, to queer, heaped-up corpses—all were comprehended. His mind took a mechanical but firm impression, so that afterward everything was pictured and explained to him, save why he himself was there.

But there was a frenzy made from this furious rush. The men, pitching forward insanely, had burst into cheerings, moblike and barbaric, but tuned in strange keys that can arouse the dullard and the stoic. It made a mad enthusiasm that, it seemed, would be incapable of checking itself before granite and brass. There was the delirium that encounters despair and death, and is heedless and blind to the odds. It is a temporary but sublime absence of selfishness. And because it was of this order was the reason, perhaps, why the youth wondered, afterward, what reasons he could have had for being there.

Presently the straining pace ate up the energies of the men. As if by agreement, the leaders began to slacken their speed. The volleys directed against them had had a seeming windlike effect. The regiment snorted and blew. Among some stolid trees it began to falter and hesitate. The men, staring intently, began to wait for some of the distant walls of smoke to move and disclose to them the scene. Since much of their strength and their breath had vanished, they returned to caution. They were become men again.

The youth had a vague belief that he had run miles, and he thought, in a way, that he was now in some new and unknown land.

The moment the regiment ceased its advance the protesting splutter of musketry became a steadied roar. Long and accurate fringes of smoke spread out. From the top of a small hill came level belchings of yellow flame that caused an inhuman whistling in the air.

The men, halted, had opportunity to see some of their comrades dropping with moans and shrieks. A few lay under foot, still or wailing. And now for an instant the men stood, their rifles slack in their hands, and watched the regiment dwindle. They appeared dazed and stupid. This spectacle seemed to paralyze them, overcome them with a fatal fascination. They stared woodenly at the sights, and, lowering their eyes, looked from face to face. It was a strange pause, and a strange silence.

Then, above the sounds of the outside commotion, arose the roar of the lieutenant. He strode suddenly forth, his infantile features black with rage.

"Come on, yeh fools!" he bellowed. "Come on! Yeh can't stay here. Yeh must come on." He said more, but much of it could not be understood.

He started rapidly forward, with his head turned toward the men. "Come on," he was shouting. The men stared with blank and yokel-like eyes at him. He was obliged to halt and retrace his steps. He stood then with his back to the enemy and delivered gigantic curses into the faces of the men. His body vibrated from the weight and force of his imprecations. And he could string oaths with the facility of a maiden who strings beads.

The friend of the youth aroused. Lurching suddenly forward and dropping to his knees, he fired an angry shot at the persistent woods. This action awakened the men. They huddled no more like sheep. They seemed suddenly to bethink them of their weapons, and at once commenced firing. Belabored by their officers, they began to move forward. The regiment, involved like a cart involved in mud and muddle, started unevenly with many jolts and jerks. The men stopped now every few paces to fire and load, and in this manner moved slowly on from trees to trees.

The flaming opposition in their front grew with their advance until it seemed that all forward ways were barred by the thin leaping tongues, and off to the right an ominous demonstration could sometimes be dimly discerned. The smoke lately generated was in confusing clouds that made it difficult for the regiment to proceed with intelligence. As he passed through each curling mass the youth wondered what would confront him on the farther side.

The command went painfully forward until an open space interposed between them and the lurid lines. Here, crouching and cowering behind some trees, the men clung with desperation, as if threatened by a wave. They looked wild-eyed, and as if amazed at this furious disturbance they had stirred. In the storm there was an ironical expression of their importance. The faces of the men, too, showed a lack of a certain feeling of responsibility for being there. It was as if they had been driven. It was the dominant animal failing to remember in the supreme moments the forceful causes of various superficial qualities. The whole affair seemed incomprehensible to many of them.

As they halted thus the lieutenant again began to bellow profanely. Regardless of the vindictive threats of the bullets, he went about coaxing, berating, and bedamning. His lips, that were habitually in a soft and childlike curve, were now writhed into unholy contortions. He swore by all possible deities.

Once he grabbed the youth by the arm. "Come on, yeh lunkhead!" he roared. "Come on! We'll all git killed if we stay here. We've on'y got t' go across that lot. An' then"— the remainder of his idea disappeared in a blue haze of curses.

The youth stretched forth his arm. "Cross there?" His mouth was puckered in doubt and awe.

"Certainly. Jest 'cross th' lot! We can't stay here," screamed the lieutenant. He poked his face close to the youth and waved his bandaged hand. "Come on!" Presently he grappled with him as if for a wrestling bout. It was as if he planned to drag the youth by the ear on to the assault.

Soldiers advancing into heavy fire were often seen to bend low as if walking into a rainstorm.

This was Color Sergeant Thomas Foley, Company C, 124th New York, who was killed while carrying the flag at Chancellorsville. His two brothers, both members of the "Orange Blossoms," also were killed.

The private felt a sudden unspeakable indignation against his officer. He wrenched fiercely and shook him off.

"Come on yerself, then," he yelled. There was a bitter challenge in his voice.

They galloped together down the regimental front. The friend scrambled after them. In front of the colors the three men began to bawl: "Come on! come on!" They danced and gyrated like tortured savages.

The flag, obedient to these appeals, bended its glittering form and swept toward them. The men wavered in indecision for a moment, and then with a long, wailful cry the dilapidated regiment surged forward and began its new journey.

Over the field went the scurrying mass. It was a handful of men splattered into the faces of the enemy. Toward it instantly sprang the yellow tongues. A vast quantity of blue smoke hung before them. A mighty banging made ears valueless.

The youth ran like a madman to reach the woods before a bullet could discover him. He ducked his head low, like a football player. In his haste his eyes almost closed, and the scene was a wild blur. Pulsating saliva stood at the corners of his mouth.

Within him, as he hurled himself forward, was born a love, a despairing fondness for this flag which was near him. It was a creation of beauty and invulnerability. It was a goddess, radiant, that bended its form with an imperious gesture to him. It was a woman, red and white, hating and loving, that called him with the voice of his hopes. Because no harm could come to it he endowed it with power. He kept near, as if it could be a saver of lives, and an imploring cry went from his mind.

In the mad scramble he was aware that the color sergeant flinched suddenly, as if struck by a bludgeon. He faltered, and then became motionless, save for his quivering knees.

He made a spring and a clutch at the pole. At the same instant his friend grabbed it from the other side. They jerked at it, stout and furious, but the color sergeant was dead, and the corpse would not relinquish its trust. For a moment there was a grim encounter. The dead man, swinging with bended back, seemed to be obstinately tugging, in ludicrous and awful ways, for the possession of the flag.

It was past in an instant of time. They wrenched the flag furiously from the dead man, and, as they turned again, the corpse swayed forward with bowed head. One arm swung high, and the curved hand fell with heavy protest on the friend's unheeding shoulder.

The scuffle for the colors between Wilson and Fleming demonstrates that, while carrying the flag is a great honor, each knows that its possession makes him a target for enemy fire.

The 304th fell back, just as the 124th had from the first charge and then returned to where the charge had begun, just as Franklin's Brigade had returned.

Col. Weygant gives the following account:
[Colonel Ellis of the 124th New York] had just discovered that ours were the only Union colors remaining on all that portion of what had been the Federal front which came within his view. Not a Union soldier was to be seen on our right; the long line on our left had fallen back out of sight; even the batteries which had been in our rear were gone, and the enemy's solid lines were moving past both our flanks.

To remain longer would have resulted in certain capture and Ellis reluctantly, and for the first time when actually engaged with the enemy, issued to his regiment the order, "Fall back;". . .

Over a hundred of our disabled comrades had already staggered off, or been borne bleeding to the rear, and nearly as many more lay dead, dying, or helpless, along the line we were leaving. Steadily the regiment fell back, carrying as many as they could of their badly wounded with them. The air now seemed filled with messengers of death.

CHAPTER XX.

WHEN THE TWO YOUTHS turned with the flag they saw that much of the regiment had crumbled away, and the dejected remnant was coming slowly back. The men, having hurled themselves in projectile fashion, had presently expended their forces. They slowly retreated, with their faces still toward the spluttering woods, and their hot rifles still replying to the din. Several officers were giving orders, their voices keyed to screams.

"Where in hell yeh goin'?" the lieutenant was asking in a sarcastic howl. And a red-bearded officer, whose voice of triple brass could plainly be heard, was commanding: "Shoot into 'em! Shoot into 'em, Gawd damn their souls!" There was a *melée* of screeches, in which the men were ordered to do conflicting and impossible things.

The youth and his friend had a small scuffle over the flag. "Give it t' me!" "No, let me keep it!" Each felt satisfied with the other's possession of it, but each felt bound to declare, by an offer to carry the emblem, his willingness to further risk himself. The youth roughly pushed his friend away.

The regiment fell back to the stolid trees. There it halted for a moment to blaze at some dark forms that had begun to steal upon its track. Presently it resumed its march again, curving among the tree trunks. By the time the depleted regiment had again reached the first open space they were receiving a fast and merciless fire. There seemed to be mobs all about them.

The greater part of the men, discouraged, their spirits worn by the turmoil, acted as if stunned. They accepted the pelting of the bullets with bowed and weary heads. It was of no purpose to strive against walls. It was of no use to batter themselves against granite. And from this consciousness that they had attempted to conquer an unconquerable thing there seemed to arise a feeling that they had been

177

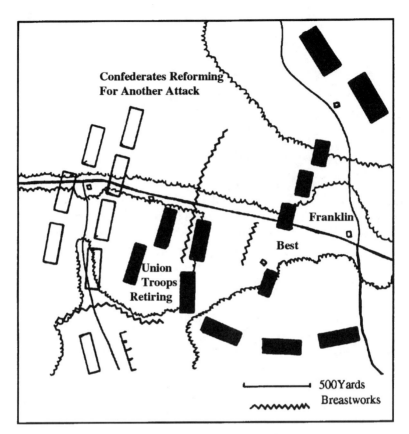

Confederates Reforming
For Another Attack

Union
Troops
Retiring

Franklin

Best

500 Yards

~~~~~~~~ Breastworks

MAP 8: SUNDAY, MAY 3, 1863, 9:00 A.M.
FRANKLIN'S BRIGADE RETURNS TO THE CLEARING

Federal infantry units ran out of ammunition and fell to the rear just as artillery ammunition also ran low. Best's line of guns at Fairview was reduced to between twenty and thirty serviceable pieces. Because their infantry had retired from the front, the Union artillerymen were free to use devastating canister charges against the advancing Rebels. On the right, Franklin's brigade found itself with no support on either flank and fell back. At about this time, Gen. Hooker was injured when a cannon ball hit a column on the Chancellor House, and a piece of the column knocked him unconscious. He recovered long enough to order the entire army back. The ever-aggressive Sickles wanted to attack and later wrote: "It would not have been difficult to regain the lost ground with the bayonet."

178

betrayed. They glowered with bent brows, but dangerously, upon some of the officers, more particularly upon the red-bearded one with the voice of triple brass.

However, the rear of the regiment was fringed with men, who continued to shoot irritably at the advancing foes. They seemed resolved to make every trouble. The youthful lieutenant was perhaps the last man in the disordered mass. His forgotten back was toward the enemy. He had been shot in the arm. It hung straight and rigid. Occasionally he would cease to remember it, and be about to emphasize an oath with a sweeping gesture. The multiplied pain caused him to swear with incredible power.

The youth went along with slipping, uncertain feet. He kept watchful eyes rearward. A scowl of mortification and rage was upon his face. He had thought of a fine revenge upon the officer who had referred to him and his fellows as mule drivers. But he saw that it could not come to pass. His dreams had collapsed when the mule drivers, dwindling rapidly, had wavered and hesitated on the little clearing, and then had recoiled. And now the retreat of the mule drivers was a march of shame to him.

A dagger-pointed gaze from without his blackened face was held toward the enemy, but his greater hatred was riveted upon the man, who, not knowing him, had called him a mule driver.

When he knew that he and his comrades had failed to do anything in successful ways that might bring the little pangs of a kind of remorse upon the officer, the youth allowed the rage of the baffled to possess him. This cold officer upon a monument, who dropped epithets unconcernedly down, would be finer as a dead man, he thought. So grievous did he think it that he could never possess the secret right to taunt truly in answer.

He had pictured red letters of curious revenge. "We *are* mule drivers, are we?" And now he was compelled to throw them away.

He presently wrapped his heart in the cloak of his pride and kept the flag erect. He harangued his fellows, pushing against their chests with his free hand. To those he knew well he made frantic appeals, beseeching them by name. Between him and the lieutenant, scolding and near to losing his mind with rage, there was felt a subtle fellowship and equality. They supported each other in all manner of hoarse, howling protests.

But the regiment was a machine run down. The two men babbled at a forceless thing. The soldiers who had heart to go slowly were continually shaken in their resolves by a knowledge that comrades were slipping with speed back to the lines. It was difficult to think of reputation when others were thinking of skins. Wounded men were left crying on this black journey.

The smoke fringes and flames blustered always. The youth, peering once through a sudden rift in a cloud, saw a brown mass of troops, interwoven and magnified until they appeared to be thousands. A fierce-hued flag flashed before his vision.

Immediately, as if the uplifting of the smoke had been prearranged, the discovered troops burst into a rasping yell, and a hundred flames jetted toward the retreating band. A rolling gray cloud again interposed as the regiment doggedly replied. The youth had to depend again upon his misused ears, which were trembling and buzzing from the *mêlée* of musketry and yells.

The way seemed eternal. In the clouded haze men became panic-stricken with the thought that the regiment had lost its path, and was proceeding in a perilous direction. Once the men who headed the wild procession turned and came pushing back against their comrades, screaming that they were being fired upon from points which they had considered to be toward their own lines. At this cry a hysterical fear and dismay beset the troops. A soldier, who heretofore had been ambitious to make the regiment into a wise little band that would proceed calmly amid the huge-appearing difficulties, suddenly sank down and buried his face in his arms with an air of bowing to a doom. From another a shrill lamentation rang out filled with profane illusions to a general. Men ran hither and thither, seeking with their eyes roads of escape. With serene regularity, as if controlled by a schedule, bullets buffed into men.

The youth walked stolidly into the midst of the mob, and with his flag in his hands took a stand as if he expected an attempt to push him to the ground. He unconsciously assumed the attitude of the color bearer in the fight of the preceding day. He passed over his brow a hand that trembled. His breath did not come freely. He was choking during this small wait for the crisis.

His friend came to him. "Well, Henry, I guess this is good-by—John."

"Oh, shut up, you damned fool!" replied the youth, and he would not look at the other.

The officers labored like politicians to beat the mass into a proper circle to face the menaces. The ground was uneven and torn. The men curled into depressions and fitted themselves snugly behind whatever would frustrate a bullet.

The youth noted with vague surprise that the lieutenant was standing mutely with his legs far apart and his sword held in the manner of a cane. The youth wondered what had happened to his vocal organs that he no more cursed.

There was something curious in this little intent pause of the lieutenant. He was like a babe which, having wept its fill, raises its eyes and fixes them upon a distant toy. He was engrossed in this contemplation, and the soft under lip quivered from self-whispered words.

Some lazy and ignorant smoke curled slowly. The men, hiding from the bullets, waited anxiously for it to lift and disclose the plight of the regiment.

The silent ranks were suddenly thrilled by the eager voice of the youthful lieutenant bawling out: "Here they come! Right onto us, b'Gawd!" His further words were lost in a roar of wicked thunder from the men's rifles.

The youth's eyes had instantly turned in the direction indicated by the awakened and agitated lieutenant, and he had seen the haze of treachery disclosing a body of soldiers of the enemy. They were so near that he could see their features. There was a recognition as he looked at the types of faces. Also he perceived with dim amazement that their uniforms were rather gay in effect, being light gray, accented with a brilliant-hued facing. Moreover, the clothes seemed new.

These troops had apparently been going forward with caution, their rifles held in readiness, when the youthful lieutenant had discovered them and their movement had been interrupted by the volley from the blue regiment. From the moment's glimpse, it was derived that they had been unaware of the proximity of their dark-suited foes or had mistaken the direction. Almost instantly they were shut utterly from the youth's sight by the smoke from the energetic rifles of his companions. He strained his vision to learn the accomplishment of the volley, but the smoke hung before him.

The two bodies of troops exchanged blows in the manner of a pair of boxers. The fast angry firings went back and forth. The men in blue were intent with the despair of their circumstances and they seized upon the revenge to be had at close range. Their thunder swelled loud and valiant. Their curving front bristled with flashes and the place resounded with the clangor of their ramrods. The youth ducked and dodged for a time and achieved a few unsatisfactory views of the enemy. There appeared to be many of them and they were replying swiftly. They seemed moving toward the blue regiment, step by step. He seated himself gloomily on the ground with his flag between his knees.

As he noted the vicious, wolflike temper of his comrades he had a sweet thought that if the enemy was about to swallow the regimental broom as a large prisoner, it could at least have the consolation of going down with bristles forward.

But the blows of the antagonist began to grow more weak. Fewer bullets ripped the air and finally, when the men slackened to learn of the fight, they could see only dark, floating smoke. The regiment lay still and gazed. Presently some chance whim came to the pestering blur, and it began to coil heavily away. The men saw a ground vacant of fighters. It would have been an empty stage if it were not for a few corpses that lay thrown and twisted into fantastic shapes upon the sward.

At sight of this tableau, many of the men in blue sprang from behind their covers and made an ungainly dance of joy. Their eyes burned and a hoarse cheer of elation broke from their dry lips.

It had begun to seem to them that events were trying to prove that they were impotent. These little battles had evidently endeavored to demonstrate that the men could not fight well. When on the verge of submission to these opinions, the small duel had showed them that the proportions were not impossible, and by it they had revenged themselves upon their misgivings and upon the foe.

The impetus of enthusiasm was theirs again. They gazed about them with looks of uplifted pride, feeling new trust in the grim, always confident weapons in their hands. And they were men.

CHAPTER XXI.

PRESENTLY THEY KNEW that no firing threatened them. All ways seemed once more opened to them. The dusty blue lines of their friends were disclosed a short distance away. In the distance there were many colossal noises, but in all this part of the field there was a sudden stillness.

They perceived that they were free. The depleted band drew a long breath of relief and gathered itself into a bunch to complete its trip.

In this last length of journey the men began to show strange emotions. They hurried with nervous fear. Some who had been dark and unfaltering in the grimmest moments now could not conceal an anxiety that made them frantic. It was perhaps that they dreaded to be killed in insignificant ways after the times for proper military deaths had passed. Or, perhaps, they thought it would be too ironical to get killed at the portals of safety. With backward looks of perturbation, they hastened.

As they approached their own lines there was some sarcasm exhibited on the part of a gaunt and bronzed regiment that lay resting in the shade of trees. Questions were wafted to them.

"Where th' hell yeh been?"

"What yeh comin' back fer?"

"Why didn't yeh stay there?"

"Was it warm out there, sonny?"

"Goin' home now, boys?"

One shouted in taunting mimicry: "Oh, mother, come quick an' look at th' sojers!"

There was no reply from the bruised and battered regiment, save that one man made broadcast challenges to fist fights and the red-bearded officer walked rather near and glared in great swashbuckler style at a tall captain in the other regiment. But the lieutenant suppressed the man who wished to fist fight, and the tall captain, flushing at the little fanfare of the red-bearded one, was obliged to look intently at some trees.

The youth's tender flesh was deeply stung by these remarks. From under his creased brows he glowered with hate at the mockers. He meditated upon a few revenges. Still, many in the regiment hung their heads in criminal fashion, so that it came to pass that the men trudged with sudden heaviness, as if they bore upon the bended shoulders the coffin of their honor. And the youthful lieutenant, recollecting himself, began to mutter softly in black curses.

They turned when they arrived at their old position to regard the ground over which they had charged.

The youth in this contemplation was smitten with a large astonishment. He discovered that the distances, as compared with the brilliant measurings of his mind, were trivial and ridiculous. The stolid trees, where much had taken place, seemed incredibly near. The time, too, now that he reflected, he saw to have been short. He wondered at the number of emotions and events that had been crowded into such little spaces. Elfin thoughts must have exaggerated and enlarged everything, he said.

It seemed, then, that there was bitter justice in the speeches of the gaunt and bronzed veterans. He veiled a glance of disdain at his fellows who strewed the ground, choking with dust, red from perspiration, misty-eyed, disheveled.

They were gulping at their canteens, fierce to wring every mite of water from them, and they polished at their swollen and watery features with coat sleeves and bunches of grass.

However, to the youth there was a considerable joy in musing upon his performances during the charge. He had had very little time previously in which to appreciate himself, so that there was now much satisfaction in quietly thinking of his actions. He recalled bits of color that in the flurry had stamped themselves unawares upon his engaged senses.

As the regiment lay heaving from its hot exertions the officer who had named them as mule drivers came galloping along the line. He had lost his cap. His tousled hair streamed wildly, and his face was dark with vexation and wrath. His temper was displayed with more clearness by the way in which he managed his horse. He jerked and wrenched savagely at his bridle, stopping the hard-breathing animal with a furious pull near the colonel of the regiment. He immediately exploded in reproaches which came unbidden to the ears of the men. They were suddenly alert, being always curious about black words between officers.

"Oh, thunder, MacChesnay, what an awful bull you made of this thing!" began the officer. He attempted low tones, but his indignation caused certain of the men to learn the sense of his words. "What an awful mess you made! Good Lord, man, you stopped about a hundred feet this side of a very pretty success! If your men had gone a hundred feet farther you would have made a great charge, but as it is—what a lot of mud diggers you've got anyway!"

The men, listening with bated breath, now turned their curious eyes upon the colonel. They had a ragamuffin interest in this affair.

The colonel was seen to straighten his form and put one hand forth in oratorical fashion. He wore an injured air; it was as if a deacon had been accused of stealing. The men were wiggling in an ecstasy of excitement.

But of a sudden the colonel's manner changed from that of a deacon to that of a Frenchman. He shrugged his shoulders. "Oh, well, general, we went as far as we could," he said calmly.

"As far as you could? Did you, b'Gawd?" snorted the other. "Well, that wasn't very far, was it?" he added, with a glance of cold contempt into the other's eyes. "Not very far, I think. You were intended to make a diversion in favor of Whiterside. How well you succeeded your own ears can now tell you." He wheeled his horse and rode stiffly away.

The colonel, bidden to hear the jarring noises of an engagement in the woods to the left, broke out in vague damnations.

The lieutenant, who had listened with an air of impotent rage to the interview, spoke suddenly in firm and undaunted tones. "I don't care what a man is—whether he is a general or what—if he says th' boys didn't put up a good fight out there he's a damned fool."

"Lieutenant," began the colonel, severely, "this is my own affair, and I'll trouble you——"

The lieutenant made an obedient gesture. "All right, colonel, all right," he said. He sat down with an air of being content with himself.

The news that the regiment had been reproached went along the line. For a time the men were bewildered by it. "Good thunder!" they ejaculated, staring at the vanishing form of the general. They conceived it to be a huge mistake.

Presently, however, they began to believe that in truth their efforts had been called light. The youth could see this conviction weigh upon the entire regiment until the men were like cuffed and cursed animals, but withal rebellious.

The friend, with a grievance in his eye, went to the youth. "I wonder what he does want," he said. "He must think we went out there an' played marbles! I never see sech a man!"

The youth developed a tranquil philosophy for these moments of irritation. "Oh, well," he rejoined, "he probably didn't see nothing of it at all and got mad as blazes, and concluded we were a lot of sheep, just because we didn't do what he wanted done. It's a pity old Grandpa Henderson got killed yestirday—he'd have known that we did our best and fought good. It's just our awful luck, that's what."

"I should say so," replied the friend. He seemed to be deeply wounded at an injustice. "I should say we did have awful luck! There's no fun in fightin' fer people when everything yeh do—no matter what—ain't done right. I have a notion t' stay behind next time an' let 'em take their ol' charge an' go t' th' devil with it."

The youth spoke soothingly to his comrade. "Well, we both did good. I'd like to see the fool what'd say we both didn't do as good as we could!"

"Of course we did," declared the friend stoutly. "An' I'd break th' feller's neck if he was as big as a church. But we're all right, anyhow, for I heard one feller say that we two fit th' best in th' reg'ment, an' they had a great argument 'bout it. Another feller, 'a course, he had t' up an' say it was a lie—he seen all what was goin' on an' he never seen us from th' beginnin' t' th' end. An' a lot more struck in an' ses it wasn't a lie—we did fight like thunder, an' they give us quite a send-off. But this is what I can't stand—these everlastin' ol' soldiers, titterin' an' laughin', an' then that general, he's crazy."

The youth exclaimed with sudden exasperation: "He's a lunk-head! He makes me mad. I wish he'd come along next time. We'd show 'im what—"

He ceased because several men had come hurrying up. Their faces expressed a bringing of great news.

"O Flem, yeh jest oughta heard!" cried one, eagerly.

"Heard what?" said the youth.

"Yeh jest oughta heard!" repeated the other, and he arranged himself to tell his tidings. The others made an excited circle. "Well, sir, th' colonel met your lieutenant right by us—it was damnedest thing I ever heard—an' he ses: 'Ahem! ahem!' he ses. 'Mr. Hasbrouck!' he ses, 'by th' way, who was that lad what carried th' flag?' he ses. There, Flemin', what d' yeh think 'a that? 'Who was th' lad what carried th' flag?' he ses, an' th' lieutenant, he speaks up right away: 'That's Flemin', an' he's a jimhickey,' he ses, right away. What? I say he did. 'A jimhickey,' he ses—those 'r his words. He did, too. I say he did. If you kin tell this story better than I kin, go ahead an' tell it. Well, then, keep yer mouth shet. Th' lieutenant, he ses: 'He's a jimhickey,' an' th' colonel, he ses: 'Ahem! ahem! he is, indeed, a very good man t' have, ahem! He kep' th' flag 'way t' th' front. I saw 'im. He's a good un,' ses th' colonel. 'You bet,' ses th' lieutenant, 'he an' a feller named Wilson was at th' head 'a th' charge, an' howlin' like Indians all th' time,' he ses. 'Head 'a th' charge all th' time,' he ses. 'A feller named Wilson,' he ses. There, Wilson, m'boy, put that in a letter an' send it hum t' yer mother, hay? 'A feller named Wilson,' he ses. An' th' colonel, he ses: 'Were they, indeed? Ahem! ahem! My sakes!' he ses. 'At th' head 'a th' reg'ment?' he ses. 'They were,' ses th' lieutenant. 'My sakes!' ses th' colonel. He ses: 'Well, well, well,' he ses, 'those two babies?' 'They were,' ses th' lieutenant. 'Well, well,' ses th' colonel, 'they deserve t' be major generals,' he ses. 'They deserve t' be major-generals.'"

The youth and his friend had said: "Huh!" "Yer lyin', Thompson." "Oh, go t' blazes!" "He never sed it." "Oh, what a lie!" "Huh!" But despite these youthful scoffings and embarrassments, they knew that their faces were deeply flushing from thrills of pleasure. They exchanged a secret glance of joy and congratulation.

They speedily forgot many things. The past held no pictures of error and disappointment. They were very happy, and their hearts swelled with grateful affection for the colonel and the youthful lieutenant.

Confederate Brigadier General James H. Lane, who led troops against Fairview, wrote the following in his official after-action report:

On Sunday morning, about sunrise, the whole brigade was wheeled a little to the left, that the line might be perpendicular to the Plank Road, and then, in obedience to orders, moved gallantly forward, with shouts, driving in the enemy's skirmishers, and handsomely charging and carrying their breastworks . . . which was fortified with a line of earthworks for twenty-eight pieces of artillery. . . . As soon as we had dislodged their infantry, these guns, with others, opened a murderous fire of shell, grape, and canister upon us, a fresh column of their infantry was thrown against us, and with our right flank completely turned, we were forced back with the loss of about one-third of the command.

As soon as the. . .brigade was reformed and replenished with ammunition, they were taken back into the woods. . . .The woods which we entered were on fire; the heat was excessive, the smoke arising from burning blankets, oilcloths, etc., very offensive. The dead and dying of the enemy could be seen on all sides enveloped in flames, and the ground on which we formed was so hot as at first to be disagreeable to our feet. . . . The men took their positions without a murmur, and notwithstanding their previous hard marching, desperate fighting, and sleepless nights, remained under arms again the whole of Sunday night in the front line, while heavy skirmishing was going on. Never have I seen men fight more gallantly and bear fatigue and hardship more cheerfully. I shall always feel proud of the noble bearing of my brigade in the battle of Chancellorsville—the bloodiest in which it has ever taken part. . . .*

* *Official Records*, XXV, Part 1, 917-18

CHAPTER XXII.

WHEN THE WOODS again began to pour forth the dark-hued masses of the enemy the youth felt serene self-confidence. He smiled briefly when he saw men dodge and duck at the long screech-ings of shells that were thrown in giant handfuls over them. He stood, erect and tranquil, watching the attack begin against a part of the line that made a blue curve along the side of an adjacent hill. His vision being unmolested by smoke from the rifles of his companions, he had opportunities to see parts of the hard fight. It was a relief to perceive at last from whence came some of these noises which had been roared into his ears.

Off a short way he saw two regiments fighting a little separate battle with two other regiments. It was in a cleared space, wearing a set-apart look. They were blazing as if upon a wager, giving and taking tremendous blows. The firings were incredibly fierce and rapid. These intent regiments apparently were oblivious of all larger purposes of war, and were slugging each other as if at a matched game.

In another direction he saw a magnificent brigade going with the evident intention of driving the enemy from a wood. They passed in out of sight and presently there was a most awe-inspiring racket in the wood. The noise was unspeakable. Having stirred this prodigious uproar, and, apparently, finding it too prodigious, the brigade, after a little time, came marching airily out again with its fine formation in nowise disturbed. There were no traces of speed in its movements. The brigade was jaunty and seemed to point a proud thumb at the yelling wood.

On a slope to the left there was a long row of guns, gruff and maddened, denouncing the enemy, who, down through the woods, were forming for another attack in the pitiless monotony of conflicts. The round red discharges from the guns made a crimson flare and a

This was Best's line of artillery and it pinpoints the location of the 304th. The house was at Fairview. The 304th was north of the road, somewhat to the rear of the line, just where Franklin's Brigade stood at 9:45 A.M. awaiting the orders that would send it forward a second time.

Union Lieutenant George B. Winslow, who commanded Battery D, First New York Light Artillery at Fairview, wrote in his after-action report:

> I. . .placed my battery in the first eligible position I could find which was upon the brow of the hill some 500 or 600 yards in rear of our advance line, my right resting upon the Plank Road. The position, as the battle developed, proved an admirable one. . .
>
> The enemy then crossed the road and came down in the woods upon our right. . . .Meanwhile the enemy continued to advance, our own troops slowly retiring before him. In a few minutes, the former came out of the woods not more than 100 yards from the muzzle of my guns, planted their colors by the side of the road, and commenced picking off my men and horses. When sufficient number had rallied around their colors, my guns having been previously loaded with canister, I gave the order to fire. In this way they were repeatedly driven back. They were, however, rapidly closing around us in the woods upon our right, not more that 25 or 30 yards from my right gun, when I received your orders to limber up and retire; besides, my ammunition was exhausted. I limbered from the left successively continuing to fire until my last piece was limbered.*

*Official Records, XXV, Part 1, p 487-88

high, thick smoke. Occasional glimpses could be caught of groups of the toiling artillerymen. In the rear of this row of guns stood a house, calm and white, amid bursting shells. A congregation of horses, tied to a long railing, were tugging frenziedly at their bridles. Men were running hither and thither.

The detached battle between the four regiments lasted for some time. There chanced to be no interference, and they settled their dispute by themselves. They struck savagely and powerfully at each other for a period of minutes, and then the lighter-hued regiments faltered and drew back, leaving the dark-blue lines shouting. The youth could see the two flags shaking with laughter amid the smoke remnants.

Presently there was a stillness, pregnant with meaning. The blue lines shifted and changed a trifle and stared expectantly at the silent woods and fields before them. The hush was solemn and churchlike, save for a distant battery that, evidently unable to remain quiet, sent a faint rolling thunder over the ground. It irritated, like the noises of unimpressed boys. The men imagined that it would prevent their perched ears from hearing the first words of the new battle.

Of a sudden the guns on the slope roared a message of warning. A spluttering sound had begun in the woods. It swelled with amazing speed to a profound clamor that involved the earth in noises. The splitting crashes swept along the lines until an interminable roar was developed. To those in the midst of it it became a din fitted to the universe. It was the whirring and thumping of gigantic machinery, complications among the smaller stars. The youth's ears were filled up. They were incapable of hearing more.

On an incline over which a road wound he saw wild and desperate rushes of men perpetually backward and forward in riotous surges. These parts of the opposing armies were two long waves that pitched upon each other madly at dictated points. To and fro they swelled. Sometimes, one side by its yells and cheers would proclaim decisive blows, but a moment later the other side would be all yells and cheers. Once the youth saw a spray of light forms go in houndlike leaps toward the waving blue lines. There was much howling, and presently it went away with a vast mouthful of prisoners. Again, he saw a blue wave dash with such thunderous force against a gray obstruction that

The ''wandering fence'' was the abandoned earthworks held earlier by the artillery.

Union Colonel William J. Sewell, who commanded the Third Brigade, Second Division, Third Corps, and who accompanied Franklin's Brigade in the charge to retake the works at Fairview, wrote in his after-action report:

> The enemy still advancing in great force, I fell back slowly in rear of the line of batteries, where, under the orders of General Sickles. . .I reformed the remnant of the brigade. . . .The batteries soon retired, their positions being immediately occupied by the enemy's infantry. The fire became so hot that to remain in that position would be only to sacrifice my men, and, having no orders to retire, I advanced once more on the double-quick, again, driving the enemy, taking possession of the small works thrown up for the protection of our guns, and planting the colors of the brigade on the parapets. My last round was fired here, and, no signs of support coming up, I retired from the field under a severe fire from the enemy's artillery and infantry, losing men at every step. . . .

*Official Records, XXV, Part 1, p. 473-74.

it seemed to clear the earth of it and leave nothing but trampled sod. And always in their swift and deadly rushes to and fro the men screamed and yelled like maniacs.

Particular pieces of fence or secure positions behind collections of trees were wrangled over, as gold thrones or pearl bedsteads. There were desperate lunges at these chosen spots seemingly every instant, and most of them were bandied like light toys between the contending forces. The youth could not tell from the battle flags flying like crimson foam in many directions which color of cloth was winning.

His emaciated regiment bustled forth with undiminished fierceness when its time came. When assaulted again by bullets, the men burst out in a barbaric cry of rage and pain. They bent their heads in aims of intent hatred behind the projected hammers of their guns. Their ramrods clanged loud with fury as their eager arms pounded the cartridges into the rifle barrels. The front of the regiment was a smoke wall penetrated by the flashing points of yellow and red.

Wallowing in the fight, they were in an astonishingly short time resmudged. They surpassed in stain and dirt all their previous appearances. Moving to and fro with strained exertion, jabbering the while, they were, with their swaying bodies, black faces, and glowing eyes, like strange and ugly friends jigging heavily in the smoke.

The lieutenant, returning from a tour after a bandage, produced from a hidden receptacle of his mind new and portentous oaths suited to the emergency. Strings of expletives he swung lashlike over the backs of his men, and it was evident that his previous efforts had in nowise impaired his resources.

The youth, still the bearer of the colors, did not feel his idleness. He was deeply absorbed as a spectator. The crash and swing of the great drama made him lean forward, intent- eyed, his face working in small contortions. Sometimes he prattled, words coming unconsciously from him in grotesque exclamations. He did not know that he breathed; that the flag hung silently over him, so absorbed was he.

A formidable line of the enemy came within dangerous range. They could be seen plainly—tall, gaunt men with excited faces running with long strides toward a wandering fence.

At sight of this danger the men suddenly ceased their cursing monotone. There was an instant of strained silence before they threw up their rifles and fired a plumping volley at the foes. There had been no order given; the men, upon recognizing the menace, had immediately let drive their flock of bullets without waiting for word of command.

But the enemy were quick to gain the protection of the wandering line of fence. They slid down behind it with remarkable celerity, and from this position they began briskly to slice up the blue men.

These latter braced their energies for a great struggle. Often, white clinched teeth shone from the dusky faces. Many heads surged to and fro, floating upon a pale sea of smoke. Those behind the fence frequently shouted and yelped in taunts and gibelike cries, but the regiment maintained a stressed silence. Perhaps, at this new assault the men recalled the fact that they had been named mud diggers, and it made their situation thrice bitter. They were breathlessly intent upon keeping the ground and thrusting away the rejoicing body of the enemy. They fought swiftly and with a despairing savageness denoted in their expressions.

The youth had resolved not to budge whatever should happen. Some arrows of scorn that had buried themselves in his heart had generated strange and unspeakable hatred. It was clear to him that his final and absolute revenge was to be achieved by his dead body lying, torn and gluttering, upon the field. This was to be a poignant retaliation upon the officer who had said "mule drivers," and later "mud diggers," for in all the wild graspings of his mind for a unit responsible for his sufferings and commotions he always seized upon the man who had dubbed him wrongly. And it was his idea, vaguely formulated, that his corpse would be for those eyes a great and salt reproach.

The regiment bled extravagantly. Grunting bundles of blue began to drop. The orderly sergeant of the youth's company was shot through the cheeks. Its supports being injured, his jaw hung afar down, disclosing in the wide cavern of his mouth a pulsing mass of blood and teeth. And with it all he made attempts to cry out. In his endeavor there was a dreadful earnestness, as if he conceived that one great shriek would make him well.

The youth saw him presently go rearward. His strength seemed in nowise impaired. He ran swiftly, casting wild glances for succor.

Others fell down about the feet of their companions. Some of the wounded crawled out and away, but many lay still, their bodies twisted into impossible shapes.

The youth looked once for his friend. He saw a vehement young man, powder smeared and frowzled, whom he knew to be him. The lieutenant, also, was unscathed in his position at the rear. He had continued to curse, but it was now with the air of a man who was using his last box of oaths.

For the fire of the regiment had begun to wane and drip. The robust voice, that had come strangely from the thin ranks, was growing rapidly weak.

CHAPTER XXIII.

THE COLONEL came running along back of the line. There were other officers following him. "We must charge'm!" they shouted. "We must charge'm!" they cried with resentful voices, as if anticipating a rebellion against this plan by the men.

The youth, upon hearing the shouts, began to study the distance between him and the enemy. He made vague calculations. He saw that to be firm soldiers they must go forward. It would be death to stay in the present place, and with all the circumstances to go backward would exalt too many others. Their hope was to push the galling foes away from the fence.

He expected that his companions, weary and stiffened, would have to be driven to this assault, but as he turned toward them he perceived with a certain surprise that they were giving quick and unqualified expressions of assent. There was an ominous, clanging overture to the charge when the shafts of the bayonets rattled upon the rifle barrels. At the yelled words of command the soldiers sprang forward in eager leaps. There was new and unexpected force in the movement of the regiment. A knowledge of its faded and jaded condition made the charge appear like a paroxysm, a display of the strength that comes before a final feebleness. The men scampered in insane fever of haste, racing as if to achieve a sudden success before an exhilarating fluid should leave them. It was a blind and despairing rush by the collection of men in dusty and tattered blue, over a green sward and under a sapphire sky, toward a fence, dimly outlined in smoke, from behind which spluttered the fierce rifles of enemies.

The youth kept the bright colors to the front. He was waving his free arm in furious circles, the while shrieking mad calls and appeals, urging on those that did not need to be urged, for it seemed that the mob of blue men hurling themselves on the dangerous group of rifles were again grown suddenly wild with an enthusiasm of unselfishness. From the many firings starting toward them, it looked as if they would merely succeed in making a great sprinkling of corpses on the grass between their former position and the fence. But they were in a state of frenzy, perhaps because of forgotten vanities, and it made an exhibition of sublime recklessness. There was no obvious questioning, nor figurings, nor diagrams. There was, apparently, no considered loopholes. It appeared that the swift wings of their desires would have shattered against the iron gates of the impossible.

He himself felt the daring spirit of a savage religion-mad. He was capable of profound sacrifices, a tremendous death. He had no time for dissections, but he knew that he thought of the bullets only as things that could prevent him from reaching the place of his endeavor. There were subtle flashings of joy within him that thus should be his mind.

He strained all his strength. His eyesight was shaken and dazzled by the tension of thought and muscle. He did not see anything excepting the mist of smoke gashed by the little knives of fire, but he knew that in it lay the aged fence of a vanished farmer protecting the snuggled bodies of the gray men.

As he ran a thought of the shock of contact gleamed in his mind. He expected a great concussion when the two bodies of troops crashed together. This became a part of his wild battle madness. He could feel the onward swing of the regiment about him and he conceived of a thunderous, crushing blow that would prostrate the resistance and spread consternation and amazement for miles. The flying regiment was going to have a catapultian effect. This dream made him run faster among his comrades, who were giving vent to hoarse and frantic cheers.

But presently he could see that many of the men in gray did not intend to abide the blow. The smoke, rolling, disclosed men who ran, their faces still turned. These grew to a crowd, who retired stubbornly. Individuals wheeled frequently to send a bullet at the blue wave.

But at one part of the line there was a grim and obdurate group that made no movement. They were settled firmly down behind posts

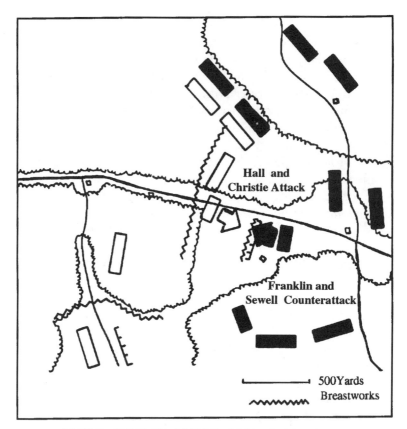

MAP 9: SUNDAY, MAY 3, 1863, 9:45 A.M.
THE SECOND CHARGE OF FRANKLIN'S BRIGADE

Confederate units under Col. J. M. Hall and Col. D. H. Christie moved up and began to lap over the Union right flank. Best pulled all of his guns out of the Fairview earthworks, but the 5th Maine battery north of the Plank Road continued to fire on the Confederates with great effect. Hall and Christie swarmed over the abandoned artillery works, but Confederate troops on their left fell back, exposing their flank. "Franklin's brigade, lately forced back and thrown into some confusion by the enemy's impetuous advance, rallies, and accompanied by a remnant of Sewell's brigade on its left, dashes back at the artillery position, recovers a number of cannon that the enemy had seized, and hurls him out of the works, taking the flags of Hall's 5th Alabama and 26th Alabama and many prisoners." *The Campaign of Chancellorsville* by John Bigelow, p. 365.

and rails. A flag ruffled and fierce, waved over them and their rifles dinned fiercely.

The blue whirl of men got very near, until it seemed that in truth there would be a close and frightful scuffle. There was an expressed disdain in the opposition of the little group, that changed the meaning of the cheers of the men in blue. They became yells of wrath, directed, personal. The cries of the two parties were now in sound an interchange of scathing insults.

They in blue showed their teeth; their eyes shone all white. They launched themselves as at the throats of those who stood resisting. The space between dwindled to an insignificant distance.

The youth had centered the gaze of his soul upon that other flag. Its possession would be high pride. It would express bloody minglings, near blows. He had a gigantic hatred for those who made great difficulties and complications. They caused it to be as a craved treasure of mythology, hung amid tasks and contrivances of danger.

He plunged like a mad horse at it. He was resolved it should not escape if wild blows and darings of blows could seize it. His own emblem, quivering and aflare, was winging toward the other. It seemed there would shortly be an encounter of strange beaks and claws, as of eagles.

The swirling body of blue men came to a sudden halt at close and disastrous range and roared a swift volley. The group in gray was split and broken by this fire, but its riddled body still fought. The men in blue yelled again and rushed in upon it.

The youth, in his leapings, saw, as through a mist, a picture of four or five men stretched upon the ground or writhing upon their knees with bowed heads as if they had been stricken by bolts from the sky. Tottering among them was the rival color bearer, whom the youth saw had been bitten vitally by the bullets of the last formidable volley. He perceived this man fighting a last struggle, the struggle of one whose legs are grasped by demons. It was a ghastly battle. Over his face was the bleach of death, but set upon it was the dark and hard lines of desperate purpose. With this terrible grin of resolution he hugged his precious flag to him and was stumbling and staggering in his design to go the way that led to safety for it.

Sgt. Sprenger of the 122nd Pa. described the scene:

It was at this juncture of affairs that Corporal Harry Hartley and the author of these historical sketches observed the advancing color-bearer, whereupon both fired simultaneously and down went the colors; however, they were immediately taken in the hands of another and planted upon the earth-works, but didn't remain there any length of time; for, considerable confusion then prevailing, Corporal Hartley and Sergeant Sprenger, both of Company K, amidst the shower of flying bullets, rushed forward in the direction of the rebel flag with the determination of capturing it, in which they succeeded as well as capturing its wounded bearer.

But his wounds always made it seem that his feet were retarded, held, and he fought a grim fight, as with invisible ghouls fastened greedily upon his limbs. Those in advance of the scampering blue men, howling cheers, leaped at the fence. The despair of the lost was in his eyes as he glanced back at them.

The youth's friend went over the obstruction in a tumbling heap and sprang at the flag as a panther at prey. He pulled at it and, wrenching it free, swung up its red brilliancy with a mad cry of exultation even as the color bearer, gasping, lurched over in a final throe and, stiffening convulsively, turned his dead face to the ground. There was much blood upon the grass blades.

At the place of success there began more wild clamorings of cheers. The men gesticulated and bellowed in an ecstasy. When they spoke it was as if they considered their listener to be a mile away. What hats and caps were left to them they often slung high in the air.

At one part of the line four men had been swooped upon, and they now sat as prisoners. Some blue men were about them in an eager and curious circle. The soldiers had trapped strange birds, and there was an examination. A flurry of fast questions was in the air.

One of the prisoners was nursing a superficial wound in the foot. He cuddled it, baby-wise, but he looked up from it often to curse with an astonishing utter abandon straight at the noses of his captors. He consigned them to red regions; he called upon the pestilential wrath of strange gods. And with it all he was singularly free from recognition of the finer points of the conduct of prisoners of war. It was as if a clumsy clod had trod upon his toe and he conceived it to be his privilege, his duty, to use deep, resentful oaths.

Another, who was a boy in years, took his plight with great calmness and apparent good nature. He conversed with the men in blue, studying their faces with his bright and keen eyes. They spoke of battles and conditions. There was an acute interest in all their faces during this exchange of view points. It seemed a great satisfaction to hear voices from where all had been darkness and speculation.

The third captive sat with a morose countenance. He preserved a stoical and cold attitude. To all advances he made one reply without variation, "Ah, go t' hell!"

A Confederate soldier in the 23rd North Carolina wrote of the fight at Fairview:

There I reckon the hardest fight of the war took place. . .This regiment never saw anything equal to it. The enemy flanked this regiment completely, and cut us up terribly. . . .the only chance to escape was running down to the right between their lines. . . .only one of my company was left. I turned to him and told him that we must try and get away from there. . .[H]ow I can't see, for it looked like nothing human could pass through such a shower and come out unhurt.
--Chancellorsville: The Souls of the Brave, by Ernest B. Furgurson, p.236

The last of the four was always silent and, for the most part, kept his face turned in unmolested directions. From the views the youth received he seemed to be in a state of absolute dejection. Shame was upon him, and with it profound regret that he was, perhaps, no more to be counted in the ranks of his fellows. The youth could detect no expression that would allow him to believe that the other was giving a thought to his narrowed future, the pictured dungeons, perhaps, and starvations and brutalities, liable to the imagination. All to be seen was shame for captivity and regret for the right to antagonize.

After the men had celebrated sufficiently they settled down behind the old rail fence, on the opposite side to the one from which their foes had been driven. A few shot perfunctorily at distant marks.

There was some long grass. The youth nestled in it and rested, making a convenient rail support the flag. His friend, jubilant and glorified, holding his treasure with vanity, came to him there. They sat side by side and congratulated each other.

The advance of Franklin's Brigade had placed it beyond supporting range of the rest of the division. Colonel Ellis, realizing that his men were almost out of ammunition, ordered his regiment to fall back.

...[T]he regiment retired toward the new Union line which was being rapidly reformed a quarter of a mile further to the rear, leaving their route over the plain marked by the blood and bodies of yet another score of Orange County's bravest sons.

Just before the regiment reached this new line, it came upon Meagher's Irish brigade, which, it was said, had been directed to prepare for a bayonet charge. They were lying down, and the 124th was ordered to form in their rear and support them. A few minutes later one of Sickles' batteries, having been resupplied with ammunition, took position but a short distance away. The enemy's artillery fire was now most terrific, and ere long another bursting caisson shook the earth, and filled the air with fragments of wood and iron, many of which fell among Meagher's men and some of them along the line of the 124th.

The enemy had halted beyond the range of our infantry, and after an hour or so the artillery firing on both sides almost entirely ceased. But we remained on the open plain until nearly four P.M., when Meagher's brigade was withdrawn and the 124th moved through, and took position behind a long line of artillery which composed the apex, or centre and most advanced portion of the new main line. At dusk the enemy made a feeble attempt, with an inconsiderable force, to reach these guns, but was speedily hurled back; and the bloody battle of Chancellorsville--so far as that portion of the Union army immediately under Hooker was concerned--was virtually at an end.
--Col. Charles Weygant, *The History of the One Hundred and Twenty-Fourth NYSV*

CHAPTER XXIV.

THE ROARINGS that had stretched in a long line of sound across the face of the forest began to grow intermittent and weaker. The stentorian speeches of the artillery continued in some distant encounter, but the crashes of the musketry had almost ceased. The youth and his friend of a sudden looked up, feeling a deadened form of distress at the waning of these noises, which had become a part of life. They could see changes going on among the troops. There were marchings this way and that way. A battery wheeled leisurely. On the crest of a small hill was the thick gleam of many departing muskets.

The youth arose. "Well, what now, I wonder?" he said. By his tone he seemed to be preparing to resent some new monstrosity in the way of dins and smashes. He shaded his eyes with his grimy hand and gazed over the field.

His friend also arose and stared. "I bet we're goin' t' git along out of this an' back over th' river," said he.

"Well, I swan!" said the youth.

They waited, watching. Within a little while the regiment received orders to retrace its way. The men got up grunting from the grass, regretting the soft repose. They jerked their stiffened legs, and stretched their arms over their heads. One man swore as he rubbed his eyes. They all groaned "O Lord!" They had as many objections to this change as they would have had to a proposal for a new battle.

They trampled slowly back over the field across which they had run in a mad scamper.

The regiment marched until it had joined its fellows. The re-formed brigade, in column, aimed through a wood at the road. Directly they were in a mass of dust-covered troops, and were trudging along in a way parallel to the enemy's lines as these had been defined by the previous turmoil.

They passed within view of a stolid white house, and saw in front of it groups of their comrades lying in wait behind a neat breastwork. A row of guns were booming at a distant enemy. Shells thrown in reply were raising clouds of dust and splinters. Horsemen dashed along the line of intrenchments.

At this point of its march the division curved away from the field and went winding off in the direction of the river. When the significance of this movement had impressed itself upon the youth he turned his head and looked over his shoulder toward the trampled and *débris*-strewed ground. He breathed a breath of new satisfaction. He finally nudged his friend. "Well, it's all over," he said to him.

His friend gazed backward. "B'Gawd, it is," he assented. They mused.

For a time the youth was obliged to reflect in a puzzled and uncertain way. His mind was undergoing a subtle change. It took moments for it to cast off its battleful ways and resume its accustomed course of thought. Gradually his brain emerged from the clogged clouds, and at last he was enabled to more closely comprehend himself and circumstance.

He understood then that the existence of shot and counter-shot was in the past. He had dwelt in a land of strange, squalling upheavals and had come forth. He had been where there was red of blood and black of passion, and he was escaped. His first thoughts were given to rejoicings at this fact.

Later he began to study his deeds, his failures, and his achievements. Thus, fresh from scenes where many of his usual machines of reflection had been idle, from where he had proceeded sheeplike, he struggled to marshal all his acts.

At last they marched before him clearly. From this present view point he was enabled to look upon them in spectator fashion and to criticize them with some correctness, for his new condition had already defeated certain sympathies.

Regarding his procession of memory he fell gleeful and unregretting, for in it his public deeds were paraded in great and shining prominence. Those performances which had been witnessed by his fellows marched now in wide purple and gold, having various deflections. They went gaily with music. It was pleasure to watch these things. He spent delightful minutes viewing the gilded images of memory.

He saw that he was good. He recalled with a thrill of joy the respectful comments of his fellows upon his conduct.

Nevertheless, the ghost of his flight from the first engagement appeared to him and danced. There were small shoutings in his brain about these matters. For a moment he blushed, and the light of his soul flickered with shame.

A specter of reproach came to him. There loomed the dogging memory of the tattered soldier—he who, gored by bullets and faint for blood, had fretted concerning an imagined wound in another; he who had loaned his last of strength and intellect for the tall soldier; he who, blind with weariness and pain, had been deserted in the field.

For an instant a wretched chill of sweat was upon him at the thought that he might be detected in the thing. As he stood persistently before his vision, he gave vent to a cry of sharp irritation and agony.

His friend turned. "What's the matter, Henry?" he demanded. The youth's reply was an outburst of crimson oaths.

As he marched along the little branch-hung roadway among his prattling companions this vision of cruelty brooded over him. It clung near him always and darkened his view of these deeds in purple and gold. Whichever way his thoughts turned they were followed by the somber phantom of the desertion in the fields. He looked stealthily at his companions, feeling sure that they must discern in his face evidences of this pursuit. But they were plodding in ragged array, discussing with quick tongues the accomplishments of the late battle.

"Oh, if a man should come up an' ask me, I'd say we got a dum good lickin'."

"Lickin'—in yer eye! We ain't licked, sonny. We're goin' down here aways, swing aroun', an' come in behint 'em."

"Oh, hush, with your comin' in behint 'em. I've seen all 'a that I wanta. Don't tell me about comin' in behint—"

"Bill Smithers, he ses he'd rather been in ten hundred battles than been in that heluva hospital. He ses they got shootin' in th' night

DIANNE DREWES

On Monday, May 4, as the men of the Army of the Potomac waited behind earthworks, there was a heavy rain storm with thunder and lightning. Civil War soldiers noted that it often rained after a battle attributing this to the tremendous heat generated by the firing of thousands of rifles and cannons.

time, an' shells dropped plum among 'em in th' hospital. He ses sech hollerin' he never see."

"Hasbrouck? He's th' best off'cer in this here reg'ment. He's a whale."

"Didn't I tell yeh we'd come aroun' in behint 'em? Didn't I tell yeh so? We—"

"Oh, shet yeh mouth!"

For a time this pursuing recollection of the tattered man took all elation from the youth's veins. He saw his vivid error, and he was afraid that it would stand before him all his life. He took no share in the chatter of his comrades, nor did he look at them or know them, save when he felt sudden suspicion that they were seeing his thoughts and scrutinizing each detail of the scene with the tattered soldier.

Yet gradually he mustered force to put the sin at a distance. And at last his eyes seemed to open to some new ways. He found that he could look back upon the brass and bombast of his earlier gospels and see them truly. He was gleeful when he discovered that he now despised them.

With this conviction came a store of assurance. He felt a quiet manhood, nonassertive but of sturdy and strong blood. He knew that he would no more quail before his guides wherever they should point. He had been to touch the great death, and found that, after all, it was but the great death. He was a man.

So it came to pass that as he trudged from the place of blood and wrath his soul changed. He came from hot plowshares to prospects of clover tranquilly, and it was as if hot plowshares were not. Scars faded as flowers.

It rained. The procession of weary soldiers became a bedraggled train, despondent and muttering, marching with churning effort in a trough of liquid brown mud under a low, wretched sky. Yet the youth smiled, for he saw that the world was a world for him, though many discovered it to be made of oaths and walking sticks. He had rid himself of the red sickness of battle. The sultry nightmare was in the past. He had been an animal blistered and sweating in the heat and pain of war. He turned now with a lover's thirst to images of tranquil skies, fresh meadows, cool brooks—an existence of soft and eternal peace.

211

Over the river a golden ray of sun came through the hosts of leaden rain clouds.

THE END.